Read This Quietly

A novel by
Stella Cadenza

Compiled by Manus Frostheart

Shifterspress

Shifterspress
Saskatoon, SK CANADA

Contents

Chapter 0:

Letter from the Editor

From Steven:

My most professional apologies. The story you were expecting to read cannot be found in this book. Plot, characters, and syntax have all escaped via an inter-dimensional portal and have now become hopelessly tangled with reality (that, and we got blood all over the cover). Your only choice is to accept the good with the bad, taking the heroes with the villains. If you choose to shut this book and place it back on the shelf, simply pray that they do not find you.

We never meant to wreck the universe. Of course, nobody ever does. If you must blame someone, the vast majority of the fault lies with fantasy novelist Reese Richardson. She was the one, after all, who dreamed up the means for the creative world to suddenly flood over into this perfectly proper existence we call the twenty-first century. Thanks to her efforts, the villains are now running about, wreaking havoc in the streets and causing nearly as much damage as the protagonists.

Once more it is up to average people like

you and me to don our grown-up underwear and do what needs to be done — the very difficult task that nobody seems to want to do: wade laboriously through the uninspired writings of Reese Richardson and face down her poorly developed characters. It's that or flee to an exotic beach somewhere and await the coming onslaught of terror with a drink in one hand and a sappy romance novel in the other. Your choice really.

Best of luck,
The Editors

Chapter 1:

Refutability

The letter glowered at Reese from the desktop across the room. She had set it there noncommittally, hoping to forget all about it in ten minutes or so. That was nine minutes ago and by now the doubt was so well burned into the back of her mind that she fancied the single and seemingly innocuous page, innocently double folded, was giving her a seriously cold stare.

After twelve minutes and twenty-three seconds, there could be no uncertainty. Reese slammed the laptop shut with a *clack* of ominous finality, pushed aside her empty teacup, and with her head in her hands, leaned over her computer and moaned four doom-laden words: "I'm a terrible writer." The time was 9:57 AM.

Seventeen minutes later (three of which were unnecessarily wasted by a talkative elderly man intent on speaking to Reese about such common and mundane things as chest pain and shortness of breath—Reese had no time for these sorts of banalities), Reese Richardson stood before a café of the type that seems to endlessly attract every variety of creative riffraff. These hoi polloi sat here and there, notebooks, cassette tape players, and chunky laptops (large enough to have the stopping power of a brick if thrown adequately) cast astrew among the empty coffee cups. Every four-seat table was taken over by a single occupant set among copious cups, saucers, plates, and crumpled napkins. The appearance of each, the clothing, the hairstyles, suggested that there was some competition on for "most original looking person". While they all looked perfectly engaged and occupied in their self-imposed creative enterprise, there was one thing Reese was certain they were not: productive. To Reese they were simply the flux that burned off as truly inspired minds were forged and shaped in the gritty fires of University Liberal Arts classes.

The man she had come to meet was already waiting for her. He sat at one of the booths near the back of the café, his chubby fingers closing about a massive sandwich. The man was wearing a dark suit, likely tailored to his unique form and not quite as pressed as it could have been. The blinds at his left partitioned his hairless face into a chimerical tiger skin. Two eyes, not fierce or keen or at all tiger-like, glanced up anticipatively.

"Gwemming unff Ffoffiber wiff habba wokk," he said in his native language, which was currently Italiano (with the addition of a very strong deli mustard). Around breakfast this man could also speak excellent Danish. The sandwich frustrating his every attempt at communication, the well-upholstered man waited a moment.

4

Eventually, he swallowed.

"Remmling and Shobisher said they will have a look," he managed, finding that he had already taken a wearisomely long break from his task of obliterating his delicious comestible opponent. He was occupied then, for some moments, as Reese sat down.

"Thank you for waiting, Earl," Reese cooed icily, ordering a cold coffee and an omelet—likely to be as cold as her coffee. The silence lasted until Earl had done away with any traces of his late culinary nemesis. If Reese were to be honest, it was not a fair duel in the least. Reese, who had known Earl for two years, cringed 0.7 seconds in anticipation before Earl commenced to licking his fingers. One, two...

"You have nothing to worry about, Reese." Three, four. "These people don't know what to look for. It will just take a bit longer than I thought." Five, six... Reese preemptively handed him a napkin.

Reese had thought the story a brilliant concept at first—something new and not at all to be compared with the infamous and shoddy writings of Gwendolyn Fairweather's *Clash of a Thousand Days*—an obviously hastily penned story of half-blood fairies who went around poisoning people.

The clock struck 10:32. At that moment, the open document on Reese' laptop, which was docilely sleeping where she left it in her apartment, had been in existence for exactly 3, 708 hours. This meant that after passing from the "what a great idea!" stage lasting for the first fifteen minutes of conception, the words she had written had already aged through the "I don't know..." phase of being (which occurs at 1, 250 hours), and exactly then was entering the "perhaps this wasn't the best story I've ever written" stage. The second hand moved once, the laptop binging to life briefly before resuming its slumber, timed precisely by the little breathing light on the front of it.

"Perhaps this wasn't the best story I've ever written," admitted Reese, looking at the small mustard-flavoured stain on the until-then pristine manuscript next to Earl's napkin. Reese wondered if Earl could consciously differentiate the two. The stain was quickly transferred to a sticky thumb and scrupulously licked up. "What do you think, Earl?"

"If you really want to know..." The economy-sized man paused. His attention was arrested by a seductive tray of cheesecake passing by. Reese waited expectantly. "Charles is the one to tell you that," Earl finished.

Reese sighed. But at the very least she could respect an agent whose only real talent was for, well, agenting.

Theodore Charles Adamson parked the entirely average, fuel efficient vehicle. Completely unadorned, fifteen-inch alloy rims scraped the curb, the wheel filing the newly-acquired markings carefully among its vast collection of scratches. To say the car appeared weathered would be on par with calling the Taj Mahal a quaint little get-away. The weathering of that particular mechanized carriage included rain, snow, sleet, desert-scorching sun, and possibly a smoldering bolt or two of lightening. The vehicle had given up any hope of ever being cleaned or maintained, and had cooperatively hunkered down to run reliably for the rest of its misunderstood and abused life span.

Two children screamed in the back seat, squeezing their juice boxes (meant to keep them busy but failing miserably in their appointed task) and spilling apple juice onto the too-cheap-to-be-real-leather seats. Theodore, or "Charles," as he went by, cleaned his glasses methodically. This action was actually a studied bid at maintaining his sanity, his mind occupied for exactly 17 seconds with imaginings of warm beaches, cool drinks, and the sounds of waves, harkened from his relaxation tape. Theodore, or "Charles," did everything methodically. According to family legend, Charles had also been rumoured to sort, compile, compartmentalize, and then consume his breakfast cereal by colour.

Charles then attempted to explain the reason for their trip to the most irrational and unthinking variant of creatures found on earth: a four-year-old daughter and a five-year-old son. Wild monkeys and tigers watched Charles from behind the eyes of the two small, energetic children.

"You get to stay with your aunt!" piped Charles. "It will be great!" was his attempt at convincing them. What he meant was: it will be great for *me*, having a quiet house all to myself for two whole days before I actually leave for my Grammatical Forms and Articulation workshop. But 4.243 years was enough for Izzy to know what daddy was really thinking at all times. His strategy immediately backfired when Izzy murmured her favourite two words, "Why, daddy?" in the most doleful of tones.

Charles said nothing further, whether by choice or simply making a wise decision to regroup his scattered forces at a less defended point. Intellect had failed in a battle of wits with two small children. Charles would now have to resort to the sheer size of his adult form to heave them out of the car, and his authoritative voice to convince himself that he was truly still in charge. Charles had heard once that a successful war campaign was grounded in deception; indeed, Charles was already nine-tenths deceived that it was he who truly ran the show.

"You two will have a lot of fun, colouring and painting. Auntie is very artistic and always gives you a culturally well-rounded experience. Did you know she has a door she painted all on her own?"

Five year-old Benton paused. He wasn't sure what a culturally well-rounded was, but he was very certain he did not need one. Izzy seemed to agree as the rest of the apple juice found Theodore's entirely tawdry (but no longer tasteless) buttoned shirt. Charles sighed, as he often did. For you see, Charles was not a man or a father, merely a large sentient calculator that found itself one day in possession of arms, legs, and two children. He tried to push aside thoughts such as INVALID QUOTIENT, or SYN. ERROR that seemed to occur so often around his children.

Instead, Charles contented himself with the reminder that at least his job made sense. Charles had gotten into editing as a means to pay the bills and feed a family, and he found the work quite linear and manageable. Stories, characters, and the indomitable magic of narrative were entirely lost on the man. He simply rearranged words, punc-ed uations, and pressed the little button that put numbers on every bottom corner. His latest project was a novel by moderately well-known fantasy author, Stella Cadenza. He did not mind that he had read the same book five times in the past month, for Charles had an objective way of picking apart sentences that allowed him to progress through the entire "book" without absorbing one iota of "story". It would not have mattered which story was set in front of him or if someone swapped the manuscript mid-way through—Charles would have continued his work without pause. Perhaps if he paused, he might remember the title, which was "Blue Moon," and if he described the plot it should have sounded something like, "well, there's this guy and a girl, and I think they're immortal. But not quite. Or. They can't be together for some reason. And they have to stop a thing that will turn the world evil, and of course he's rich and she has communication issues, and yeah."

Charles approached the old house, two recalcitrant children in tow. An uncanny shade of door yawned expectantly.

It was not an ordinary train ride across town for Reese. However, it presented sixty-four normal sixty-fifths of an uneventful commute, excepting one very awkward minute when an ill-coordinated man in a smoky suit spilled his suitcase of drug money on a man entirely not bristling with concealed weapons. Slightly embarrassed, an off-duty narcotics officer coughed loudly and politely got off one stop early, feeling dizzy at the thought of all the paperwork that could have ensued, particularly since his pen had run dry at quarter past noon.

"Very sorry. Seven, eight, nine... hundred thousand. All here. Thanks, my good chap," the man muttered, collecting the dirty folds of cash. The mugger was entirely too surprised to do anything save stutter, "goodness me", and help the poor fool.

Reese noticed none of this because she sat two seats forward. In her mind, publishing agents in drab suits had tied her career to a rough wooden chair and were dousing it with entirely more accelerant than necessary. An old-fashioned interrogation was about to begin, the kind performed in a dark room with a single dangling light bulb. The kind where "thug 1" and "thug 2" nibble matches and massage large caliber firearms in the corner. The smell of gasoline would soon permeate the room and one break of the single bulb would prompt an explosion that would make a nuclear melt-down appear a small spark, eliminating Reese' career and leaving not the slightest evidence of its existence. The anxiety did not subside as Reese stepped onto the train platform. Had a match struck within her hearing, she may have entirely broken down then and there.

Two more city blocks were traversed in relative uneventfulness until Reese arrived at the towering offices of Harbour Darlings Publishing — a rather audacious falsification of a name since the "Harbour" was made of concrete and situated in a green-space as man-made as the bricks forming it. Right on the waterfront, the building offered a voluptuous view of the sultry shoreline for all the trite and desaturated businessmen and women who never credited it one thought. A vice-publishing secretary had looked out a window once, in 1952.

The air in the building smelled of dated carpet and false hardwood, because who ever walked on the real stuff and left significantly more productive and satisfied than before they entered anyway? The entire lobby décor seemed timeless, as if the architect had known thirty years ago which drab patterns and moldings would, in thirty years, remain utterly innocuous. Perhaps the company had sought to avoid the need to remodel. Heels clacked periodically across the lobby, and boring neckties undulated meanderingly about as they preceded their various owners. Reese was sure that many of the solid coloured neckties had more personality than their slightly less bold human counterparts. Reese' mind chambered a thought, priming her focus on the present.

DING.

The Elevator creaked open. Inside, a man stood with a folded docket of papers. He was tall, thin, and clad in a graying suit. In his unoccupied hand the man held something that looked rather like the offspring of a union between a loudspeaker and a cinderblock. It twanged insidiously.

"What is that?" Reese asked.

"Just came out. It's a mobile phone. Mr. Johnson insisted I have one."

"But it hasn't any cables," Reese objected.

"Quite right. I just can't see them catching on. Like carrying a yappy Chihuahua." The man frowned depreciably at the dastardly device.

The Elevator made no comment. It simply DINGed again with signature smugness, secure in its keen technological foresight. It also considered the occupants of the building disinteresting and certainly obsolete, and quite longed to move up in the world.

Reese Richardson did not leave the elevator. The woman who stepped out of the elevator and strode confidently onto the twenty-fifth floor was known as Stella Cadenza, fantasy sci-fi romance writer of moderate caliber in the literary world. She had eleven titles to her name, all published and arranged on a shelf in her apartment. Among these were various other books she had enjoyed, as well as a very haggard and hole-riddled Holy Bible. Stella considered it her most holey book, and also the one that had seen the most mileage.

Taking a deep breath, Stella strode into the office where she was convinced her career would shortly become an incendiary catastrophe. She could almost hear its cries for mercy emanating from behind the door just before she opened it.

The room failed her grisly expectations. Instead of a lone light bulb there were several, arranged in brass-implying wall sconces and one overly pretentious chandelier. The false brass shone cheaply in a halogen glow. There was no sign of Thug 1 or 2. Perhaps they were out for more matches, gasoline and 11.4-millimeter bullets. Rather, behind a dark brown desk sat Thompson, the Supreme Executive Dancing Monkey himself.

"I'm sorry, Stella," said Thompson, an elderly man with a white, droopy moustache who had long since lost any vestige of insight regarding the interests of the present-day reader.

"We signed on for your last series, but now that you've killed off your main character, that contract has expired. We just can't take a chance on something unprecedented when we have several very clever and not very creative authors, who continue to write more of their familiar stories again and again. That is what people want, Stella: more of the same. My father once lost the key to a lock. He had the smith make him a new one, but a week later he found the old key. Do you know which he kept?"

The rhetorical question came bouncing back from the opposing wall.

"Of course he kept the old key, it already had a heavy following in a very competitive market. Anything new or different will only put off readers. Perhaps you could change your last draft—it's still with your editor? Keep your hero alive for one more book, eh? Maybe two? We would certainly back that."

Stella was sure that this villain had, through the oft-times used expository monologue-ing, just exposed his plot for dominating the written world, and that after a scathing interrogation, her future would be unceremoniously flung from the window. From there, blandly attired minions and secretaries (with stark lipstick and fake eyelashes, not to mention other fake bits) would fill the world with the same book, over and over. It would be bound in every colour, branded under every title, yet it would remain constant. Thompson would win and claim hundreds of millions of dollars. He would, of course, buy a large, impractical car with a tacky hardwood dash and a built-in car phone that sounded the car horn when it rang. Literary discretion would slowly die an ignominious death at his hands, and the citizens themselves would slowly degenerate into mindless zombies.

Yet no hero burst in to stop the tirade and rescue Stella (nor her ill-fated new novel), and Thompson continued. Stella had created many heroes, some traditional, some tragic, and a few... ironic? Bionic? One of the two. She now realized that they were all very rhetorical, only diced vegetables that still taste like the can from which they came. Nobody was going to save her or her literary work, she realized with a dour, perfectly-executed pout.

Stella suspected Thompson was still talking; his moustache wagged as his mouth presumably articulated coherent phrases and words; the intermittent jiggling of his second chin was a staunch additional hint. However, Stella had ceased to heed his ramblings. Indeed, she was beginning to realize that those four words she had despairingly uttered were proving to be true after all.

Twenty-two minutes of cold refutability hence found a very downcast Stella Cadenza returning to the street. As if on cue, a cold drizzle started up from the gloomy heavens, the clouds toying with the idea of snow. It seemed a most uncanny coincidence, something that would only happen in a badly written screenplay or paperback: *Exterior, Street, Day: Conditions: rain. Enter heroine, screen right.* Stella wondered how, in one week, she had gone from her role as reputable author to playing the part of her own down-and-out, misunderstood anti-hero. Celebrated author to rejected wanna-be in seven short days. Perhaps she ought to write a How-To book on that, she mused.

Nonsense, Stella told herself. If I were in a book, my life would certainly benefit from better pacing. Life isn't a story, and I am on my own.

"Stella Cadenza?"

The voice barely penetrated the veil of self-induced gloom that enveloped Reese. She looked up, for a moment alarmed.

"Yes?" she responded.

Before her stood a young man in clean, sharp clothes. His long, dark hair was restrained in a ponytail, and his dark eyes gleamed with something that could easily pass for friendliness.

"So it is you," the young man went on in a silken, rich voice. "What a coincidence. Did you know, I have here one of your works?" The young man produced, from a very dark and very long coat, a brand-new book. In its condition, Reese doubted that the copy had been given time to get comfortable on the shelf. The title, *The Penultimate Graeling*, glinted forth in faux gold leaf of a very low cost and slightly less durable variant.

Reese, out of mere habit, held out her hand for the book. She knew what came next: the endless torrent of "sign this for my aunt," or "say something to my darling nephew," or even, "write it in the ancient *Graeling* tongue!". (For such occasions, Stella always carried in her wallet a genuine Creative License to be used without restraint.)

But what happened next was none of these things.

"What can I write for you?" asked Reese, the book in hand. The virgin spine made a sickening, nerve-grating CRINKLE as Reese opened the cover for the first time. The young man laughed, as if Stella had just related a vaguely inappropriate joke.

"It is far too late to write in this book. Say what you will. However, I trust you have a happy ending in mind for Duchess Alina, now that Prince Azalion has defeated all of her potential suitors and rescued her safely from the Isle of the Maiden-devouring Mandibles."

Reese paused. She eyed the man curiously. She did not like to discuss storylines with fans, yet she had the faint foreboding that this man did not quite belong in the 'fan' queue.

"I haven't thought about it yet. To be honest, I haven't started writing the next one." That wasn't, even in the stretchiest, spandex-clad sense of the word, true, of course. The manuscript was well past the cursing, agonizing, heartbreak and exhilaration of writing. It was, in fact, presently in the hands of Reese's editor, having been reviewed by the publishers and given a limited stamp of approval—a judicious editing was needed according to Remmling—with all the best parts to be surgically removed, without benefit of anesthesia.

As it happened, Reese had, in a rather adolescent show of rebellion, killed off the fans' most beloved main character—a rather seductive and poutingly charming prince Azalion. This was not something Reese ordinarily did, of course—she hated killing her favourite characters. It had been a decisively strategic move on her part: if the popular series was brought to an end (and what more definitive way to conclude it than to kill most of the main characters?) then the publishers would be forced to look at Reese' other works. Wouldn't they? Reese sighed. Not according to Thompson. She supposed she would have to consider a severe revision of her work and let the poor prince live if she wanted to pay her rent...

"And does it not burn you, Cadenza," the youth went on, pulling Reese away from her self-inflicted morass, "to live without knowing what has befallen your most dear, if not fully material, friends? At any rate, thank you. Please do take care. These are strange times." With his long coat fluttering, he snapped the book shut and turned to walk away. Reese had absent-mindedly scrawled something along the lines of "best wishes, tell your uncle to get well soon, don't be afraid to dream, Alex- wait what?"

"I didn't get your name," Reese inquired. She offered her hand, though still holding the pen, and the young man shook it.

"You are not mistaken. I did not give it," the young man grinned. By the time the boy had disappeared around the corner, Reese' mind had thawed from a lethargic confusion. But in her hand, where the pen had been only a second earlier, she now held an exquisitely formed black rose with a sickeningly sweet pink smell. The rain wet her face with cool kisses as she walked slowly back to the train station, considering the rose, its fragrance heightened by the moisture in the air.

It was certainly true: Reese' life was not well-paced. She proceeded to dejectedly and despondently droop home and in fact, spend the next five hours unhappily watching her television set. She only had to tweak the rabbit ears twice in that time to stabilize the picture.

"You never did have the guts for this job, Rachel," said a dapper man in a dark suit.

"Don't put that blame on me, Rich. I have been here for you through the thick and thin of it, and all I get…" the woman drew up her fabulously colour-coordinated rain jacket, long blonde hair shying her eyes into shadow. She stifled a daintily affected sniffle.

"And you're all right with never knowing what we could have had if we stuck it through?"

"Rich, I've stuck through quite enough. Not knowing is the greatest thing you could give me now."

Click.

To preserve the flow of narrative, and offer Reese a semblitude of privacy, these five hours shall go undocumented.

Earl hung up the phone. The offices of Remmling and Shobisher, known citywide for punctuality and promptness, were not answering. He sighed. It was a heavy sound, disdainful of even the smallest disturbance in the daily schedule that had been so nicely laid out.

Earl had been in contact with them that morning, two minutes after Reese had left her apartment to meet him for their delayed breakfast (or early lunch). It had been agreed that the next morning at eight, Earl and Reese could meet with their people to discuss a publishing arrangement. Earl found no trouble dismissing the trivial matter with which he had just called. He rose from his large, leather desk chair. The wooden desk shifted moodily as he stood.

The gravity was amiss in Earl's house. He found that, no matter where he started from, he could always bank on being slowly drawn to a single square meter next to the fridge. It was here that Earl opened a white door and withdrew, from the frigid depths, a plate of cold ham and potatoes. Following this, a sandwich, some soup, a soda pop and a bag of chips (Earl believed that flavour molecules, like water, expanded when cold). He made his way to a large sofa that undeniably slouched in the middle. It gave utterance to an Atlantean groan as it struggled to hold up its burden. It had once met a handsome young sofa, and tricked it into taking on his role.

The scheme had worked until the clever devil had said, "you've tricked me fair and square. So just hold Earl for one minute while I adjust my cushions and prepare for an eternity of be-burdenment". The ancient couch was still stiff over the matter of falling for a trick he had seen before.

One remote control sat on the glass coffee table. The buttons had seen constant use for months, not to mention the incident with the pet rabbit (which had chewed off the "off" button). Earl had been grateful the rabbit had not damaged anything important.

A warm glow absolved Earl then of all doubt, all thought, and the need to do anything but bask for several hours in the televised radiance. He told himself: oh well, the meeting will proceed as planned in the morning, and this book will be a success because...oh gosh, we're down three oh already.

While the meal took merely two minutes, the game accounted for Earl's next hour and a half. Earl did not have a conscious thought for the duration of either.

The television obstinately ceased to hold a clear picture, apparently having better things to do with itself. Reese turned it off and walked to her apartment balcony. No clouds in sight, and certainly no thunderstorm. Reese was not very distraught by this occurrence; she had watched nothing but poorly written soap operas and game shows, and now she was ready to do something else. Besides, they all seemed so very depressing, even the romantic comedies. Why should she watch people falling in love when the real thing eluded her? The characters were all so shallow, and despite their mistakes they were always preserved by a miraculous fate and granted happiness for the most superficial of reasons. For Reese, her writing was not the telling of a story, but mere wishful thinking. Her unspoken quest, deep down, was to write and refine the perfect hero. However, Reese knew that no matter how strong, or how gentlemanly, these characters would never be more than just that. Even her best heroes seemed pale and hollow in the light of the past two days. Real people, she concluded, had real problems. Non-people would never be able to help her.

Thus, it was 7:24 PM when the phone rang. Reese lifted the receiver casually, in fact a little too casually. She could not know it then, but that single phone call had just set in motion a string of events that had the potential to change her life forever. The Voice of Destiny called out to Reese from another world.

In a carefree feminine voice, it said: "Hey Reesey, were we still going out tonight?"

Reese responded to the Voice of Destiny with all the pomp and ceremony it warranted: "Uh, sorry. I kind of forgot you were going to call."

Destiny covered its face with one palm and

tried to salvage what was left of the situation.

"Still up for dinner then?"

"Um, of course. I'll just get dressed."

"Ok. I'll pick you up shortly."

Click.

Reese struggled to find something appropriate to wear. Meeting her oldest friend, Macy, took a rather disagreeable amount of energy. Reese found that some people had an unlimited inner spring of optimism and drive. Reese generally found these people quite annoying, and now knew to avoid these sorts at all cost. It was a lesson learned the hard way but a friendship that had weathered the murky, winding, teenage-angst riddled trenches of high school is not lightly cast aside. By now Reese was quite used to her friend's animated way of talking. In fact, Reese often thought that a monkey in an energy drink factory would have a hard time keeping up with Macy.

Reese picked out a plainly dark, yet subtly affectatious dress. In a few minutes, she was at the curb below her apartment, watching her friend's small car pull up. In a collision with a shopping cart, Macy would no doubt find her 5.5 hp econo-hatch entirely obliterated. It seemed to Reese the vehicle had been created by someone who had never actually seen a wheel.

"Hey there!" Macy smiled, lighting up instantly.

"Hi Mace," Reese replied.

"How was that meeting? Knock 'em

dead?"

"Would that I could," Reese replied drearily, having a sudden mental picture of Thompson's expression if suddenly handed a primed grenade. It had been an awful week, comprised almost solely of ineffective writing followed by ignominious rejection of said writing, and Reese wondered if she would wake up tomorrow in a dismal gloom and kill off one of her favourite characters out of sheer bitterness.

Reese almost felt badly, being unable to match Macy's level of cheerfulness. Some people are just born with optimal levels of happiness, and using any of that up on someone as negative as Reese might upset the balance. Reese often wondered if she could, without meaning to, discourage someone as unshakeable as Macy, thus reaching an ominous critical mass that would tip the entire world into a pandemic of despondency.

"Aw, no worries. Dinner's on me," Macy purred. Reese decided Macy had definitely remained unfazed, and wondered if anything could truly dampen Macy's indomitable optimism. Raining fire, scorching famine, and rivers of blood were the only things that seemed remotely able. Regardless, for now, universal laws remained upheld.

"Don't you dare cheer me up," Reese threatened.

"But it's so easy!" laughed Macy.

True to her word, Macy treated Reese to a

wonderful dinner while they talked — or rather, while Macy talked. Macy related a date with Mr. Thisandthat (whom she would never see again on account of his lack of genuine affection and commitment), a job interview that ended in embarrassment for all, and best of all, the grisly demise of her late microwave oven — evidently Macy did not succeed in loosening a metal ketchup lid by heating the entire bottle, cap included. Reese was astounded that her friend could flawlessly articulate an endless stream of verbiage, all the while devouring her savoury pasta plate. The food seemed to simply disappear as Macy monologued in perfect syntax and rhythm. Reese wished her writing flowed as smoothly, and said comparatively little.

"How about you, Reese?" tagged Macy, waiting expectantly. Having just awoken from a glazed, blank void, Reese vaguely inferred that it was finally her turn to articulate. The topic was likely fairly beside the point, as was usually the case with Macy.

"I don't know. I had this idea of where I'd be by now, and this isn't quite it. I don't feel like I'm any good at what I do. I don't feel like I'm any good at anything."

"But of course you are! I adored the book about the magical prince! I'm still just waiting for him to burst into my life and whisk me off, you know. I can't believe he died like that. I mean, a thousand arrows. Wow. One will do it good enough, you know? That Duke really overreacted. I mean, I'd only torture someone for say four years, not a full decade!"

"That's what I mean. It's just not GOOD writing. Really, if my life were a book, I hope someone would put a lot more effort into it than that." Reese stopped, her thoughts trailing off in a foggy... whatever it was that fog usually occupied. It was too late. Macy dropped to her level of frankness. Her sudden change in demeanor had the same effect as the aftershock of twenty warheads: crumbling remains of conversation in a perfect silence.

"You know, when I met Parker, I thought that life was this big, cosmic story and I was sure that the bad part of the story was over. But maybe it's more than that. Characters in a story don't change or adapt, they just *are*. But we people get to learn—we're not as (sorry) but ... fake. Canned."

"Fictitious?"

"Yeah. Fake-tishes."

The two were quiet then, for the first time that evening in a stillness that would have welcomed silence as a pleasant interruption. It was for this reason that they noticed the older man at the next table, and then were quite surprised that neither had noticed him up to that point.

The man held a vintage pipe, which he was currently packing with tobacco. A soot-stained sailor's cap—the Shirley Temple sort—and a grime-encumbered jacket, buttoned in brass, were his most remarkable attire. He muttered to himself in an unending string of unintelligible sounds, punctuated here and there with a louder syllable.

Reese found that if she listened only to the edges of the words, it sounded something like the following:

"T'were naught lyk et." The sailor's strange accent mingled with the hot, buttered crab that dribbled from his mouth. "Ai, naught lyk et an de 'ole see, me dear. Whirrin' and a'glimmerin, heavin' and a-shimmyin'! Lights of yon deerk ahbyss as the ole gal went daen a'twixt sea an' t'under!"

Macy laughed. "I've never seen a better Mate McAnderly act!" she whispered to Reese. Reese rolled her eyes with a practiced grace.

"These fans find me wherever I go, just today even..." she groaned and left the remainder of the sentence up to Macy's prolific imagination.

"At least you're popular. A lot of people would kill for that. I mean, he's even got that necklace from his Spanish love! The one he never did see again. A copper cross with the saviour on it — his is tarnished though."

"Everyone has a hobby, I guess," Reese deflected unfeelingly. The man was clearly, Reese thought, a little too lost in his books — *her* books. She wondered briefly if she ought to be a little more appreciative of that, but decided not. Some authors gained readers so easily, like the perpetrator of all those t-shirts that read "slightly colder weather will likely occur within the near future". Reese couldn't stand that type of mainstream crowd-pleasing, but then again, she never read a book unless the author had been dead at least twenty years, and possibly kicked out of the Christian church for no reason at all. Reese tried not to let her audience dictate what she wrote; if she had written a book for everyone, it would be very different and more than a little boring. She would rather write the book she wanted to read herself, at the cost of a little popularity.

Conversewise, Reese found herself at the head of a strangely fanatical following—people who actually immersed themselves in her characters as though they were real. Her stories did not attract the casual reader, but mainly the outlying obsessive types that devoted hours to decoding her *Graeling* tongue in poster-plastered basements of their parents' homes. These fans would push up their large glasses, don a pointy wizard hat, and spend hours at small desks made of milk crates. Reese did not have the heart to tell these devoted followers that contrary to popular belief, there was no rhyme or reason to the elegant language she had made up—that bit of reality foist on the basement-dwelling, icon-t-shirt wearing, wanna-be linguist would be tantamount to kicking a puppy.

The man at the next table carried on, seemingly without noticing the two women eating dinner. In his buttery hand he grasped a rugged proto-pencil, sketching out something on the back of a pamphlet.

"Twas tha nite of da greet fure... ain't ne'er der ben a fure lyk et. Yardarms ablaze wit all da furry a' da pits! Blaiss ma baerd. In 'is raight the gleaming amulet, an' 'is left a'grippin yon maightey sweerd. Fyre an waeter taek me, nae but fyurr 'o blue."

The two women giggled as they asked for their bill. Reese happened to glance over the man's shoulder as they left the restaurant. He had drawn a strange tetrahedron, covered in symbols and hieroglyphs.

The man was silent then, and Reese could feel his gaze burning at the back of her skull. Macy did not seem to notice. The two left the restaurant, their stomachs full of high-priced pasta and designer cheesecake.

Reese was, despite her best efforts, thoroughly cheered up by the time she reached her apartment and once again feared for the cosmic balance of things. Macy went home, and the blackened city awoke in a gale-force flurry of scattered amber lights. The hazy glow, stymied by a low-flying cloud, boldly tinted the entire night sky a stomach-turning shade of starless mauve.

And in a darkly embroidered pocket, on a coat, on a young man, who was not too terribly far away, the signed copy of *The Penultimate Graeling* had begun to *glow* with a *white heat*. The book hissed a little as the black text burned a dull orange. The boy knew then, without checking his watch, that it was *time*. His pace quickened.

Chapter 2:

Sanguiscanes

The ancient relic threw no pale light, dull with ages of disuse. The only light in the dark cavern was that of a steady, blue flame. Runic silver markings were scarcely discernible on the smooth, black, obsidianite surface. The object rested on a pedestal of black basalt, shying into the (if anything) slightly lighter-coloured darkness. It fit in a triangular depression in the stone, unmoved for five thousand years. It took a slightly unsettling trapezoidal form.

A gloved hand reached out slowly and touched the cool surface. No traps sprung. No hell-hounds bounded from hidden chambers. No maniacal laughter rang from the subterranean passages. Count Ignes turned the object over in his hand. He smiled, and the blue light grew stronger.

A hundred leagues away, over mountain and valley, gorge and forest, a battle had raged for a night and a day. In the rugged Northern Region, men of the Central Landemasse had flocked to standard, spear and steel. The invading force would not be stopped, and barely slowed under the heaviest of onslaughts. A many-scaled, silver serpent of men had, that morning, marched a straight path for the citadel.

The snow now glimmered with the blood of

countless slain warriors. Gnarled and bare, grey trees clawed at the sky like the withered hands of long dead ancestors and of those more recently deceased. Ahead, the road to the mountain palace was aglaze with red ice. Noble, highly engraved swords and armour lay scattered about, useless in the murk. Arrows sprouted from the ground like tall, late-summer grass. Even the wolves shunned the plain, leaving the doomed to slowly return to the earth on their own. A damp snow flitted on a breeze laden with the scent of death. The battle had ended, and the war was soon to be won.

Weary footprints, through snow and mud, dogged their way into the town. A mighty force of invaders had passed onward. Scorched stones and walls marked their path to violence; blood dried black along the walls. The town of Ehud had become a looting ground.

At the center of the town stood a massive tower, many-spired, cold battlements glaring down on intruders like scorched sockets where eyes had once been. The palace itself, a frozen citadel, was seated on a small hill. Cold eyes kept watch from the frigid heights. Sinister black smoke, coiling like a serpent, wound its way from the surrounding townhouses. The blood of the town guard, keen defenders, ran in the gutters and between the cobblestones sliding under clanking metal feet.

A body of soldiers, glistening in war-gear and ring-coat, surrounded the gate to the citadel. Among the host were cries of hate and urgency, vying for carnage and violence. They heaved a massive tree betwixt them, assailing the mighty black iron doors.

A warrior, extremely well-muscled, clad in boots and furs, stood near them. This man watched the progress of the men working to batter the doors. His windswept chestnut-coloured hair caught in a contradictingly warm errant mountain breeze. The man was evidently a leader and a noble, for his gear and harness bespoke him to be of high rank. From his boots, finely punched in bear-hide, to the gleaming bronzanium torc at his neck, this man was the stock of mighty warriors. The gleaming longsword at his side had already drunk of the enemy's blood, but would continue to thirst for the battle-drink of one enemy only. Bainan, son of Balaan Wolfblood, sought vengeance this night.

Bainan was growing impatient. Imprisoned at the peak of the tower was his long-lost love, the most beautiful woman in all Kaemundus: Tsarmina Pulcharis. Hers was the only royal right to rule the shining city of Aotz, and her aging father had spurred Bainan to her rescue as the only hero who could hope to preserve her from the clutches of King Sven.

Even now King Sven was preparing the wedding ceremony that would forever separate Bainan from his beloved princess. Secure in his icy fortress, the king had no need to fear. For try as they would, the men Bainan commanded could not breach the gate. There was only one option left. Bainan drew his long, keen sword and bid it a solemn farewell as he dropped it in the snow.

"My faithful friends," Bainan addressed his comrades, "now is the hour of requital for the hideous acts of treachery with which King Sven has beset us. Yet alone, and only alone, may I win the day. Await you my coming from this high tower, my bride in hand, for it shall be a most glorious and memorable occasion. Now leave me, friends."

"My captain," spoke a voice, "shall we abandon you to torment and death at the hands of these immoral pagans?"

The speaker approached as the men of the South stood back before him. His garb was of silver armour, handsomely strapped to a solidly-muscled frame. Boots lined with fur, a wolfhide cloak trailing at his heels, he opposed Bainan not with the air of an enemy, but that of a true friend.

"No, Ulf the Ever Warlike, you shall leave me because I ask it of you."

The captain did not argue. For he knew the tone in which his captain uttered the doleful words; a voice half pleading, half desperate, but lacking none of its authority and edge. Cloak splaying in a harsh wind, Ulf trudged yonder, looking back as he went. All he saw through the smoke of battle, the haze of tears, and the murk of a blinding snow was his lord and captain roughly dragged, bound in heavy inconium chains, into the dark tower.

Anthony closed the book, pushing up his glasses for a closer, squinty-eyed look. A scarcely clad, fabulously athletic man grinned sardonically at him from the front cover. In one hand, he held a beautiful woman, also nearly unclothed, adorned primarily with golden jewelry. In the other hand, the man gripped the hilt of a sword buried gilded-ricasso deep in the torso of a monster with six claw-sporting arms and a hideously pained expression.

Anthony blinked.

Perhaps mom was right. Anthony re-shelved the book and left the library with the other fourth graders. However, it was already too late. A masculinity complex had just been triggered by that very book, and Anthony would either grow up to be a firefighter armed day and night with a moustache comb, or else a lumberjack who would later in life kill a bear by clubbing it with a moose's jaw bone. In either scenario he would once, in 1995, take a slightly longer route home from work and stop for a crossing jogger. Everyone is destined to one or two inevitable, unstoppable events of debatable significance.

If ever he were asked, Anthony would never be able to name what exactly drove him to bench press small vehicles or carry kittens and swooning girls from burning buildings — at the same time. Yet in some small way, certain events that we may deem inconsequential or of little import can prove to be defining and pivotal points in an undeveloped personality. The people who know this think very slowly and carefully before reaching down for a chocolate bar at the till, and always answer cautiously and deliberately when the clerk asks them if they brought their such-and-such points card.

Yet the words in the closed book carried on, though nobody was there to know of it — much like a tree falling unseen in a forest. For a thousand miles from the fortress of Ehud where Bainan was captured, what had been Lost had just been Found. However, Destiny can be a little objective at times; it does not so much care who does the finding, so long as all the T's are crossed and the I's dotted in the all-encompassing Book of Fate. After the incident involving the "Book of Fale", the act had been entirely cleaned up.

Something awful had happened.

Reese, cocooned in a warm, pleasant dream of country sunsets and a wonderfully toned, tanned farmhand, had quite woken up. Reese had only 3.24 seconds to wonder what had woken her before the phone rang again, insolently demanding her attention.

Shoot! I missed the meeting!

Reese leaped out of bed — or should have. The bedclothes catching her ankle, she clumsily tottered out of the bed in a landslide of pillows and downy duvet. With an involuntary "Eep!" she was devoured by a cascade of navy velvet and pink cotton, narrowly escaping the previously ascertained 1 in 42, 000 risk of injury due to bedclothes. (The victims from whom the statistics had been carefully studied, measured, and established had mostly survived but were subsequently left incurable insomniacs, the cause of which should be obvious to anyone paying attention.)

Intermittent 3.24 seconds. RING. Intermittent 3.24 second. RI—

"Reese here," she answered, the phone cable trailing to an arm protruding from the layers of cushions. Reese had often laughed when watching badly written movies, in which the actress repeats the lines supposedly relayed over the telephone for the benefit of the audience (who cannot hear the distant caller). She was not laughing now, though had an audience been watching from couches around the country, they would have understood the call perfectly.

"Something awful has happened," came an urgent voice, garbled through the miles of telephone line.

"Something awful?" Reese muttered, still half-asleep.

"Reese, it happened at the meeting."

"I see. What happened at the meeting?"

"It's Earl. He's missing."

"Earl is missing?!"

"Just get down here as soon as you can."

"Right. I'll be there as soon as I can."

The call was terminated. Reese sighed, the day ahead appearing before her as a many-headed serpent of missteps, ill timing, and fatally flawed decision making.

First things first. Pants.

Great time to take a spontaneous trip for

authentic Mexican sopes, *Earl*, Reese thought to herself as she scrambled to collect, organize, and don her clothing in the correct order.

Reese spent the brief train ride in suspense. When she reached the offices of Remmling and Shobisher, the first floor was in chaos as the building chewed up its occupants then spat them out one or two at a time. Reese made her way through the scattering of drab business suits and dresses in the lobby, barely dodging the bodies that hurried out the front door. She moved up a dingy staircase, escorted by the stout policeman who had been waiting for her just inside the foyer. His presence was her first hint that something was very wrong.

The second clue came from the blood, appearing in amounts that absolutely justified the use of the word 'copious' and 'plentitudinous'. Police officers and what looked like forensic investigators wearing coke-bottle examining glasses milled about, sipping coffee or writing in notepads (one was actually sketching a nearby potted plant out of sheer boredom), but none of the uniformed mass appeared the least affected by their surroundings.

The scene before Reese would have made any horror film writer faint of both envy and shock at once. Indeed, any decent mass murderer, power saw in hand, would have pushed up his hockey mask and sat down with a pen to take notes. Moreover, the very devil ought to be proud, if he wasn't already. Insufferably so. This was one of the many reasons that his heavenly department had been suddenly downsized. Few other job terminations since had involved sacred flaming swords and legions of Latin-chanting, winged warriors, although some of the most influential businesses had come close.

Facedown at a desk, where a coat of crimson paint was slowly drying, slouched the figure of (so Reese could only assume) Remmling. A knife protruded at a precisely measured picturesque angle from the back of his neck. The hilt and pommel were of a very early 1930s design, and highly engraved. The man had clearly been dead for a while, unless he could manage to comfortably spare sixteen liters of blood. Many experts had already concluded that the amount of red which adorned the walls, the floor, the ceiling, the desk, and even the keys of the desktop computer, was completely too voluminous to have been contained in the body of one thin and elderly man.

In the hand of the cold corpse rested a book, the title "Triple Condemnation" facing up. Below, plainly visible, was the author's name: Stella Cadenza.

Reese gasped. She had seen this grisly scene before. Sweeping up the sopping wet book from the dead man's hand, she passed quickly to page 134 where she read the following:

Facedown at a desk, where a crimson coat of paint was slowly drying, slouched the figure of (so Jim could only assume) Rowlings. A knife protruded at a picturesque angle from the back of his neck. The hilt and pommel were of a very modern design, and highly engraved. The man had clearly been dead for a while, unless he could manage to comfortably spare sixteen liters of blood. Dr. Ronald Howe had already commented that the amount of red which adorned the walls, the floor, the ceiling, the desk, and even the keys of the typewriter, was completely too voluminous to have been contained in the body of one thin and elderly man.

Jim donned his fedora, muttering around a smouldering cigarette, "It's alright, doc. You better get home. I have this feeling that from here on things only get … stranger."

"Think, Jim," returned Dr. Howe, putting away his stethoscope, "you know who did this. We have to stop him before he acts again."

Jim glowered at the disturbing scene. At times like this, he was grateful for faithful friends like Bremington, always there when you need them. Always holstered with utmost loyalty. Drawing forth his diminutive, 1918 model, semi-automatic friend, Jim chambered a fresh magazine. "Jack Grendel," he spat malignantly.

Reese sat down several minutes later, in a large break-room three floors down, with yet another policeman. Reese was in a panicked state—not the run screaming down the hallway sort of panic, but rather the type that makes one slow and obtuse. The lieutenant had explained in perfectly rational and reasonable terms that this unanticipated murder was likely the work of over-zealous fans. His routine, this-is-the-third-body-I've-seen-this-week (and-it's-only-Monday) voice droned on in its pedantic course. He described a potential suspect with too much time at his disposal, not much creativity, and access to a nigh limitless medical blood supply. This explanation would have satisfied most people.

Reese, however, was still hyperventilating and not truly paying attention to such things as explanations, no matter how reasonable. She hated to think that someone had taken her work as license — or worse, encouragement — to commit murder. She wrote stories to entertain, not to inspire! Her mind flashed back to the Mate McAnderly in the restaurant and she almost lost what little hold on her composure she still possessed.

Reading the anxiety on her face, the lieutenant began his pre-recorded anti-shock message. It was probably all very reassuring, but to Reese it sounded much like, "now this geezer is dead, it's all your fault, and since we can't find the murderer, we shall just put you on trial for thinking up the murder scheme in the first place. After all, you planned every detail, leaving only the question of execution, which makes you practically an accomplice. By the way, your career was found earlier this morning in the river, hands bound together and fifty pounds of steel about the ankle. And if you ever write another book, men in black will be on site shortly, one hand in a suspiciously rectangular-shaped coat pocket". Sometimes Reese wished she could be less imaginative and more attentive.

"What?" she choked when the officer's lips stopped moving and he sat, watching her as though he were waiting for his microwave dinner to *ding*.

"I said, if you ever start to feel threatened, we can have officers over shortly," the man repeated.

"Before that. About my career?" Reese blinked.

"Um…I don't know what you mean. I never said anything about your career."

"That's convenient." Reese was sure he had mentioned it.

"I'm sorry?"

The interview continued in like manner. The questions focused on her interactions with Earl and Remmling, and when or where she had last seen the two men. Reese was focused on anything but. The lieutenant asked questions in a very plain, overly calm manner, using the sort of tone and pace one would use in talking a person off a building ledge. Reese answered less so. She was eventually allowed to leave.

The officer sighed. He was looking forward to seeing his wife and son at the end of the day and having a conversation that was neither pre-recorded, rehearsed, or routine. They have cassette recorders smart enough to do my job, he thought.

And he was right. In actuality, a tape recorder would have been as much use to Reese and might have spared the man the previous 87 minutes. Still rattled by the incident, Reese walked quickly as she left the building. The officer's presence did little to calm her. She briefly considered stopping for an espresso latte, but then pictured her nerve centers tripping all down the wire like circuit breakers one after the other, finally reaching her brain, where...

Reese stopped.

The sky slept fitfully beneath a heavy blanket of grey. A cold wind whispered omens in a tongue no mortal understood. Finding her way blocked by a wall of orange signs and grimy men in reflective vests, Reese turned down a side street. If she hurried, she could still make the 1:00 train.

An oblique doorway spat forth the form of a man. Clad in a long, dust-spattered leather coat and a wide hat, he stepped squarely into Reese's path, planting his feet firmly. His face was be-scruffen and haggard, his eyes alight with something west of desperation.

Reese stopped, reluctant to approach or pass the man in such a narrow street.

"Ma'am," was his salutation, as he touched a finger to his hat brim. "I'm a-lookin' for a woman, name o' Cadenza."

Reese' half-choked utterances would not have qualified as a response in the proper sense of the word, but evidently, it was sufficient for the man to glean some remote understanding. Having all the confirmation of her identity he needed, the man pulled aside his long coat. From his hip, he drew a classic 'army' Sam Bronco revolver.

Reese' jaw dropped. A *cowboy* stood in the *crosswalk* with a *revolver*. What was wrong with this week? Evidently, someone had torn the wheels off it and her days were now sliding uncontrollably sideways.

CLICK. The pull of the tempered steel hammer said more than Reese could have disclosed in a two-page, tightly composed submission letter.

Reese knew something had to happen, and within the next two and a half seconds. Her mind sped up under the sudden influence of adrenaline, as if she had pressed pause on her (quite new) VCR and was now watching her life move forward with a halting stop-action motion. The world around her slowed, excepting the grainy static horizontal bars. It was at moments like this, when no ideas immediately presented themselves, that Reese would stop writing. She usually took a long walk to her habitual café where she would think for three hours, watching the sun slowly set. This did not appear to be among her options just then.

Plan B: call for help. The street was strangely deserted. There was nobody to hear. She looked back at the construction site: only one worker was in sight. However, Reese doubted he would hear her past the whine of his pneumatic reciprocating jackhammer, or more importantly, his earplugs.

Reese would have next reached into her pocket for her cell phone, but ten years of un-happened technological development precluded this action. Besides, she didn't have a suitcase big enough to carry a mobile phone of the times. Where was she? Right, the gunslinger standing before the convenience store. Reese still had to figure that one out.

Reese had plenty of experience weaseling out of tough situations. She wrote characters who did it every day. Choosing a character at random, she tried to picture what he would do in a situation like this. Her mind, for no particular reason, settled on Claude.

Claude was a character in a corny (even Reese admitted it) romance she had written three years ago. It had been a B-list best seller. Boy and girl, Claude and Iris, had fallen deeply in love and had sought to get engaged. This was one month after they had both been diagnosed with one of the most terminal diseases known to man. They had spent the remainder of their fatally messed up lives moping, their characters stagnating, until Reese had grown tired and depressed and simply brought their suffering—and her own—to an end. The characters spent all their money in a reckless blur of abandon, and by the time Iris died, their love was still unconsummated; as if teenagers these days needed more ill influence.

Reese was never sure why she had written the book, perhaps just to rip out her audience' hearts and watch them continue to beat on library and bookstore counters—not entirely unreasonable as that was the only way in which a story of that caliber would have any forward momentum. It certainly had nothing to do with her at-the-time breakup with a particularly successful photographer. So there was her solution: Claude would lie down and die of pulmonary cardiomyitis. This revelation, however, was unhelpful. Reese had now arrived at plan C.

What was plan C? Her mind came up blank. Through the jittering analogue noise that screened Reese' furiously racing mind from reality, she could see the menacing gunslinger fairly clearly. He mouthed words that Reese neither heeded nor comprehended. Her time was running out.

Ducking!

Ducking was a good plan. To her right, Reese could see a large, heavy, entirely steel truck. It could only be one thing: an anachronistic Farmermobile, dredged up from the dusty barn depths of a bygone era. Reese could well imagine it belonging to Farm-man, who was constantly swooping in at the last moment to save the harvest. Holy rusted fenders, Farm-man! It looked like an excellent beachhead. Maybe it would even stem a tide of lead.

Reese was halfway to the truck when a better Plan C emerged from a doorway, striding in slow motion while a dramatic chorale interlude played heroically in the background. (Reese had a mind that was very good at editing in the little details.)

Plan C was wearing a dark, fitted coat. His polished shoes clacked resoundingly in the concrete side-street. His vaguely familiar long black hair was tied back but somehow still managed to blow majestically in the breeze. Before Reese could wonder where the sudden breeze swept in from, or look about for a set crew with a large fan, both ponytail and long coat were stuttering imperiously in the gust of mysterious origin.

Plan C smiled grimly. Reese resolved, at a future point that did not involve imminent small arm fire, to ask his name. She suspected it was much more intriguing than "Plan C" but was nonetheless grateful for his timely interruption. Indeed, Reese could not imagine his entrance being better timed even if a writer in reading glasses had orchestrated the entire thing from a keyboard before a glowing computer monitor somewhere in the wee small hours of the night (and then got up to stretch his legs and grab a sandwich from the fridge).

At any rate, the present plan had the highest chance of success given the long line of afore-mentioned plans. The gun was no longer pointed at Reese. To her horror, Reese saw the gun now leveled at the young man — the same one who had, only a day earlier, asked her to sign his book. Reese had a vague inkling that his presence was more than coincidence. This suspicion was overrun by her conscious trail of thought, the frantic profanities of which would have made the most swaggering sailor appear a well-mannered schoolboy.

Reese and the world were still out of sync; she watched in perfectly focused 500 fps slow motion as the gunslinger pulled the trigger.

The youth moved also; his hands coming up, flicking aside long sleeves in a neat gesture that appeared very rehearsed.

BLANG.

The bronco revolver spoke in words all men understand. 9.1 millimeters of high velocity lead split the distance between the two men. Smoke coiled from an octagonal barrel, the tang of burnt powder spewing out and lingering in the air.

The boy clapped his hands together, extending one arm toward the gunslinger in the classic gesture of 'halt'.

The bullet had no time to consider this request. It simply exploded in a spray of flower petals, an arm's length from the boy. The smoking flower petals drifted to the ground.

The wrangler grunted, adjusting his large hat and chambering another equally potent argument to persuade the young man to lie down and ooze red fluid.

Then something extraordinary happened. Without drinking one cup of tea or watching a single corny romance film, Reese had an *idea*. The three-letter revelation came to her in the form of an insistent, miraculous bold-italic typeface: **_RUN_**. (It should be noted that Reese thought in regular, *italics*, and when things were very urgent, in an imperious **bold** but had never had the occasion to use multiple styles in combination until that moment and had certainly never before underlined any of these.)

Reese **_RAN_**. She clambered out from behind the Farmermobile, breaking away down the street. Despite her on-and-off-again relationship with the treadmill, Reese managed to distance herself very well from the unpleasantness unfolding.

The young man watched her go with a smirk of self-congratulatory satisfaction. The gritty wrangler, however, only grew more agitated. He fired the powerful revolver again and again, yet every round burst harmlessly into multi-coloured flower petals before the boy. Hand outstretched, the youth sneered at his adversary. Superheated brass casings tinkled to earth among the flower petals.

By this time Reese had resumed her synchronization relative to the rest of the twenty-first century. She reached the train station and simply boarded the first, most immediately departing train, heedless of its destination. Ending up in the wrong side of town was no issue; Reese' only concern just then was to remain on the right side of mortality. At the latter she had so far succeeded. She tried to calm her breathing and heart rate as the train left the station. She looked back only eleven times to ensure that nobody pursued her.

Calling the police did not cross Reese' mind. She had talked enough with officers that day to know the vague and unassuming manner in which they conducted their affairs. The events in the alleyway had been so surreal that Reese could not, for the moment, accept them as fact. It puzzled her greatly, and she wondered if her senses had lied to her after her horrible shock of the scene she had witnessed earlier that morning. However, she had calmed herself enough to realize that this may not be the case, and that something very strange was going on. Reese got off the train and caught another one, this time to return home from the southern district of town. She reached her apartment and lay down in a daze.

Reese must have lost consciousness, for it was dark when she awoke. Checking the clock, she saw the obdurately glaring red numbers assume the dim shape of 11:30 PM.

Reese donned a pair of pants and a long-sleeved shirt, walking to the kitchen for a glass of water and something to eat. The day had been most horrifying, and Reese needed to do what she always did to relax: listen to a soft jazz record while scribbling and sketching in a ragged notebook. Who knew, perhaps the day's events might inspire the next runaway best seller — something like Kevin Sting's story about a rabid cat that stalks the people of a small town, dragging them down into its lair in the sewers (how a rabid cat would have the sense to do that would require a rather lengthy explanation — one which would ruin the flow of the narrative if it hasn't already).

Reese' notebook, however, was nowhere to be found. Reese fumed frustratedly. It had surely been on THIS TABLE twelve hours ago when she had last seen it. Reese fumed about for a brief period until her focus waned. What had she been looking for? Oh well. Reese filled a glass, leaving the fridge a jar. The fridge had no use for the jar, but by now it was used to Reese' odd behaviour and did not object.

"Turn off the light, or they'll find you," came a voice from the dark. Reese jumped, her thoughts returning to rabid cats. She grabbed an object at random from the countertop, brandishing it menacingly at the darkness. However, it is difficult to look menacing whilst holding a pink silicone spatula.

A dry chuckle issued from unseen lips. Reese looked down disappointedly at her improvised weapon, wondering whether she had in the apartment a large breadknife, and who first thought to make a knife out of bread anyway.

"We don't have much time. I can explain, but they will find us if you don't put out that light."

"Was that you in the alley? Who are you? I've never seen you before in my life!" Reese clung frantically to a rapidly moving linear passage of thought as it sought to throw her.

"That is quite true, you have never seen me before yesterday. But nonetheless you do know me, Ms. Cadenza." Half-visible now in the light of the open refrigerator door stood the dark-haired youth from the alley.

Reese looked again upon the boy. His facial features were strong and smooth, and he had no beard whatsoever. On one finger he wore a silver ring which glittered in the ethereal glow of half-eaten sandwiches and cold, left-over pasta. His dark clothes were a conservative take on styling that might have been of a pseudo-eighteenth century fashion. His garb was like that of an old B movie, set in a period on which the costume designers had done no real research.

"No. You're lying. You can't be him." Reese had not put up her threatening kitchen implement, folding the air tenaciously with flamboyant pink Teflon.

"I thought you would need some convincing. Proceed," the boy shot back in a tired, impatient tone. He crossed his arms and leaned back a pace. Reese did not fail to note that he glanced at the windows importunately.

"Where did you get that ring?" Reese demanded.

"It was bequeathed unto me by the father

of Alina."

"You've studied," Reese shot back. "That doesn't prove anything."

"Then ask me that which cannot be found in any book."

"There is a manuscript in my office right now. It hasn't been published, and not even my editor has seen it. On page 34, Damean asks you why you fight for his people. What was your answer?"

"I would rather perish in the boiling fires of Kenol than live in a world in which the mighty tread on the backs of the weak."

Reese lowered the spatula, but did not release her grip on it. "Prince Azalion?"

"It is I."

Reese opened her mouth but found that her brain had put her on hold. Resolving to call on her frazzled mind again later, she shut the receiver. She simply stood, stupefied. Azalion was likely about to explain the situation, to the great benefit of Reese, but was forthwith interrupted.

A dazzling light swept the room, laying bare its occupants in a scouring glare of brilliance. Azalion was quick to act, pulling Reese behind the sturdiest structure in the apartment: the single brick column that occupied what would have been a most convenient side table space.

The lights, shining in at the tenth floor on which Reese lived, could belong to nothing short of a flying machine. Peering out the window,

Reese caught sight of a scowling prow and a metal-shod hull. From the ship, a muffled voice uttered tense, hostile words in the same tinny and incomprehensible language spoken over department store, airport, and hospital loudspeakers. (The language is a conspiracy, of course, made up by those perverse people who want to waylay you and then say 'Well, we told you what to do'.)

Shapes of men lined the upper deck, swaggering menacingly. Azalion pulled Reese behind the column as the first volley of electrified cannon fire smote the apartment building. If Reese had ever looked distastefully at the column of tawdry brick, or berated the thing for interrupting the view of the next room, she repented instantly.

Reese was not known for her timing. She had once, in grade three, stepped in front of a vehicle on a rural road and broken her arm falling to the graveled drive. She was less than rushed to the hospital. The Good Lord, said her father, has given us two of every body part for a reason. Shortly after the "work incident" he amended this to two reasons: the second being soda bottles, which evidently require two hands to open. What the doctor, her parents, and even Reese had not known was that the elderly Mr. Edmond had been driving the only vehicle that would pass over that road in the span of twenty-two hours. He had, at 7:46 that morning, broken his glasses planing some lumber in his garage. Forthwith he had set off to the optometrist, broken glasses on the passenger seat beside him. In his haste, he forgot that the brakes on his elderly Suick Quinthentury had not been bled of air pockets, leaving the ineffective brake pedal with a rather spongy feel.

Had Reese eaten a frozen waffle (preparation time two and a half minutes) instead of making oatmeal (five for the kettle, three to cool) before school that day, she should have never heard an engine in her entire eleven-minute walk to school. And had her malicious shoelace not troubled her with a particularly nasty and inexplicably intractable knot, she should have given Mr. Edmond 57 additional seconds to stop the crippled vehicle. But she hadn't, and it did, and therefore she couldn't.

However, it is important to note that due to being so long in the hospital, Reese had not returned to school that day. Rather, she had been taken home to watch cartoons and thereby avoided the gargantuan tree that inexplicably collapsed on her homeward route later that afternoon at precisely the time Reese would have been passing under it. It was one second a tree, and the next, splinters and a shattered four-thousand-pound trunk upon the road. The furiously apologizing Mr. Edmond would have been much relieved to learn that sometimes the meager bad occurrences unfold simply to prevent us from stumbling headlong into the truly awful. Thus, it happened that, true to her haphazard sense of timing, Reese chose a moment rife with cannon fire to find the words to address her present situation.

Azalion, deafened by the roar of the guns, heard none of the eighteen questions Reese shouted sequentially into his ear. Rather, he took her to be alarmed and panicked, and determined to with her flee the scene, a puzzled yet concerned look on his face. Reese decided she would like very much to very soon get some answers from Azalion regarding the spaceship hovering about the building, the cowboy in the alley, and writing implement-to-flower transformation methods — to say nothing about the bullets. Maybe, just maybe, logic would be able to negotiate the circuitous labyrinth that was Monday morning and bring some clarity to her muddled world.

Then all at once, silence descended like dandelion fuzz.

"Shhh, listen!" Azalion muttered.

"They've stopped firing," Reese deduced brilliantly and with no small degree of relief.

"That's not a good thing," returned the prince.

And, indeed, they soon found it was not.

Chapter 3:

Caerulembus

Jed stopped the patrol car, its brakes giving off an alarmed squeal. The car had never intended to go into law enforcement—it had rather aspired to Grand Prix racing. Unfortunately, the thing had quickly learned through a rather ignominious street race that its box-like form did not lend itself well to racing. Following a high-speed chase resulting from engine-seizing despair it had given itself over to the police to serve its sentence.

The engine quieted, letting through for the first time the light plinking sound of raindrops on the steel panels. Leaning out the window, Jed looked to the sky. He blinked, ignoring the cold splatters of rain on his cheeks. He blinked again, harder this time. It didn't work. He then checked his coffee; perhaps Joyce, the barista at the café he regularly stopped at, had slipped something extra into it. Coffee, cream, sugar. Nope, it was clean. He took a slow sip and ran his mind over the past few days—there had been no hallucinations on this scale. Besides, his slightly dyslexic imagination usually just mixed up letters and scrambled sentences. He had even, quite

Spooneriffically, seen a billboard early Saturday morning that read, "Fight your Liars with Wally's Matches". All he could picture for the rest of that day was people running around with their pants alight.

In the end, Jed decided that there must, in fact, be a colossal space galleon floating above 6th Avenue. Very odd, he thought. If aliens had invaded, he hardly expected them to do it here — or in a craft of that make and model. Many better places existed in town, like the downtown area. Or the freeway bridge — monster movies always had a bridge in them. Jed reached for the vehicle's radio then set it down again. Headquarters would know about this soon enough, he reasoned. Jed did not feel like playing the madman just yet — and certainly not until he got a closer look. He slowly eased himself out of the car. He then wondered if this tremendous floating apparition had anything to do with the other wild story he had heard that day.

The break room had been in shambles that morning. All were excited by a rather unique murder scene in the downtown area. Burnt coffee and day-old donuts tainted the atmosphere inside the station.

Jed sat with two others, a cold beef sandwich clutched tightly in his fist as he tried rather desperately to hold it together despite its tendency to slide away from itself. The sandwich consisted of one scanty slab of pseudo-meat dangling out of either side of the two mustard-drenched bread slices that presently provided a thin layer of protection for the hands of its ingestor. A dash of colour was added by the single leaf of wilted lettuce — homage by the sandwich's maker to a complete meal in the dietetic sense of the term. Anyone who took more than a cursory glance at the meager meal would conclude in a hurry that Jed lived alone, did his own grocery shopping (which only occasionally entailed giving the neighbourhood teenager a list and having her fetch a few items), and did most of his own cooking (when he wasn't consuming the fine cuisine of a local pizza establishment).

At the moment, however, a hurried game of cards was underway, and Jed's only thought for his lunch was that of keeping the mustard from staining the cards so that the others would not know what hand he held in the next round.

"What card did you lay, Jed?" Officer Simon asked, not paying attention.

"Ho'r o' farts," Jed returned absentmindedly, his poor brain twiddling all the words about as he tried to chew a mouthful of sandwich and count his cards at the same time. Grins were exchanged, but Jed was too entertaining for anyone to let on and spoil the fun. Another hand was played.

"No, before that," Officer Simon pushed.

"Dive of Fiamonds. Keep up, Simon." Jed clutched the remains of his sandwich more tightly as the meat slid another degree. He held a momentary silent debate with himself, weighing his options, then shoved the remainder in his mouth all at once, trying to lick his fingers at the same time.

The grins about the table grew wider. Jed gave no indication that he was catching on, determinedly chewing the last soggy crust of what we must, by mere association with noontime, term his 'lunch'. Somewhere a snicker escaped. The card game ran its course, and Jed rose to leave.

"No time for another hand?" goaded Officer Stewart, flashing her patented mocking smile.

"Patrolling near 7th Avenue. See you fellows later," Jed explained, interrupted only by a final lick of mustardy fingers. He finally exited the station, clambering heavily into a patrol car. Voices muttered on the radio as the engine turned over and over. Number 117 tended to be persnickety and was clearly due for a check-up. Dearly clue for a check-up indeed, thought Jed as the timing belt gave one low squeal. Jed set off, scraping the front bumper on the ground as he exited the steeply sloped parking lot.

The patrol had seen a full 27.5 minutes of un-eventivity when Jed stopped at his favourite coffee joint. The aroma in the small café was similar to that of the station, but far fresher. The woman behind the counter, who also coincidentally came to the coffee shop every day, had Jed's usual drink ready by the time he reached the till. She handed it over before accepting the three coins he passed her. Exact change, as usual.

"Anything exciting going on, Jed?" the woman asked with a perky smile.

"Just some big crime scene downtown. How about you?" Jed ventured a glance at the attractive barista. She probably still smelled like coffee after work, Jed thought. He took a moment to ponder the attraction of that concept.

"Mostly regulars. Toque Man ordered his quadruple espresso, those three business goobers were here with laptop computers, and Mr. Yin is still in the corner with his third newspaper. So what was the big mystery then?" Joyce smiled, seemingly unaware of the three people lined up behind Jed.

"Wouldn't know. I wasn't called in for it," Jed returned briefly, adding a "Thanks, Joyce" as he lifted the cup to her in salute and turned to leave.

Halfway through the parking lot, Jed braked hard. It appeared that his patrol car had just been hit by a small boy on a bicycle. A grimy man with a beard was following closely, wrench in hand. The child suppressed a flicker of horror that played across his face when he saw the approaching officer. Turning from Jed, the boy addressed the bicycle mechanic in a saccharinely innocent tone.

"Was this the bike that was stolen?" asked the child. The bicycle mechanic had caught up, and snatched the handlebars from the boy.

"That depends," he grunted, "are you stealing it?"

Jed had his hands full for a while after that. It was not until some time later that he rounded the corner of 6th avenue and glimpsed the steel behemoth floating between buildings like some spectral zeppelin of a bygone war.

It appeared to be a large steel hull with several small fin-like masts — a bizarre combination of submarine, space shuttle, and Spanish galleon. The hulk seemed to propel itself with white-hot jets of flame that issued from the sides and rear of the ship, bursting forth with a hiss and a cloud of smoke.

As Jed watched, the flying machine let out a tremendous volley of laser cannon fire from the port side, directly into the 6th Avenue apartment building. The radio receiver fell from Jed's shaking hand.

Glass rained down on the street below. Flying saucers, Jed had no experience with, but glass he could handle. He began to empty the street of passersby, clearing people away from the newly declared urban warzone. Finding his inner voice of authority (the tone of which sounded much like a lifeguard on deck with juvenile delinquents wreaking havoc in the pool) Jed did not utter a single spoonerism while herding the citizens to safety.

More tenants were shortly pouring from the front doors of the building. Among them were a boy and a woman. A few blocks from the disaster area, they paused.

"So, was that magic or something? Where did you learn that?"

"I went to Dogfleaz wizard school," the boy half-jested in a dry tone, casting his gaze about and looking for street signs.

"So, like, a school where special people are chosen if they have the ability to learn magic? With wands and all?"

"Don't be daft. There's no such thing as a magic school. Now think. Who else came in contact with your latest manuscript?" Azalion turned his attention back to Reese.

"Earl, Shobisher, and…" Reese struggled to slow her racing heart, or to speed up her lagging mind. Either one would have been extremely helpful.

"AND?"

"Charles! My editor. He's had it for the past few months."

It occurred to Reese then that her manuscript seemed to meet all the requirements of a major plague: if you were in contact with it long enough, you eventually died. Reese gasped for air; she had done more running in that one day than in the entire past month. She collapsed on the pavement for a breather.

"Then he will be next." Azalion muttered. "We have to find him before Grendel does."

Reese' face drained of colour, turning a vomitous grey shade. "Grendel?" she choked.

"You saw the crime scene. What do you

think." Azalion posed the question really more like a statement. When he chose, he could also phrase statements that one felt inclined to answer—it was a gift.

Reese was suddenly jolted from the seductive flow of Azalion's logic, and her suspension of disbelief utterly snapped.

"This makes no sense. Why are you here? Why are all my characters suddenly real? No offense, but *YOU'RE MADE UP!* This has to be some kind of game, and one I don't want to play!"

"I know I am not real, although I do not know how I came to be here. Regardless, I am present. We have to find out what's happening quickly, before another act of violence is committed." Azalion pulled Reese to her feet.

"If I can summon my royal protector," Azalion continued, "my great winged lion, we will be able to fly across the city to find your friend. The buildings will shelter us from cannon fire as long as we can stay ahead of these pirates. However, navigation may be a challenge, these stars are entirely foreign to me." Azalion looked at the partially overcast sky, exasperated.

"The underground train comes in five minutes, on the hour. They can't fly that thing underground. The thirteen will get us there. And it's less obvious," Reese suggested. Having no vehicle, she was quite adept at planning train schedules on the fly.

Azalion thought for a moment. "Right. We'll take the train."

Five minutes elapsed. The Prince frowned
deeply, muttering unintelligibly as he sank into a
hard, cheap plastic seat. His displeasure
deepened to a devout distaste. An offensive word
scrawled on the wall next to his ear sizzled
slightly, made a nasty smell, and was gone.

"What's the matter," Reese teased, "had
you been expecting a cohort of shield bearers and
winged foxes to escort you?"

The Prince smirked. "Is it not unfair," he
returned, "to know everything there is to know
about me, when I know absolutely nothing about
you?"

"Oh, it gets better: the bits about you that
you don't know are only because I haven't made
them up yet," Reese replied. She then chuckled at
the fuming look of appall that crossed the young
man's face.

"Hardly. I get on fine," he objected.

"Really?" Reese challenged. "What's your
favourite colour?" Reese' question was met with
silence. She smiled widely at the speechless boy.

"I don't have one," Azalion finally
answered.

"You don't have one, because I haven't
needed to add that bit — haven't written it… Wait.
I'm going to try something," Reese said,
producing from her pocket a very abused
notebook. She scrawled one sentence, facing
Azalion from the opposite side of the train. She
crossed the last *T*, and a puzzled look crossed the

Prince's face. He looked over at Reese.

"Magenta," he said with a surprised edge to his voice. "My favourite colour is magenta!" He groaned. Reese let out an amazed gasp and looked back at the sentence she had just written. The Prince issued an exasperated sigh and muttered about requiring a manlier favourite colour.

AHEM, said a roughly polite voice near Reese.

Looking up, Reese saw a portly train conductor passing by. She bought a ticket, managing to find a few refugee coins in her coat pocket. The conductor turned to Azalion. The Prince raised an eyebrow, sighed deeply, and produced several very large, extremely heavy copper coins. Each one was intricately engraved, and on each appeared a face like to the features of Azalion, but with more facial hair. The conductor stood dumbfounded. Azalion plucked the ticket from the conductor's outstretched hand while the man stared stupidly at the coins. Azalion turned his attention from the train-man and back to Reese.

"Hang onto that notebook," Azalion warned, setting a grim look on Reese.

The train-man, for reasons he could not comprehend, judged himself to be in the presence of a very influential individual, and realized in the same instant that he had been dismissed.

Reese contemplated Azalion for a moment then quickly scribbled in the notebook again. She looked up and watched expectantly, but Azalion only sat, the same smouldering pout on his face as he scanned the passengers surrounding him — he made no monkey noises, however. She had written that the Prince would suddenly burst out making monkey noises, but...nothing. Reese scribbled in the book again. This time, Azalion immediately stood, offering his seat to a young man who was walking past. The man declined and continued on his way and Azalion resumed his seat. Well, that had worked, Reese thought. Why not the monkey noises? But then...she had written Azalion's character to be dignified. He had, in fact, died a splendidly stately, even honourable death. It would be out of character for him to act like a monkey. Evidently, the notebook had its limits...

Charles stood at his balcony, watching with puzzled interest what appeared to be a historical fair being acted out in the park across the street from his two-story house. Men in armour brandished swords and spears, forming up and breaking rank again. Their clothing and weapons seemed entirely historical. Horses brayed. Horses. Was that even legal in city parks? Who gets to clean up all the — wait, is that a ballista? Charles had a healthy appetite for history books, and had read quite a few in his school years. The siege engine gleamed on the walking path, looking quite brand new. A man with a dog turned onto the walking path, then for some reason spun on his heel and exited the park immediately. The costumed men appeared aimless, as if they were warming up to begin the real performance. They continued to train and parade. How odd. Charles went back inside.

Swift, loud, and furious, came the knock on the door. After a two second hiatus, came another, and louder. Charles shoved the dirty dishes into the washer, then made his way to the front porch. The aged door creaked.

"Reese. What brought you?"

Reese bounded into the small porch, shutting the door and locking it after a young man in black had entered along with her.

"Who is this?" Charles asked, puzzled.

Reese more or less explained the situation. She started with something about a murder and the bit about a spaceship and her apartment exploding then ended the tale with pursuing space pirates and it's likely we will die, and did I mention Grendel exists and he's likely to be the one who will kill us all?

The explanation had rather the same effect on Charles as if someone had slapped his face with a boned fish. He stood there in a state of rational dubiousness, donning a mask of very polite disbelief, as if waiting for an apology for having been just slapped with aforementioned hypothetical halibut.

Azalion determined to take matters into his own hands at that point. "We have no time to explain *properly*," he put in. "For now, let it suffice to say it is vital we repair to a safe location. If you have any—"

Azalion was interrupted by an impertinent yet imposing knock at the door. A knock so loud it may have, in fact, been caused by a group of men swinging a lamppost into the door.

The patterned glass showed only glinting steel and black night beyond. Approaching a nearby window, Azalion slowly tilted the blinds. He immediately replaced them—again, slowly.

"It looks like a party of warriors. They are likely the ones sent to kill Charles," Azalion inferred calmly.

"Sent to—I say. How now, sir?" Charles stuttered out a vague response.

"All we know," Reese explained, "is that everyone who has seen my latest manuscript is ending up dead, or perhaps worse." Reese added, wondering where Earl was. She pictured him cuffed to a chair, left for days in the greasy kitchen of an Asian buffet, unable to eat a thing— his own personal hell.

"Well why would anyone want something so trivial as your manuscript?" Charles' sentence was, at the very least, coherent this time, even if it was espoused in a sort of high-pitched squeal.

"Whatever the reason," Azalion wisely surmised, "the clue to their purpose lies in the manuscript itself. Find it, now. We have to leave," Azalion commanded.

Charles walked halfway to the stairs, returned for his hat and coat which he donned quickly thanks in large part to a pattern learned well through rather obsessive habit, then led the way upstairs to his study.

A thunderous crash echoed throughout the first floor. Charles scooped up the entire manuscript, and in a moment of foresight (plus one extra moment to perfectly line up every page corner) he stapled it all together.

"What now?" Charles queried.

"Is this the highest level of the house?" Azalion asked in a very business-like tone. Chairs could be heard crying out, which was a sure sign of trouble. Save for a minute groan when dragged over a clean floor, chairs generally had no penchant for complaining. But Charles' chairs could be heard writhing in splintered agony on the hardwood floor as they were smashed for entirely no reason what-so-ever by the invading marauders below. Maybe the activity was outlined in the *Ye Olde Requirements As Be Applicated To Pillaging* instruction book that all marauders carried on their person for such times as these, Reese thought.

The only (semi) word that could be torn from Charles' chattering lips was "a-a-attic".

The three were on the stairs again in an instant. They came to a door, not very wide, at the top of a completely wood-coloured, curving staircase. Above was a single round window, as small as a woman's fist, which let in a solitary ray of moonlight, that now illuminated the sole aperture in the wooden door: a keyhole. Charles drew forth a key, but his shaking hands could not find the keyhole. Azalion snatched the key and unlocked the door in a single fluid motion. The door moved easily inward, having no knob, and Azalion then noted how extremely thick the door was. Perhaps the house was older than he would have guessed.

They locked the door behind them, as it seemed the best course of action. The attic was dark, save the diffuse and somewhat meandering moonlight that filtered in from the double French doors at the far side. A balcony extended thither. About the room were scattered boxes and covered furniture, equally scattered. Just off-center of the room, trying its best to look inconspicuous, stood a complete suit of armour. Charles could have sworn he saw it take a self-conscious step backward as all eyes fell on it.

"Funny," Charles began, "I haven't been in this room since I inherited the place from my father, or since he inherited it from his father." Charles composed himself as he spoke. No sound was heard on the steps. Perhaps the medieval men were still busy demolishing the furniture, although no wooden cries of agony were presently heard. Perhaps they were standing around, staring at a magical glowing screen, completely enraptured by the pictures and sounds emanating from it.

"Did your father collect armour?" Reese asked.

"I do not recollect so. Isn't it odd? It surely

is strange to see a cuirass of modern hot-rolled steel. I do not believe it antique."

"Step back," Azalion urged. "There is no dust on that suit of armour."

The two others stood for a moment, trying to figure out just what that might mean. As comprehension dawned, both heads turned slowly to the metal man silhouetted in moonlight.

All at once, a startlingly white light illuminated the apertures in the steel helm, giving the metal face the appearance of a glowing, grinning agent of hell. A mechanical whirring smote the silence. At the same time a voice rang out.

Imagine a voice as sweet as honey topped with more honey, the fairest voice of the purest maiden to ever wander the greenest glades aflutter with white butterflies edged in crimson sunset. Now discard the idea immediately, because this was not that voice.

Like a hue in a colour wheel, so does sound know its antithesis. Conjure up then, the complete complementary opposite of the voice just described. What one hears is a voice, barely so, rasping hoarsely on the eardrums like a file dragged across a violin's strings. What the three heard issue forth from the darkness of the helmet was a sound as oxidized and pitted as rusted metal itself, as though emerging from a corroded throat coated with fine steel dust.

WHO DOTH TRESPASS IN THE

RIGHTFUL DOMAIN OF THE BLOOD ORDER?

The voice demanded an accounting. It also clearly said, in and between those few words, "whoever does not oblige this instant shall be painfully and slowly dismembered through the ages by the most slow and tortuous terrors imaginable". The words could have put a fine edge on a dull knife.

Reese and Charles stood stock-still, staring at the thing with mouths agape. Azalion took one cautionary step forward, placing himself between the two parties. He had lost none of his nerve, wit, or cool aloofness. If he knew fear or doubt, there was absolutely no trace of it in his fierce, boyish eyes (largely because these things had never been written into his character — and a good thing, too, as it happened).

A tense silence ensued. To describe it could have filled three chapters. (For the sake of the Narrative it has been pared down to these two sentences): Freshly disturbed dust drifted through the haze of moonlight that spackled the back wall with a mosaic of window-squares. Three frozen forms faced one, the space in between heavy with unspoken doubts and fears.

"The blood order?" came a second voice. "Give me a break, how do you come up with this crap?" It was an entirely average, strong male voice. It chuckled with incredulous good humour from within the suit of armour.

IT WAS PRETTY GOOD, WASN'T IT? LOOK AT THEIR FACES! The grating voice shambled on, laughing in a manner I shall not describe, for it was a sound so awful and terrifying that it should never be published, even in type form.

"You scared the torque shivs out of them," said the human voice. The suit of armour stepped forward with a clunk, lifting the visor of the helm. Behind the protective armour, lit by an eerie white light cast by several unnatural, diminutive diodes, was the face of a man.

"My name's Matt," he said plainly.

AND I AM SERAIAH, said the other voice.

"If your plan does not involve killing us," said Azalion, "then may I suggest we all adjourn to a safer place immediately." There was both urgency and annoyance in his voice.

Plated feet clanked on the steps. Charles wondered if the siege engine he had seen earlier would fit in the staircase. He ended the consideration with a "probably not" and turned his attention back to finding a means of escape.

"How do we do that? We can't just fly off the third storey," Reese pointed out.

Azalion grinned. "Do you really think we cannot?" was his reply.

The iron plated boots belonging to iron laden men sporting iron-plaited beards could be heard advancing up the narrow stairway among a great deal of jostling of metal. They carried swords and struggled to fit their spears and standards into the small area. Many of the

74

banners displayed frightening arms and fantastic, horrifying creatures. A horse had backed into a closet and could not move for all the pressed bodies on the first floor. The ranks parted, and from the midst of the horde emerged a large middle-aged man, bearded and long-haired. He was dressed in a full suit of plate maille, finely crafted in blued steel. Engraved upon bracer and greave, in a long-dead runic alphabet, were curses of every variety.

"Kepten," he began in a thick accent that lay somewhere South of Norwegian but west of Russian. "Hwhere did dey go?"

"Through this door, My Lord. Three of them," the captain offered just before he stepped back.

"Iss time we hed summ enswers. Bring bettering rem," he commanded.

"Sir, this cloister be much too small. It will not fit," returned the captain.

"Very hwell then," said the large man, scowling a scowl that would have smote the most hardened biker rebel convict into myocardial infarctions. He reached into a sheath at his side, drawing forth a miniscule, less than a pinky-length replica, of a sword. This he proceeded to insert into the keyhole and wiggle about for some minutes, his ear stuck to the ancient wooden door.

A cab pulled up before the house that, while seemingly innocuous by appearance (save the small group of brawny men milling about outside the front door) was, at that moment, brimming with marauders, horses, several assorted people, and one stray dog that had followed the group inside, hoping for a morsel of food. The man in the cab paid the driver, thanked him perfunctorily, and stepped into the sordid pool of amber light pouring down from the nearby streetlamp. The cab pulled away, the cabbie fortunate enough to escape further involvement in events presently unfolding within the unobtrusive-looking house.

The man left standing in the thin beam of anemic light was tall, thin, and as cold as a winter's day on the Canadian prairies. He strode ominously to the door, the ranks of soldiers parting before him like his own personal Red Sea. The hardened battle-veterans who had had the misfortune of meeting this man before were taking particular care to give him space, a fact which, in itself, did not bode well.

Clad in a long grey coat, that matched his long grey suit, the tall pipe cleaner of a man ascended the four steps to the front door. He removed a suspiciously dated-looking fedora and stooped to enter the house.

He said not a word, and not a word was needed in order to make his way through the pressing cluster of men inside. His presence seemed to precede his form like a sickly shadow. A pathway opened before him, whether or not there was room to make one, and brought him to the stairs.

Thmp. Thmp. THMP. The man ascended to the second floor, stopping to observe the study. His fingertips came to rest on the 88 square inches clearly no longer occupied by the manuscript; its outline could be seen in the thin layer of cookie crumbs on the tabletop and the abrupt edge of a coffee stain. A grimly dissatisfied sigh was the only sound to be heard as the man made his way to the third storey.

"Sven, my friend," said the man in a voice thick with duplicity, "how is it that for seven minutes, you have been unable to open this door?"

"Iss too closed fur bettering rem," grumbled the armoured man. "Und du, Jeck, how hest thou feeled to keel thes weakling writer?"

"Firstly, oaf, my name is Jack. Jack Grendel. Do try to enunciate please. Secondly, what in the hell is that?" Jack gestured to the tiny sword.

"Iss door-sword," replied Sven, hearing a small but immensely satisfying click. The door swung inward a fraction. Sven stepped forth to enter, sheathing the door-sword, but Jack placed a hand on his shoulder and easily pulled him back despite Sven's substantial mass.

Jack Grendel drew out a long, shining, and very sharp knife. It was of the full-tang, clipped-tip, single-edged, triple-fullered persuasion, typical of knives used for guerrilla warfare, hunting grizzly bears, or storming trenches at the blood-soaked prows of lever action rifles. It had absolutely no business being in the quiet suburban neighbourhood where Charles lived. Whether or not Jack had had occasion to use it to its full potential on previous escapades is fodder for a different sort of story.

Jack entered the attic, the darkness enveloping him. He welcomed the blackness; he felt that by now it was a familiar part of himself, just as was his shadow. Well used to the inky sightless void, Jack had no trouble seeing the contents of the room, easily reading the titles of the shelved books to his left, and comprehending at a glance that the attic was plainly abandoned. He saw naught but stacked boxes, covered furniture, and a suit of armour standing conspicuously in the center of the room. It seemed to be trying its best to be noticeable in the dim light.

Jack closed the door behind himself, seeking to investigate the escape route taken by his quarry without the bumbling interference of his cretinous counterparts. He advanced two steps into the room, inhaling sharply through his nose. They had been here — most certainly.

Jack stopped. He looked questioningly at the armour. The visor was suddenly aglow with spectral white light. It was then that Jack heard the voice.

WHAT KNAVE DOTH ADVANCE AGAINST THE CLAW OF THE BEAST, THE MOST RAUCOUS RIGHT HAND OF RUIN?

The knife flashed to hand. "That sure is a

nice trick, you audacious automaton," Jack hissed in a snide tone.

The supposedly unoccupied suit struck Jack squarely in the jaw, and he staggered back a pace.

"It's no trick!" Matt jibed from within the armour. The greedy knife lashed twice, but could drink none of the pulsing red life-wine it craved. Rather the cruel blade twanged harmlessly off a sternly wrought brigandine.

A great gauntlet clasped the knife, but Jack would not accede to let go until insistently persuaded to do so by a second iron fist. Clump. Clump. As Jack Grendel pondered whether anything could be done to save his nose (or would have had he retained his powers of ponderality), Matt (or possibly it was Seraiah) clenched the fist that shattered the murderous weapon.

THOU SHALT NOT PURSUE US IF THOU HAST VALUE FOR THY LOATHSOME AND MOST URCHIN-LIKE EXISTENCE. THE BLOOD ORDER SHALL—

"He 'nose' already," Matt mocked the prone attacker. "Let's give him a 'break' shall we?" Matt broke into a bout of unfettered laughter.

I FIND YOUR MODE OF HUMOUR MOST APPALLING.

"Whatever, Sera. Let's get out of here and catch up with the others."

After fumbling unsuccessfully with the

knob for some moments, Matt shouldered his way through the glass balcony door, clumsily apologizing. The suit had a few inconveniences; Matt found himself most days incapable of minute motor functions including the ability to press one button at a time on a television remote and, most inconveniently, using the restroom.

The suit began to shimmy, and rust shook from the back of it in a trail of fine orange powder. From two small apertures on the back of the cuirass sprouted two fin-like wings. Steel feathers, grating like blades, projected as Matt and Seraiah prepared for flight. In a white-hot burst of flame, they were airborne.

King Sven would pick the lock once more in seven minutes, and enter the attic to find the prone form of Jack Grendel, knocked to by a steel-plated right hook. Jack Grendel would rise, spewing blood-spattered curses across the room, and draw another and (if possible) even more cruel knife from his coat.

Troy forsook the warm glow of the record shop, making his way through the cool, moist evening. He was very pleased with his new acquisition: the latest album by new-age electronic-pop-rock group Stereo Bread — on Compact Disc at that. Troy had a brand new Disc player in his apartment — a shoddy two-bedroom he shared with — Nevermind, she left.

Right.

Troy wore a dark leather jacket, jeans

shredded nearly to unrecognizability (well before it was fashionable to wear torn apparel), partially tinted glasses (despite the lack of sunshine) and a pair of worn, beaten, but still brand name Multiversewalk sneakers (kept solely because he liked them too much to throw them out). He owned a car — ten years old, but still running — yet he had chosen to walk the eight blocks to the record shop. The night air was pleasant on his face, and Troy honestly had nothing better to do since — Nevermind, she left. A few raindrops chilled his cheek. Troy looked again at the Disc cover, and because he was fumbling for the next minute to fit the case in his all-leather fanny pack, Troy did not once see the massive battleship sailing above 8th street. As it happened, he also missed the flying man in armour.

Troy reached his apartment and climbed through the halls that smelled not at all like stale cigarette smoke and the inside of old beer bottles. A few uninterpretable black marks decorated the no smoking sign. Troy opened the door (apartment 476) and kicked aside Nevermind's shoes — she hadn't collected much of anything when she had stormed out early last week. She would likely be back, Troy inferred. Maybe he ought to clean up the place, he thought, considering it as the thirteenth herculean task.

Troy cared for the girl — heaven knows — but life with Nevermind was one long, sadistic magic trick: now she wanted him, now she didn't. Unfortunately for Troy, the girl was entirely too attractive and wily to give him any slim hope of not being sawn in half. Finally, he had said 'no' to her. He had stated that it wouldn't last (just like last time) and that he did not want to be her passive plaything (again, like last time). That 'no' had lasted 46.25 hours before Troy had dialed her number.

Troy and Nevermind had known each other since high school — and — wow — were they bad at romance back then. Things were somewhat different now — or were they, Troy wondered. Probably not. Nevermind claimed to want to be with Troy, yet could never say the three words he needed to hear.

So what if he had broken up with her on her birthday — stuff happens, right? The circumstances had been extenuating, and Troy had very much needed a break and time to think. The two were soon back together. Troy had thought she was over it, after all it had been eight months ago, and they had been doing all right since then. He had even bought her flowers — he had never bought flowers in his life!

Perhaps the breakup had shaken her faith in Troy. Her attitude for the past few weeks had been cold and toneless. Her efforts at holding up the relationship were on par with those of a wet string. Not that Troy held himself blameless — there were plenty of times he had not been there for her and he would very much have liked to apologize to her for that.

Instead, Troy had given up.

If any of his friends had asked him if he were over her now, he would have replied with confident indifference, but he was only too keenly aware that Nevermind would continue to hurt him more deeply than she knew. Again, Troy blamed himself unreservedly — this time he blamed himself for being such a fool.

I guess I won't get another crack at her birthday. I wonder how much that ring will go for.

Troy collapsed on his decaying couch. He was on a self-imposed hiatus from friends, from work, even from his regular espresso habit, and he now had the headache to prove it. He had scarce left the apartment and the television save to procure more instant food and soda pop. He had, however, considered going to the arcade sometime. Heaven forbid someone should beat one of his high scores without Troy being there to defend it. Troy was quite shut off from the world, left alone with an old and abused guitar, and he had no intention of leaving his fortress of solitude any time soon.

Troy's descent into sloth was clearly evident. The coffee table was littered with empty beverage containers and chip boxes. Candy wrappers marked a trail, bread-crumb style, to the kitchen lest Troy should become lost amidst the moldering Asian food containers and be unable to locate the mostly empty bowl that harboured the candy. Dead pizza boxes were slowly accumulating in a stone wall / battlement formation surrounding the garbage can to stave off any thoughts of productivity, and a spray-pattern of cookie crumbs provided the necessary insulation from intruding phone calls for the couch's lone occupant. Sanitation workers would likely have bagged and shipped off the apartment's entire contents — perhaps even Troy himself.

Piles of videocassettes lined a few shelves, most of them recorded from the television and labeled in a wretchedly faded off-black marker that was more of a purple colour after a day or two. Troy liked to think he had everything he could need — a stereo with cassette and disc player, VCR, a large tube television set and, of course, the computer. An oversized grey box, the thing sat on a desk and did little most days except eject what were then called, Flimsy Discs, and play a strange matching game. Troy reveled in the new frontier he had discovered, and had read three books on computers so far.

Troy knew, however, that his life was still missing one thing. Troy reached for one of the many pop cans on the table, but found it empty. Make that two things. He sighed, and for the next 57.4 minutes, Stereo Bread echoed his feelings satisfyingly concisely in a screeching blast of guitar with a wicked back beat on the drums.

Reese paused to wonder if fictitious winged lions, like fairies, died if you doubted their existence. She decided she did not want to risk finding out just at that moment as that would mean a sudden suspension at 80 000 feet with only one means of landing: abruptly. Instead she clung to Azalion and hoped that he, at least, would remain tangible until she was safely on the ground again.

The lion had appeared just when Reese thought the marauders would force the door in. Alighting on the balcony with an incredible *swoosh,* and leaving room there for naught else, the creature had greeted Azalion with a friendly growl. The beast stood at least half again as tall as a regular lion, and was snowy white everywhere except the wingtips which boasted all the pastel water colour shades that might appear in any nice children's story book. The eyes of the huge lion, though black as night, seemed ablaze with a latent fire of ancient wisdom.

Azalion easily swung onto the lion's back. The beast pranced and bucked, as if eager to fly or simply glad to see its master. Azalion muttered a few strange words in its ear and it calmed, waiting for the next two passengers. Reese and Charles scrambled, fighting one another for second place in boarding.

Charles pushed Reese forward and she hesitantly touched the lion's fur: though bristly, it was nevertheless soft to the touch. The animal was quite well groomed. Her hand on its flank, Reese could feel the vibrations of its deep breathing resonating through its colossal frame. She stepped up unsteadily, and clung to Azalion.

It had taken some minutes to convince

Charles to actually clamber aboard the majestic creature's back. The lion had watched Charles comprehendingly as he took his place behind Reese. Charles stuttered and issued several unintelligible sounds that might loosely have been interpreted as a generalized misgiving regarding the entire idea. Abrupt footsteps were heard on the stairs and Reese pulled Charles on behind her. The trio was airborne before he had finished his incomprehensible, utterly nonsensical non-sentence.

The steady wing-beat held Azalion, Reese, and Charles aloft. Naught could be seen before or behind, clouds obscuring all visibility. The wind raced through hair and danced under coats, deathly chill at their present altitude. Reese may have shrieked, for sheer delight or terror she knew not, but the force of the wind shoved the unborn cry back down her throat with a halting breath.

Charles was gasping for air behind her, his breathing amounting to mere gulps of air, punctuated in his own head by the throbbing beat in his temples. He briefly wondered if the others heard it too. Azalion seemed entirely unperturbed, like a cold, emotionless theme park veteran boarding a roller coaster with a class of queasy kindergarteners.

The lion continued to gain altitude, clawing at the air with massive paws. The handsome beast proved a most capable steward of its three charges.

A short distance away, an airline pilot looked out a window and three days later resigned for medical reasons.

Somewhere else again, long spindly fingers were pressed together before a sly mouth that spoke but one word, married to a maniacal chuckle: "Eh-he-he-xcellent".

Chapter 4:

Indeprecabilis

The barbed cat 'o nine tails descended upon the resolutely unfortunate war-prisoner, its nails and frayed leather slicing into the cords of his defiantly-muscled back. *Forty-seven*. The unshakably rugged warrior knelt silently, giving voice to not one cry of the agony written upon every observing face. *Forty-eight*. The white marble floors became spattered with a vivid red. Still the torturer did not let up. The torturer believed that pain was a means to edify the souls of men. *Forty-nine*. In the corner of the room, a man smiled wickedly, tightly gripping a trapezoid hidden in the folds of his cloak. *Fifty*. The torturer and his two attendants retired, allowing the beaten man to sink to the cold floor amidst his own blood.

King Sven watched from a throne of chiseled stone, his eyes portraying no emotion. Standing near to the throne was the most beautiful woman in the entire city of Aotz: Tsarmina Pulcharis—a prisoner despite her lack of restraints. Of all the observers, her eyes only were brimmed with tears.

"You see, frind. My min hev teken everyting you hev. Your frinds hev deserted you. Your war was fought for nothingk. Why do you continue to defy me?" King Sven drawled in his thick accent, a mix of every televised portrayal of mid-European cinema villains.

The bloodied warrior struggled to rise, despite collapsing upon his first effort. He pushed himself up again. Stripped of weapons, of nearly all clothing, he grimaced for the fresh stripes on his back. The only answer he made was a blend of blood and saliva, projected in the general direction of the throne. He looked to his beautiful betrothed, as if waiting for her approval. She nodded imperceptibly.

A fighter to the bone, Bainan strode toward his enemy. As Bainan predicted, nay depended upon, a guard intercepted him. Pulling the armoured guard close by the shoulder, Bainan landed a fist on the large man's jaw, but he may as well have struck the Celestial Citadel itself. The guard, appearing not to notice the blow, dealt Bainan a mighty requital with the brass hilt of his sword. Bainan stumbled and collapsed face down on the floor.

"Und what hev you accomplished, my frind?" came a mocking voice. Bainan loosed his bloodied lips, uttering a hoarse and satisfied laugh. Tears freely flowed down the pale cheeks of the captive princess, as she watched her helpless beloved stain the floor red with his heart's love for her.

"As long as my princess and I both live, neither will have any other," Bainan was confident, convinced, convicted. The woman before him, even when persecuted, was faithful through and through. The grim set of her jaw, despite the tears staining her lovely face, only confirmed his assertion. King Sven scowled.

"Tekk hem ewey," came the pronunciation of doom. For when Sven uttered these words, scarce was a victim ever seen again. The preferred method of execution was a swift beheading with a square-tipped sword, specially made for the purpose. The trend later shifted to dungeon torture, or when Sven was in a particularly bad mood, live incineration.

Tsarmina felt her stomach leap and her heart stutter. Were her hero taken beneath the castle, she could very possibly never see him again. Could her love be so easily defeated? Had Bainan Wolfblood, slayer of armies, conqueror of castles, been stymied thusly by a mere citadel guard? She stared with a pained and longing expression at the wounded man on the floor. No, he wouldn't be. The princess decided it could not be. Tsarmina knew that his courage and bravery were far too great to be contained in the torturous pit beneath the tower. If it took him ten lonely years, thirty even, he would find her again.

The guard sheathed his sword, approaching the prone prisoner prince. Reaching down, the guard dragged Bainan harshly to his feet.

Pulling the guard suddenly close, Bainan hissed out a hoarse war-cry, heard by only a single man. The guard gasped and collapsed to the floor, his own dagger protruding from his breast. Already in Bainan's hand, the guard's faithless cut-and-thrust sword gleamed lustily, anxious to redeem its name. Bainan gave vent to a tremendous, crazed laugh, determined to give a mighty account for himself. This would, if not save his princess, go down in lore as the bloodiest battle for revenge ever undertaken by mortal man.

Armoured figures flooded in through every entrance, and the real battle began. Bainan leapt and dodged, hacking and hewing left and right. The swordplay rang from cold walls and echoed in the towers. The palace guard seemed unable to match the half-mad warrior, yet Bainan knew it was only a matter of time before his own mangled and lacerated corpse adorned the palace floor for the sport of his assembled enemies. The notion only spurred him to fight as he never had fought before.

A neon sign proclaimed the restaurant to be "pen". Despite the late hour, the greasy fires continued to fill the air with a smell that announced, "you may die if you eat this stuff, but we all know you really want it and you're going to anyway". At any rate, the owner appreciated the free advertising that wafted into the street, luring weak-willed customers to their protracted deaths while at the same time repeatedly filling his cash drawer.

A man sitting alone at the bar (let's call him Bill), well known in the area for being a loudmouth and one quick to bicker, felt a soft and likely accidental shove on his shoulder. He whirled in a flurry of self-righteous indignation, made slightly less intimidating by the blur of alcohol that spun the room groggily around him.

About to thoroughly berate his presumed adversary, Let's-Call-Him-Bill stopped short when he noticed the five-foot claymore hanging at the other man's side. Let's-Call-Him-Bill considered his options, then mumbled a quick "m'sorry" and bumbled out the door. He made out quite well, considering he was wide of the mark by eight feet or so. Somehow he managed to locate the door and exit the building, not even breaking the window in his unwitting act of defenestration.

The burly newcomer slammed a large, empty tumbler noisily upon the counter. His long chestnut hair, looking more like something a cat had played to death, rolled on, and dragged through the mud before actually dragging it in, partially covered his cold, keen eyes. A group of men he had with him, all doughty, stocky men with the build of war-galley oarsmen. The apparent leader grinned, all white teeth, and drooling only slightly onto an unshaven chin.

"Most honorable inn-keep! Let the ale be as plentiful as the water of the Norr, the mighty river, home to the Naiads of Nerenola!" The other men, rattling shortswords in their sheaths, cheered heartily. The barman, thinking this to be simply another drunken college party, obliged without the slightest acknowledgement for the strange manner and dress of his guests.

Bainan the Bold, conqueror of the Seven Realms, Prince of Perennia, continued to consume cheap, partially alcoholic beverages in

"Bertram's Brewery" on Leonard Street. Indeed, he had drunk enough to put five men on the grimy floor, and to the barman's astonishment showed no sign of slowing or of any change in temperament. Nor did any of his companions. This suited the barman quite nicely as he anticipated their ongoing consumption and a quickly filled till.

Could any man fathom the mind of Bainan Wolfblood, he would discern nothing but a vague fog containing these three notions: must drink; must fight; must princess rescue. It was more or less the same regardless of his level of sobriety. The case was not that when drunk he could function in a sober manner; rather, even when sober, his mind was nothing but a vague, vacuous den, not unlike an empty mead hall.

However, one must only weigh the means and the end. It could also be said to his credit that he knew no fear, nor did he know any cowardice. In fact, he had not a cowardly bone in his body; his mother had removed them with a flint knife when Bainan was only two days old.

Yet, glancing down at his empty glass, Bainan was, for the first time in his life, at an impasse. It seemed that his princess could not be found and, thusly, could not be rescued, leaving him only two directives to pursue. This posed somewhat of a problem for Bainan, for the men under Bainan's command, you must understand, were good at only two things: drinking and fighting—and they were nearly finished the former.

Reese caught a glimpse, through the airborne fog, of something quite otherworldly. This new development was wrought in wood, with a sleek, graceful hull and three masts set to full sail. It was exceedingly strange, Reese thought, to see an old-timey galleon in this day and age. The truly more odd fact that it was flying only just then occurred to her. She deliberated what laws of physics she could muster from her ignoble attempt at high-school science, but the ship apparently also did not understand physics itself, and so ignored the laws out of hand.

How is it flying?

Reese did not get an answer for quite a while. When she finally did, it came from a grimy sailor garbed in clothes that seemed entirely the colour of used oil. Possibly, if thoroughly washed, this man would be found to wear no clothing whatsoever beneath the grime. His accent, utterly foreign to Reese, made any sensible answer he may have given completely incomprehensible. Reese merely smiled vaguely, thanked the engineer sweetly, and left. The first engineer turned to the second.

"Opp schwey unnace wannn, enthci tink?"

"Orrtink ooshaw oryorworrk," griped his superior.

Yet none of this was of relevance as all physics and even common sense was steadfastly overwritten and the winged lion on which Reese and the others rode continued to fly toward the great soaring galleon. As they were drawing steadily nearer to the ship, Reese deduced that they might indeed be landing on it.

Reese wondered if the crew were friends or foes. Shifting her logic into reverse, Reese figured that since she was currently riding a lion belonging to Azalion, who had rescued her, and who was also the one who chose the destination, it ought to be all right—he could have left her to the space-pirates, after all. Besides, had he wished her harm he could have turned her into a potted plant or something worse.

Shoot, it would suck to be a potted plant. I would have to just sit there and hope Macy came around with a watering can now and then.

However, Reese' overly imaginative brain was unwilling to simply stop at the "if he had meant to harm me" cop-out. It continued down the following rabbit hole: a victim is always more agreeable when he or she volunteers, despite minor doubts, to follow one who merely wishes to harm him or her at their own convenience. Perhaps he was under orders to kidnap her, or bring her to his leader. Reese' head popped back up out of the warren and she was left back where she started, wondering optimistically about what manner of people she was about to meet.

"What is the meaning of this?" asked Charles, who seemed to have found his wits, though where, nobody knew—he rarely kept them on his person. His question evidently did not warrant an answer. Instead, Azalion merely guided the lion into a steep dive, alighting effortlessly on the deck of the craft.

The galleon was larger than it appeared. Much larger. Had the titanic been looking up from its watery, shark-infested mooring, it should have turned green with envy (had it not already been so from the corrosion). It would then resume its own business of slowly decaying, muttering grimly that any boat worth its salty keel ought to have at least one pool on board, and drat that scurvy owner who dared God to sink the largest ship ever built. But for that, He likely wouldn't have hidden that iceberg in light reflections of his own creation and doomed the pawn of a ship. Thanks indeed.

The flying galleon was squarely two city blocks long, and seven decks deep. However, the sheer breadth of sailcloth dwarfed the hull completely, affording the craft an impressive canopy of golden cloth. Had any shipwright been present, he should have remarked upon the remedial nature of the fore'ard topgallant. However ostentatious, the ship soared along gracefully.

The lion touched down, softly as a kitten despite its weighty load, upon the deck of the galleon. The arriving party was quickly surrounded by uniformed officials, all of whom were bristling with musketry and various friendly-looking bladed implements eager to make one's acquaintance.

"Azalion..." Reese said dubiously, leaving him to extrapolate her unfinished question.

In answer, the prince slid from the lion's back, patting it amiably. The ranks of men parted, the officials briefly dropping to one knee.

"Hail, prince!" came the hoarse, haughty cry of many hearty sailors. The little finger of a cold dawn, as though atomized in a gracefully colour-corrected sepia mist, managed to touch the scene. Morning light gleamed coolly from the steel accoutrements adorning the assembled men-at-arms.

Reese exhaled in surprise, at a loss for words. How did she not recognize the splendid airborne carrack? Of course, it was the *Aura Regency Hide*! The ship had appeared in one of her early science fiction-fantasy novels. It had met its demise ablaze, downed to shatter against a mountain having finally destroyed the enemy but not without meeting a sacrificial end itself.

The ranks parted, revealing a silent figure, silhouetted in a solemn haze. Striding forward, the looming figure called out:

"My prince! Where art thou?" The speaker, now that they could see him, was clad like the others; he wore a cloak of velvety navy, so inky blue it was almost black. His helm, removed in deference to his master, shone of gilt silver. His face was adorned with every mark of wisdom, tracing white lines of cherished experience of the most arduous kind. His mail and plate armour was of a light metal that did not glimmer.

"Uncle!" returned Azalion. The two shook hands, then the elder drew the younger into an embrace. A cry went up among the sailors.

"Hail, the king's son returns! Hail, the king's son returns!" Their deep voices rang out across the deck.

The custodian of Azalion turned to Reese, addressing her in a tone so serious it was nearly severe. "Art thou the storyteller, lady?"

A silence descended upon the decks and all eyes pinned Reese to the spot. Reese's gaze darted about, reading in each helmeted face what she could not tell. They regarded her with looks of perhaps curiosity, or possibly fear. Reese became very afraid, and looked to Azalion, who only stood silently beside his uncle, awaiting her answer along with the others.

"Y-yes. I-I am," Reese replied quietly, not knowing what the reaction would be.

Silence reigned. Will they blame me, Reese wondered, for everything that had gone wrong in the city this week? Will they blame me for being suddenly jolted from their own lives by some impossibly supernatural force? It could hardly be *her* fault that they were here! This could have happened to any mediocre, demi-popular novelist. She found herself suddenly grateful that this type of thing never happened to horror-thriller, blood-spilling action writers like Ken Peghints, who wrote books about psychotically convincing rapists and murderers. In fact, it made one wonder what that man really did when not writing books. Was his fictional life just a cover to boast of otherwise untold atrocities? At any rate, Reese was glad that there were no power-tool hockey-mask men running about.

Right. Back to the present. *I think someone's talking to me*, Reese thought.

" —if you will come with me, there is something you may wish to see," finished Azalion's uncle.

Reese made no reply and offered no resistance (given the scores of men toting halberds she immediately discounted the idea of refusing), simply falling in line behind the tall man. Charles glanced about and, appearing to choose the rock as opposed to the hard place, followed behind Reese.

Azalion's uncle led the way to a lower deck, Azalion at his heels. This is definitely bad, Reese thought. Have I escaped the pirates, or just run right to them? They will likely try to ransom me, then kill me when they find out I'm not actually worth anything. How much money does Macy have? Shoot. The most I could afford to ransom her with, were our places reversed, is a mere couple hundred dollars. Perhaps if that amount were cashed in one dollar coins, it would look more impressive in a steel chest. These buffoons likely won't know they have been duped—I was never very specific about their treasure. That is likely the best option. Reese decided she would get the amount in one and five cent coins, just to be on the safe side.

The room below was dim and claustrophobically close. Reese' fears escalated from kidnapping to torture. Did she know anything that she shouldn't? She could simply volunteer the information now, to save every one the time, effort and well, pain. She'd certainly blab anything at even the sight of a drill or tooth-puller. Hmmm... Political science classes probably aren't the stuff of valuable intelligence. Perhaps it was something she didn't know she knew, something she had witnessed in the past week. *What do I not know?*

To Reese' devout relief, she found herself not in a blood-soaked, light choked torture chamber. Rather, looking about the room she realized it was actually the ship's mess hall. Three rows of simple wooden tables lined the great hall; even below, the ship was colossal. Several officers sat eating, evidently on break. Among them, laughing, wearing a blue cloak that could only just barely be said to fit him, was Earl. Reese nearly cried out with delight and relief, two emotions suddenly thrust upon her in a cascade of surprise and shock.

Earl was engaged in his favourite pastimes (laughing, story-telling, and eating) with three of the ship's officers. He looked up when Reese called his name, and laughed out a light greeting. Charles also greeted him warmly.

After that, Reese and Charles sat with Earl and the officers for a number of hours. They were brought food and drink of a strange yet delicious variety, and were soon full and comfortable. They told each other the tales of the past day and a half, of escapes and chases and new friends. Eventually they retired for the night, were shown to separate guest quarters (of which there were many) and fell fast asleep. For eighty thousand feet above the surface of earth, there is no seasickness or difficulty sailing. Azalion watched them leave the mess hall from a shadow in the corner; in fact, the only gloomy shadow in the whole room was the one he chose to occupy.

"Come, uncle Quercius. We have plans to discuss."

Jed reached his apartment building. In a shoddy neighbourhood, Jed had received exactly what he paid for. It was that, or end up like officer Jennings, remorse and despair passing through his mind only brief moments before the bullet. The fatal shot had been fired by Jenning's own hand, owing to the homicidal interest rates he had faced buying his first house and the resulting mortgage payments only finalized after the sale. No, Jed thought, he couldn't end up like Jennings. And Richard. And Dickson. And...

The eternally unchanging hallway lighting, independent of any sunlight and disrespectful of open doors, coaxed Jed into believing that it could still be four in the afternoon. He could have just left the office, sunlight glinting blindingly on every glass surface and automobile. He let his mind wander.

Perhaps he had stopped in at the coffee shop, and Joyce had smiled sweetly at him. Maybe she even slipped her number in with his change, or Jed could have finally collected the nerve to ask her out.

Reality, however, was a drifting schooner of a different cut of sail.

What a day it had been. The dark apartment greeted Jed coldly and with some reluctance, the door protesting Jed's arrival with a resonating scrape against its frame. It didn't much like to be disturbed by being called into action, and it recognized Jed as both the only person who ever interrupted its internal musings (the previous tenant had been a philosophy major and had given the door quite a lot to think about) and also a person with very cold hands. Jed was going to turn the bolt, but due to the dark he couldn't quite find it on the bookshelf next to the door. In the end, his inadvertent security tactic was to accidentally knock over the recycling bin, filling the doorway with empty soda cans. At least they would make noise, Jed rationalized.

The time was 1:34 am. Jed stroked the back of his sleek, black cat. The porcelain cat did not feel his touch nor in any way acknowledge that its master was home, but then, neither did it beg for food, claw at his drapery (such as they were) or vomit on his carpet (again, such as it was), so Jed considered it a fair trade-off.

"This place is a mess," Jed observed to his cat. "Pretty pathetic existence, hey puss?"

The porcelain cat wisely made no reply.

The bedroom was lit by a vacant, blue television screen. It must have been left on. Jed flopped face down on a cot that scarce supported his weight, sinking into a stupor and letting the events of his evening roil up around him in a cloud of swirling thoughts.

It had been a normal day until he had spotted the soaring space ship. In fact, the occurrence had rather contrarily defibrillated Jed's day, shocking it out of its rhythm. Jed had been involved in crowd control for the next 3.9 hours, plus organizing a cleanup after that. The army had considered showing up, but as it turned out, they had a prior engagement meddling in the affairs of a foreign country. They decided that their time, blood and bullets would be better expended elsewhere and left the problem of a massive space sloop sallying over Sixth Street to the diligent efforts of the local constabulary. After sifting through all the rubble and calming the chaos, Jed still wondered if he had dreamed the entire affair, but no matter how hard he tried, he was unsuccessful in washing his brain of the memory.

After the initial volley of artillery and obliterating one side of the apartment building, the ship had circled the complex twice. Jed had watched, on the radio with one of his superiors, lacking both the words and the diction to describe the situation accurately. Jed found his imagination as well as his vocabulary stretched to its absolute limit.

"That's right sir. A space ship. Yes, sir. Downtown. No, I haven't been sir, not a drop…" Jed put down the radio. He tested his coffee once more. Unfortunately, it was certainly not the culprit. Jed searched the sky again, and the bones in his neck made a wretched crunching noise that echoed about his head, not unlike that of rubber tires on loose gravel. The ship had vanished. Jed looked all about, just to be sure. Then he looked again. Where a moment ago the sky was filled with groaning metal, hissing pipes, and screaming engines, only the stars could now be seen, stabbing faintly through a layer of sickly grey cloud.

"Hucking fell," Jed didn't quite manage to swear under his breath. He wondered then how he ought to explain calling in a disappearing spaceship to his superiors. Very slowly, he decided — and carefully too, maybe.

The scene took 3.75 more hours to wrap up. Present had been plenty of witnesses, and they testified alongside the cavernous craters in the building, the remaining pieces of which seemed to be queuing up to protest its recent treatment. All the evidence summed up, vaguely implicated that Jed wasn't quite a lying lunatic, nor in fact, inebriated. Jed was very grateful for that. For this reason, he was spared the skin-searing, soul-searching, over-the-glasses glare from Officer Chambers. The old man must live for that glare, thought Jed, he does it better than he does his job.

A staring contest had ensued between Chambers and his unruly subordinate, Hanson. Chambers had always held an odious suspicion that Hanson harboured ideas far above his station. Hanson also used words like *obsequious* and *fatuous* — words Chambers didn't particularly care for — largely because he had no idea what they meant. He had pinned Hanson with his icy gaze, daring him to utter a single adjective with more than four letters. Those spectating the event had soon become bored from all the waiting around and left. Hanson and Chambers remained, likely with no idea what they had originally disagreed about as their veins bulged in their temples. Faces red, and foreheads streaming with sweat, the two men glared each other down long into the night. Naught could be confirmed later about the subsequent events of that night, save that the four-a.m. custodian arrived to find an unconscious Hanson sprawled on the floor.

Jed sighed. The ride back to the station was wearisome. The radio blathered on about some madman in the park with a broadsword and a great lot about a marauding hoard. Or something. Jed tried to come up with a second reason to like the city. What would be next? Cowboys maybe? It would be a welcome relief and might be mildly entertaining. From sheer exhaustion, Jed chuckled an octave or two higher than normal. He immediately decided that he had been awake for far too long. He held firmly to that idea until 1:46, right before he passed out for the night.

A few miles and several hours' drive away stood an innocuous looking warehouse. A shambling wreck of a building, which could only have been barely engineered by some half-wit first year architecture student, as it seemed in danger of imminent collapse. Yet this was not the most notable feature of this steel shack, buried in a long-deserted industrial district. What struck one the most was the lack of anything at all striking about the warehouse; the building seemed to have no recommendable, objectionable, redeemable, or discernable features whatsoever. The fact was plain: the building looked too obviously abandoned to be truly empty.

Nor was it.

Headlights approached, piercing the rain-speckled fog with despondent yellow eyes, a black gaping socket where one of the running lights ought to have been—an unfortunate result of the bicycle incident. In all fairness, the car (in that instance, at least) was blameless, which made the injury all the more egregious. The car was still churlish about it.

The taxi stopped before the absolutely featureless building, allowing for the egress of a tall man in dark attire—the sort that drips into the shadows cast at its owner's feet. The cab remained for some minutes, the driver presumably counting the rather large tip the man had left him — then was gone.

Jack Grendel knocked faintly at a slightly open door. Pushing the steel door to with a cringingly loud creak, Jack entered the dark space beyond.

Perhaps an anemic light painted the obsidianite blackness a faint grey, and perhaps the under-stimulated eyes of Grendel were simply guilty of wishful looking. Yet there were other senses with which to penetrate the darkness. Grendel strained his hearing, discerning a shuffle somewhere to his left. So, the board has been set and the game was on.

My move.

Grendel crouched, scuffling his foot too clearly to be mistaken. From the darkness came the sound of footsteps. They clacked confidently on the floor, coming straight toward Jack. *The fools*, Grendel thought, smirking, *they took the bait.*

"Here he is," came a voice, "Mr. Grendel, allow us to —"

SWOOSH. SWCKCHCH.

A gut-wrenching sound split the darkness, requiring only consonants to convey its chilling effect. Grendel's blade spoke quietly but assertively, staining his assailant's clothing with a grisly and presumably (it was quite dark) red stain. A dampened *thud* reached the sharp ears of the killer. Many more feet could now be heard, and Grendel perceived that he was surrounded.

Just then a match was struck, a lantern lit.

Jack found himself standing dumbly over the form of a man dressed in a tunic, sword still sheathed. Glancing up he saw, King Sven and his host, along with a group of men with holstered revolvers, mud-caked boots and impressively large hats. Jack averted his eyes from their invariably soiled neckerchiefs.

"Well, that was unfortunate," came a sly female voice, dripping with irony and gleeful spite. "Threatened beasts truly hold no loyalty." A seductive snicker followed.

Jack stared remorselessly down at the bleeding form lying prone on the cement at his feet. King Sven did the same, as did all his men. An unspoken "oops" did not drift through the dead air and was not heard by Sven's men. Furthermore, their eyes did not turn accusingly on Jack, who therefore did not ignore the glares. King Sven removed his helm, turning with deference toward the woman who had spoken.

Perched with impeccable, perfectly poised posture on a wooden crate, the woman crooned callously over the cold corpse. She was young in appearance, possessing a sultry visage, sweeping raven hair, a slender figure that was round enough in just the right places, and an expression in her eyes devoid of all warmth or depth. Her dark eyes glinted with an animated malice and a keen cunning.

"This must be the notorious Jack Grendel," she cooed coaxingly, pandering pitilessly to Grendel's pride and ego.

Of course he was proud of his notoriety. But distrust had sown deeper roots in his heart.

"And I suppose we are all waiting for Cadenza to simply hand herself over?" Jack groused in a steely voice, cleaning his bloodied knife on the tunic of a nearby man-at-arms. The soldier wisely made no protest nor, in fact, did he seem to mind. The stain was at home among many others of the same congealing brown colour.

The woman laughed, deigning to finally relinquish her station on the crate. She executed a flawless slide from her makeshift throne. Contrary to many laws of physics, she landed solidly and without hesitancy on a single stiletto heel (she tended to ignore the laws of physics, having encountered them once. The less said of that tryst, the better) and strode forward with complete confidence in the 5-inch spikes on which she moved. The ranks of soldiers parted before her, an undertaking which savoured strongly of fear.

"Peace, dearest Grendel," she beamed, "or have you lost your faith in us so soon?" Her tone was mockingly petulant.

"My faith lies in hardened steel," muttered the killer, "and the results I see before me." Grendel still clutched the long, slender knife. The blade looked sinisterly incomplete, as if it ought to have a bloodied lever-action rifle attached to the pommel.

"Normally I would punish a disobedient

animal, but then we've not been properly introduced so I may pardon you — this time," mused the woman casually. "My Lord Ignes has left such decisions to my sole judgment. I, Ustrina of the Frozen Flame, could smite you for such arrogance," the sorceress teased toyingly.

Ustrina stalked toward Jack, her long dress clinging to her form like a shadow. The dress was a midnight blue, and interrupted briefly at her shoulders before the cascade of dark fabric was resumed by a matching pair of long gloves. Trapped by his fraudulent confidence, Jack would betray no weakness by backing down. Instead, he merely crossed his arms and adopted a passive stance, the blade in his hand, unaggressively palmed yet dangerously present.

Ustrina stood but two feet from Jack. He would never show it, but something in her depthless, piercing eyes made him very uncomfortable. Stock still he stood, betraying no sign of fear — or so he thought.

Ustrina tilted her head and smiled sagaciously. Reaching out she stroked Jack's cheek like a mother petting an adorable child. Jack shuddered — her touch was deadly cold! Even gloved, her fingers seemed like cascading ice-water as she traced his living skin. Ustrina gripped the bare knife blade. Jack hissed and let go as the temperature of the metal dropped several dozen degrees in the space of a second. With a smug grin, Ustrina fiddled with the confiscated weapon. The metal was seen to condensate, then steam as when ice meets warm water. Jack glared. Ustrina blinked. She dropped the knife to the floor, and smiled when she heard it shatter.

"Very well, sweet Jack. Judge with your eyes and your heart, and you shall know the truth."

The woman stalked off.

"We hev contingency." The interlocutor was King Sven.

"A *contingency*, you say?" Jack sneered. "And could they, you brutish knave, even articulate that word in your world of savages?"

King Sven fumed silently, glaring at Grendel. The latter only smirked in reply, fingering another long knife sheathed inside his coat.

"We vill get the story-teller and her peppers," Sven insisted. "She vill do whet we want. We hev *contingency*."

Chapter 5:

Morbochalyb

That's right. My name is Matt Ferren. Up until yesterday, I was just a station security officer on the District 65 space station colony. I had a date last night, too. Never happened. Who knows, she might have been the one. I'll never know now.

Outer space is a lifeless void, a hurtling maelstrom of fire and ice. The searing radiation afterglow cuts a balmy minus 233 degrees like a knife. Living in a pressurized can, many days at a time are spent breathing recycled air in minimal gravity conditions. But as bad as that is, earth was in worse shape. Our end was not brought about by aliens, zombies, or mindless robots like every science fiction movie predicted. Our undoing was ultimately our humanity, leading to a world overpopulated with bad decisions and starving multitudes.

Work had been chaos lately, but that morning was normal. Strangely normal. I had woken up, unstrapped myself from a wall-cot in the minimum-gravity wing, and made some coffee (I won't even tell you how hard that is in a powerless artificial gravity setting, nor will I describe the taste of the stuff). As I reached the core decks, the gravity got stronger. I put on my uniform and seldom-used sidearm—electric of course, no hurtling lead allowed in a sealed tin of oxygen and carbon/hydrogen-based life forms—and checked in at the security depot. It's about a ten-minute walk from my quarters. There are no vehicles on the station, just elevators and a few rail lines.

Everybody on board is there to work. The focus is building the D65 colony, on some small nowhere planet (it was actually more of a meteor) found hurtling through the void. Colonists, like cattle, would eventually be herded to the planet for propagation and preservation. Ice was present in small quantities on the barren rock, as well as iron, so the 'planet' was deemed inhabitable. Sometimes I wondered if I made the right choice, leaving 43 and coming here, but you have to pick the pile of rock you want to die on. When humanity picks up and exits earth in every direction, it's hard to know which direction is the right one.

Trent was already at the station. He was tearing through his standard breakfast of one protein bar and a glass of dehydrated milk. If there is any good thing about deep space life, it is that the lifestyle rather eliminates the burden of decision-making. One set of clothes, one meal, one job. That's all you get. That's all there's room for. The last time Trent had an original idea, it had been a disaster—you could still see the dent in the ceiling.

The first order of business: security duty. Check these forty workers, repatriate lost prox cards, confiscate unauthorized tools and weaponry—the usual. A shuttle would shortly embark to the planet's surface, taking the poor fools down for the non-negotiable thirty-hour shift. I rather humbly appreciated my job. The only complaint I could make most days alone in the security post was that my legs fell asleep from all the sitting around.

The shift had hitherto gone smoothly, considering that some of our beloved workers were barely better than cosmic ex-con castaways.

The security crews consisted mainly of military rejects. These were the guys that never quite cut it for the real deal: the heart-breaking, life-taking Interstellar Naval corps. Sometimes I felt the entire station was just a landfill for all the garbage cast off by society, and that I had wandered into by mistake. At least, I fervently hoped I didn't belong here.

My story was little better, though. I left a decaying earth thinking that subsisting in space might be less of a misery. After my father was laid in the earth-resembling silicon dust, there was no reason to stay. I had seen enough of earth to sadden any man's soul. On Earth, life was cheaper than the air needed to sustain it. Humans, children even, had become just a resource. Nobody seemed to care for anything anymore. All those virtues I had read about—courage, loyalty, and honour—seemed to be little more than ideas called on to pardon violence and crime. No one could find a love worth fighting for, and the very word had only become a euphemism for its physical counterpart. I suppose as bad as the station was, it was still better than what I left behind. I would never return to the Earth I had left.

The real problem began around noontime: the vending machine in the hall next to the security station had eaten my ration token without dispensing any snacks—that and a minor issue with the returning shuttle. It was supposed to bring back the last batch of colony contractors, but it never came. We waited around. The shuttle never showed up, but something else sure did.

"Matt, you need to see this," Trent woke me from the violent, vending-machine-throttling thoughts that enveloped me, my eyes slowly opening. Trent, his lightly bearded face now pale, gestured to a display monitor.

The feed showed an image from dock B12, a security channel meant to help officers guide in docking craft. The sight it now displayed chilled me to the bone.

A dark shape, like a sinister cosmic slug, was stationed squarely in the center of the screen. Many smaller objects orbited the craft, spiraling about in aimless circles.

"What ship is that?" I asked Trent. He made no reply, simply shaking his head. I slid my chair next to Trent, grabbing the camera toggle knob from his cold hand. Pounding the zoom button repeatedly, I soon had a closer view. The blood rushed to my face, boiling red in my veins. Anger escaped my lips in a wordless choking groan.

What I saw before me was a pirate sloop. Low and fast, it could handle perhaps a crew of twenty, likely less. Drifting in idle, eerily sprawling circles about the craft were the frozen bodies of perhaps thirty colony workers. Taking a deep, shuddering breath, I seized the communications microphone.

"This is D65 hailing unidentified craft, identify yourself," my voice strained as I tried to stay calm. Silence slowly ticked by. "Unidentified craft, respond or you will be fired upon." I was bluffing, of course, but I was also desperate. Weapons decks on the 65 had been stripped bare after a civil turf war two years back. There was nothing to stop the pirates from commencing a forced docking, boarding the station, and overpowering us lightly armed guards. I really doubted they were just here ordering a take-out meal, so I loaded a new fuel cell into my sidearm and pulled three more taze rifles off the weapons rack. Authorization or no, I would not go down without a fight.

The ship began a slow approach, refusing to answer any communications. While Trent notified the bridge staff of our situation, I brainstormed a way to keep the brigands from boarding the station. Of course, that was only half the problem. They would likely open fire as soon as their access was denied. It was a risk worth taking.

My fingers had not been idle. Clacking away at a keyboard, I had managed to access the docking port security panels using an administration password that sure wasn't mine. In a few minutes every port was locked down, fortifying the station adequately against a forced docking. But as I would shortly find out, the situation was not quite so bad that it couldn't get worse.

GREETINGS, FEEBLE OXYGEN CONSUMING PARASITES.

The voice came through every electrical device in the room—miraculously including the microphone. Trent clutched his ear, throwing off his headphones.

"What is that?" Trent gasped.

"I would rather we didn't find out," I replied. "Kill every communication link out of this station."

Trent obliged. The intercom static was eliminated. This was the day I learned that sometimes even our best plans only amount to a faint struggling against an unstoppable force constricting our efforts to frustration and futility.

SHALL I TAKE THIS TO MEAN YOU FIND MY CONVERSATION DISINTERESTING? The voice was back.

"Who are you?" I shouted in no particular direction. I primed my hopelessly underpowered electric sidearm. Like I said: I was desperate.

I WOULD APOLOGIZE FOR MY LACK OF MANNERS, BUT I AM EMOTIONALLY INCAPABLE OF DOING SO. I AM SERAIAH.

The computer made a pinging noise, indicating that the docking bay had just been remotely opened.

"It's a virus," Trent deduced. "The pirates are using it to break into the station," the younger man paced the room, flustered.

"Trent, think. We can stop them."

"The manual airlock coupling."

"Find it on the schematics. I'm getting the EVA suit."

Trent leaped to the computer as I descended to the maintenance deck. White steel walls gave way to exposed steel pipes and cables. Circuit breakers sprouted from the floor and walls like some multicoloured electrical fungal forest. Given all the wires and buttons, I was quite amazed that the station was able to function as long as it did.

The suit stood in its port, gleaming a sullen, chilling smile to anyone who looked at it too long. The two charging lights adding in make-shift glowing eyes (just in case you missed the malevolent grin). I had always thought the thing looked positively archaic, more like a mediaeval suit of armour than anything I would want to step into space wearing. I wondered if the designer had been afflicted by dis-inspiration the day he conceived it and had turned to a medieval novel for his creative muse—or maybe he was just a history buff. It was the only suit in the security post, owing to budget cuts and administrators who didn't give a flying something-I'm-not-proud-to-repeat about the little guy.

Did it even still work?

I tapped the helm and was astonished to receive a glowing white response when the visor light came to life. The vanadium-steel dinner jacket popped open animatronically, and I laid myself in the humanoid steel coffin, allowing it to close about me. I experienced only a moment of dark-as-pitch claustrophobia before the visor powered up and I was able to see, the heads-up control panel lighting up in front of me.

Lights of all colours came on about me, endless readings displaying power levels, oxygen levels, and something that looked a little like a water meter readout.

"Are you outside, Matt?" Trent's voice droned through the helm's intercom.

"Nearly," I said as I closed myself into the airlock. I took a deep breath. This was always the worst part. I cracked the hatch, and was hit by a shock and a vicious swoosh as the oxygen drained from the chamber.

Every station has a series of ladder-like bars lining the exterior of the hull (I never knew if I was going up or down on the things—like I was in some futuristic game of snakes and ladders). Had I been wearing a newer unit, I would have had magnetic soles built into my boots. I now clung to the grown-up monkey bars, a mile of security tether paying out behind me, static in formation. Out here, floating, I had little protection from micrometeorites or bursts of radiation. I continued to suck in the life-giving 4.7 psi of atmosphere within my metal container. Hand over hand, I slowly made my way to my goal.

"The manual coupling will be adjacent to the main hardline. Once you throw the switch, nothing electronic will be able to open the door."

"You can't beat the mechanics, mate," I returned. Within a few minutes, I had reached the dock. Looking up, I perceived the pirate sloop drawing closer. A dull clunk was heard, or rather felt. The visor began to fog. Something was wrong.

"Trent, is this thing supposed to fog up?" I asked.

"I'm not sure. The last time I used that thing was back in 3042. I don't remember it doing that then…"

"Quiet for a second," I whispered, straining my ears. A low hissing reached my ears. Spinning around, I saw a small trail of vapour following me.

"Shoot. My tank has a leak. I'm running out of oxygen," I took a slow breath, savouring the sensation of drawing air into my lungs, for how much longer I wouldn't hazard a guess. Air is a privilege, my father used to say—turned out he was right.

"Turn back, man. You can still make it inside," Trent sounded nervous. Trent never sounded nervous.

"Then what? If those pirates get in, we'll all end up out here and not with suits on either. No, I have to lock down that door. Listen, you're in charge 'til I'm back."

Silence was the only response.

Taking the lack of response for assent, I plugged on. The main sewage duct was now visible, and I traced it to the locking mechanism. A few meters from the conduit, the helm was completely fogged up. Ice crystals formed on the glass. Furiously I scraped at the visor with my free hand, but it was no use. The frost had formed on the inside.

"Trent, I can't see anything. Am I close?" I felt

my way forward. Trent did not reply. Perhaps a radiation flare had scrambled the frequency. It could happen—maybe.

Grasping what I assumed to be the lever, I pulled with all my might.

Nothing. The lever refused to move.

Feeling about, I groped for what I hoped might be a locking pin. At length, I found it. It had become a struggle to keep my breathing steady. The air I drew in was colder now and much less nurturing, like the heady atmosphere on a mountain peak.

Where was that pin!?

I vainly swiped at the visor again. If it cleared the ice forming on the helm, the fog within was still to be reckoned with. One option left.

I switched the visor to thermal imaging, despite the knowledge that this method was quite useless. At minus 236 degrees, everything is frozen and would therefore appear black, but this technique combined with an infrared heat gun on the EVA suit just might help. Turning the heat gun to full throttle, I pointed it at the lever. Within one suspenseful minute, the conduit was a visible dull red, the metal superheated by the gun.

From there, throwing the switch was no problem. One thing left.

I accessed the conduit's control panel to disengage the computer from the lock—the wires from the gears and metal. I soon discovered my error as a voice rang out, directly in my ears.

MANY THANKS, EARTH HUMAN. YOU HAVE

PROVIDED ME WITH A POWERFUL DEVICE WITH WHICH TO ACCESS THE STATION: THE VERY SUIT YOU ARE WEARING.

"No! Get out, darn it!" I was out of options. Within wireless range of the station, the viral intelligence would be able to access any computer system within minutes. This range would be limited to one or two hundred meters.

A moment of deliberation. It was my life, or every life on the station. I checked the tank. Two minutes of oxygen left. I could see nothing but the faint heat reading of a few closer stars. Hands shaking, perhaps from stress or from lack of oxygen, I finally made up my mind.

No one would harm my colonists. Not on my watch. Even if nobody ever knew that I drowned in the dry depths of space, I would at least have the satisfaction of knowing that I made possible the living of their ignorant lives.

I swiftly unclipped my harness, and the safety tether drifted away, a mere snake of shining cable in a black void. With one last mighty push, I leaped headfirst into space.

Not one person moved as Matt finished his story. The wooden ship creaked sympathetically, and the wind raced past the partially open porthole, whispering as though offering its condolences. No other sound could be heard. Reese was practically in tears. Everything that happened to Matt, to everyone present, was entirely her fault. It had come at her own hand.

Azalion seemed to observe the turmoil behind her distraught eyes. General Quercius was the first to speak, his deep yet soft voice broaching the almost palpable lament.

"Thank you, Matt Ferren," he said simply. "To you we owe our clearest description of these modern pirates. It is evident that these men do not hesitate to open fire upon peaceful folk. That is something which I abhor." The approbation of everyone present was manifest in the nods and hushed murmurs. Quercius sat quite still, a brooding darkness gathering behind his eyes.

"We shall set a course for interception at once. Not idly does the wind stir in the sails of the *Aura Regency Hide*. Give orders forthwith. All men are to assume battle positions. Captain Lee, brief this assembly regarding our refugee situation."

A young woman rose, her hair closely cropped in military fashion, save her blonde bangs, which tumbled listlessly over one eye. She wore the garb of a soldier, the ensemble complete with a sabre, knife, and brace of pistols.

"As you may know, this ship has become a refuge for any characters we discover. We do know that excepting our guests, all persons on this ship are entirely fictional. We have all been *removed* from our own worlds, if you will, and now find ourselves at the mercy of a strange land and people. This ship is currently home to just over three hundred characters, all from various works of literature written by our wordsmith creator: Stella Cadenza. The ship's harvesting equipment, though improvised, maintains our cloud cover, an effective camouflage for our operations. This vessel continues to welcome Displaced Fictional Persons, or DFPs, on a daily basis as said fictional works are read." The woman stood stock still as she spoke, her posture a formal mockery of ease and nonchalance.

"Very good, Captain Lee," said Quercius, "and what of your research?"

"There is another thing we all have in common," Captain Lee continued. She gestured to a pile of books before her. "This is a collection of works by Stella Cadenza. I have taken the time to read through them all, to garner as much knowledge as I can regarding our backgrounds, strengths, weaknesses, and even our darkest secrets—as well as our enemies'. Through the course of my research, it has become apparent that every character on this ship, every DFP that has been removed to this world..." she paused, perhaps for dramatic effect, perhaps for the trepidation shrouding her eyes.

A stage director could not have better captivated his audience than did Captain Lee. Twenty-four souls leaned closer, waiting to hear what would come next. Eyes peered quizzically over glasses, or inquiringly from behind glasses, or through no glasses at all (these were the least curious members present). The shoulders of Captain Lee sagged ever so imperceptibly.

"Once again, excepting our human

guests — we — all fictional characters — are deceased — as intentionally written by Stella Cadenza and unwittingly read into the collective knowledge by her readers. It appears the world we are in is, for us at least, the afterlife."

The room burst into a state of panicked confusion.

Eyes began to look to Reese. Some were distraught while some wore a mildly offended expression. Reese began to feel quite uncomfortable.

"But, but," Reese stammered in the only utterance she could command at that moment. "You're all characters I kil—" Reese halted abruptly. "I mean you're characters I wrote out of my books?" Reese did not miss the sharp and penetrating glance of Azalion at that moment as he stepped forward.

"I died?"

Really, there ought to have been a bit more exclamation in the question (and the accompanying punctuation), but Azalion asked Reese in a tone that was polite to the point that it would really have been less threatening had he simply chosen to scream at her.

"You killed me in the next book?"

Reese reluctantly raised her gaze to that of her accuser then glanced at the faces surrounding her. She briefly wondered if she could write herself out of the present story, but didn't have time to pursue that idea.

"Well??" demanded Azalion.

"Y-yes. I did. I mean…" Not for the first time did Reese Richardson wrestle with word choice. How would this conversation go in one of her stories? Reese thought. "You have to understand — they wouldn't let me stop writing your story. I needed to do something else — wanted to write a different story, but they wouldn't look at anything unless it was another installment of *The Penultimate Graeling*. I — " Reese stopped. It was no use. "Fine," she huffed. "I'll write you back in. Will that make you happy? You would get along great with my publisher. Look, I'll do it right now." Reese grabbed for her notebook, pulled the pen from where she had jammed it into the coiled spine, and scribbled two lines:

For some inexplicable reason, Azalion didn't die. He returned to his beloved and they lived a long and happy life together.

"There," Reese pouted, shoving the notebook under Azalion's nose. He glanced briefly at the notebook. All eyes fell on Azalion who only stood now with his arms crossed, giving Reese the haughtiest of looks.

"Well?" Reese asked. "Why aren't you back in your book?" She turned a questioning look on Captain Lee, as though the Captain should surely know the answer.

"If I may?" Captain Lee began with a glance at Quercius. Quercius assented with a nod of his head. "I believe stories that have become common knowledge cannot be changed. Ms.

Cadenza cannot alter that which had already been read and become known."

A low murmur had begun in the wooden chamber. The voices raised about the room escalated into a frustrated tumult (*we're all stuck here then; even SHE can't fix this; how on earth do we get back; etc.*). Reese choked in a shaky breath. One figure, hitherto seated at the far end of the table, rose suddenly.

"Peace," boomed General Quercius, "do the very rocks and trees question their creator? Nor shall we. Whoever we once were, and whatever our stories had been or were going to be, are now at an end. Our paths have converged here, in this moment of communal interface. The only question we face is what to do now that we are here."

There was a shamed hush about the table. Eventually a man spoke. His name was Aeolus.

"Sir," he addressed General Quercius, "Speaking for myself, Sir, I would like to make the most of whatever existence has been extended to me. What means are at our disposal to rid all worlds of these villains permanently?"

Quercius squinted into the table, as if trying to see through the dense wood plane, or perhaps a deeper wooded plain further in his mind. He must be able to see through Earl and Charles well enough, Reese mused gloomily. This man was a searing beam of truth, clothed in a brightness that put all compared to him in a dim and disrespectable light. She ought to know—she had first imagined him.

"Azalion, my nephew, do show us what you have discovered."

The young man rose, and gestured to Reese.

"You may have guessed that this woman we have included in our otherwise closed council is Stella Cadenza herself. To her we owe our very existence and, as my uncle has pointed out, our sincere gratitude for the lives we have been privileged to live out in lore. This woman—for better or worse—is our creator, and thus she commands a power over even the strongest of us. Lady Cadenza, if you would show us the notebook," Azalion concluded.

Reese offered forth the battered notebook.

"A demonstration if you will," Azalion intoned.

Reese pondered a moment then scribbled a line in the notebook.

Suddenly the cloaks of all present fell to the floor. There was pointing and gasping, and everyone scrambled to replace their garments before turning amused glances on Reese.

"Very well," came a voice, from the corner, "now that we are all quite embarrassed, what else may this wondrous gift do for us?" The speaker was a captain by the name of Perfuga. He was dark-haired, with a rather goat-ish curl of hair sprouting from his chin.

Reese smiled, glad that she was no longer an object of fear or of animosity. She thought for a moment then proceeded to scribble "and the party dined on the finest meat, bread and drink". And so it appeared, laid out on the table in a glittering array of splendid silverware.

"Go on, friends" Reese addressed the crowd, "this banquet is for you."

A few faces eyed the delectable dinner dubiously. General Quercius was quick to save the day, gallantly piling high a silver plate and shoveling a bite appreciatively into his mouth.

"T'is wonderful," he praised, "I hereby grant the cooks a night off!"

The party began to dine, marveling in the power of their creator. Cheerful banter pervaded in the council chamber.

"Marvelous! Wonderful!" croaked Captain Perfuga from the end of the table. His voice was the loudest and most unreserved in praise of the author's abilities.

Azalion alone adopted an attentive air; attaining an aloof, affected abstemiousness. He ate sparingly, glancing gloomily about the table. He did not doubt that a non-discreet display of power on this level was sure to bring trouble. Could he trust those assembled to contain the secret? Azalion trusted nobody to keep a secret, not even the dead — and especially not this many of them. He glanced to his uncle, who smiled reservedly.

The sails had been set; the future naught but a fickle wind boldly driving the *Aura Regency Hide*. Quercius quietly quelled querulous quandaries, quiescently quaffing quality quartered quahog.

Meanwhile, maindecks, at the port bow, two figures leaned casually against a railing. Earl looked to Charles, who was fumbling with a small notebook.

"The food is good enough, Charles, quit your shuddering and have a hot cocoa," Earl tried.

Earl had known Charles some years, well enough to know that the man was timid and rather lacked confidence. More than once had Earl advised Charles on a matter for which (so he thought) an answer was plain to see—or was plain enough for anyone except Charles, Earl mused.

"I have already eaten, Earl. It's just—this place, how did we end up here? I had a normal existence this morning, and one I intend to return to." Charles furiously scrawled a few lines in his journal. "People don't have lives like this—they don't get chased by barbarians with swords or talk to programs from outer space or soar about on air-ships!"

"Don't forget to mention the flying lion," Earl jibed, cradling a warm cup between his hands. Charles turned a funny colour, choking slightly, then slammed the book shut.

"That's just what I mean: how did any of this happen? These people aren't *real*!" Charles, in his excitement, spoke perhaps a bit too loudly. A few passers-by paused to glance at this intrusive interlocutor.

"Now Charles," Earl sighed, "do remain calm. Don't think of this as a calamity, rather, an opportunity. When Reese wrote the *Penultimate Graeling*, she described the feasts in detail. I never thought I would get to sample the cooking of the Coasting Guardsmen! This is quite spectacular!"

"She also, Earl, described the terrible villains in detail, as well as the awful things they do to their enemies! An opportunity, you say, only you mean aside from the fact that people who don't exist (my apologies, ma'am) are trying to kill us and likely via the most violent and grisly of means!" Charles was clearly not approving, even under the guidance of Earl's sound, if simple, logic. Earl tried a new tactic.

"Time to sleep on it, my friend. We've had a long day."

"You intend to repair to your quarters?"

"Right after a trip to the galley. They leave the hot stew out for the night watch!"

"You are truly predictable, my good Earl. Good night, you glutton." Charles nocked the Parthian shot, fired from the saddle, and sauntered to his quarters.

Chapter 6:

Frigis Iracundia

It finally happened. Destiny and Fate had eagerly anticipated this moment for weeks. It had taken a monumental effort on the part of both as they strove together in this singular project. Between the two of them, they had orchestrated a few deaths and weddings, many comings and goings, one rigged election, two assassinations, and an inconvenient water system shutdown. All of this took place in a communal effort comparable to moving one little red car slowly but steadily through erratically darting traffic toward the end goal. (Destiny and Fate both happened to hate that little board game, having been in the business for so long.)

None of these events, however, involved butterflies flippantly fluttering their wings in foreign lands. Contrary to popular belief, fate is not so fickle, to within a few degrees, as to toss a coin based on the twittering of one insignificant insect. For in the right circumstance, Inevitability will fight for us all; nobody is allowed to be quit of their fate. One who deceives him or herself into believing they have escaped their calling is only walking further along their appointed path, however involuntarily.

The time had arrived.

Troy had left his beachhead.

The daylight glared from chalky pavement; Troy blinked after the stygian blackness of his apartment. He was done hiding. He would rejoin the masses and reclaim his life — he deserved no less. This revelation happened to coincide with an empty pantry. The fact was: Troy was completely out of anything edible save one thing: a nasty jar of pickles so old, Troy had no recollection of either purchasing them or owning them.

Troy was dressed and shaved; he thought that since he was at last out in public, someone might actually see him and he ought to be prepared for the occurrence.

Troy approached the grocery store. A cold wind stirred, and Troy paused momentarily to pull his thin coat a little tighter about himself. He watched as one slow breath came as a cloud of vapour.

This pause was crucial to the plans of Fate and Destiny — it was a timing thing. That singularly minute facet of the plan was, in fact, so pivotal to their collective scheme they had enlisted the help of Predestination, a rather A-Type Right-Hand-Of-God sort who was quite obsessed with the fine details of things — and he insisted everyone else be cognizant of them too.

Following the pause, Troy entered the

store, double glass doors parting before him. His sneakers seemed to clack a little too dramatically on the hard floor and he unconsciously slowed his pace (another important particular of the plan).

The first item: blank. Troy had attempted to find his shopping list, but it was lost among the shelves of Stereo Bread lyrics somewhere in the labyrinthian depths of Troy's mind. Seizing a basket, Troy gathered a few random items. Cheese is a good start, who isn't always out of cheese? A forklift bleeped in the next aisle.

After a few common-sense items, (cereal, cereal, cereal, oh, and milk) Troy meandered aimlessly into the canned soup aisle. At least he thought it was on his own whim. In truth, Troy was meant to enter that aisle, at precisely that moment, no matter which circumstances brought him there. Had he, that morning, sought to drive as far as Iqaluit, he still would have, with absolute certainly, entered aisle 9 at 10:42 a.m. The only difference would have been a minor collateral death toll and the momentary rewriting of a few pivotal cosmic and physical laws.

That is when Troy saw her.

The young woman strode into the aisle from the opposite end, carrying a basket half full of produce. Her fair hair waved shoulder-length about a keen, comely face. Eyes bright, not from their virulent shade of blue but from the life that shone forth from them, alighted on Troy. He prayed sincerely at that moment that he had, that morning, donned a shirt with no swear words on it.

Troy had two smiles: one for general laughter and one for feigned politeness. Neither surfaced; he attempted to affect a cheerful, greeting half-grin. Perhaps it was a success, though not for the reasons he had hoped. The woman smiled back, suddenly wishing for a reason to casually enter into a conversation. She looked about noncommittally. Canned soup. Could not two people hold an intellectual conversation on that topic? Fortunately, or not so fortunately as you will have to decide, there was no call to test that hypothesis.

The forklift beeped on; Troy could see the mast raised to the highest shelf. The operator was attempting to shelve a skid piled high with extra-large ketchup cans.

Looking up, Troy perceived that something was very wrong. The operator drove the forklift at the shelf, from his low position unaware that it was already occupied by a similar skid of cans. A skid of cans which loomed over aisle 9, directly above the lovely young lady Troy had just smiled at. She had seen nothing of the impending disaster, presently contemplating exactly how to begin a conversation involving canned soup. It would have helped her greatly if she first had seen which soup Troy had reached for.

Understanding the imminent danger, Troy felt his heart double its regular pace. Without command or instruction from Troy, his feet burst into a run. Troy followed, praying he would be in time. Two thousand pounds of canned condiment tottered precariously at the edge of the top-most shelf.

Troy reached the young woman, and stretching one arm about her waist, used his momentum to bear her backwards five paces or so, where they both collapsed on the floor in a shower of corn flakes and fresh parsley.

Troy's running force was exactly enough (of course). The crate made a hideous screeching scrape, and crashed down upon the floor right where the woman had been standing. From their perspective on the floor two meters away, the two frightened shoppers watched the wreckage leak a bloodied, ketchupy red, like some macabre war-time mass grave.

Troy looked in alarm at the girl's face, which was partly covered in a splotchy red. "Are you hurt?" he asked, eyeing the suspicious scarlet on her face.

"No, just ketchup I think," she replied, smudging a finger across her cheek and tasting cautiously. She looked at Troy and nodded.

The shock lasted 14.8 seconds before both chuckled nervously.

"Thank you," the woman offered. "I suppose dinner might not make us even," she chuckled again, still shaken, "but it's a start."

"As long as you don't use any ketchup," Troy returned. "I'm Troy. Sorry I tackled you there."

"I'm very glad you did, Troy," returned the young lady. "My name is Macy."

"I've heard that hot chocolate helps with shock," Troy suggested, noting the flustered state of the other. He pulled open the package of napkins he had intended to buy and handed a few to Macy.

"That's a very good idea," Macy said. "I do sort of owe you — forever."

Troy smiled.

The two made their way to the food court. By the time the careless forklift operator rounded the corner, the pair had gone. Long thereafter, aisle 9 had a faint vinegar-y odour, though neither Troy nor Macy ever returned to learn that.

The light was already on when Troy arrived back at his apartment, the door unlocked. Troy pushed through the door cautiously, a few glass jars clinking together inside the paper grocery bags he carried. The door had been closed and locked when Troy had left the building (or at least it was highly probable) which, by process of deduction, meant that someone else had entered. Troy set down the groceries as silently as he could, picking up the phone and rather wishing it fired armour-piercing rounds as opposed to simple electronic milquetoast beeps.

He was 33.33333~% finished dialing 9-1-1 when he spotted her: Nevermind, sitting on his couch (having first cleared at least one cushion of the refuse that was a by-product of Troy's recent existence as a self-proclaimed recluse). Troy set the phone down and simply waited for the tempest of emotion, bracing himself for the onset of the coming dark clouds blowing in on an arctic wind and spewing ice crystals.

"This place could use some serious help, Troy," Tessa said quietly.

The look in her eyes was something Troy had never seen before. Troy wondered at it momentarily. If he hadn't known better, Troy might have mistaken Tessa's expression for humility, almost meekness, but if a list of all Tessa's qualities and traits were tallied, humility and meekness would not be found among them.

"It seems like we all could," Troy returned cautiously. He was convinced that the girl was a loaded musket — the kind that typically backfired out of spite. "Your stuff is still here. Thought you would be back for it," Troy offered.

"That's not why I'm here," Tessa attempted a shy smile. "I think things got out of hand. I wanted to say that I'm s... sure you didn't deserve what happened."

Troy chuckled. Not in the least. Nor did he miss the way she ducked out of saying what he really needed to hear her say. Close, but no cigar...

"You've always deserved the words I have never been able to say," she went on.

Troy did not laugh this time, at least not out loud. He was curious to see how far her feigned amiability would go.

"Then why is it so hard for you to say? You could never say what mattered." Troy prodded.

"I don't know. Things with you are just… different," she finished lamely.

"Different how? That makes no sense," Troy regarded her with a look of incredulity.

"I don't know."

Troy moved past the couch, intending to put the groceries in the fridge. Tessa stood and stopped him with a hand on his arm.

"I want to find out where this goes," she said.

"You said that when we met, Tessa. That was four years ago. I need more than that if this is going to work. This isn't your train ride. You have to put in what you want to get out of it. I need you to go."

"He hit me, Troy." Tessa felt her voice shake.

Troy sighed.

"Kind of reminds you of all the times I didn't, hey?" Troy didn't doubt that the girl could effortlessly attract the worst of men.

"I have a history of jerks in my life," Tessa stuttered, "you weren't one of them."

"I keep hearing you say that. Here's the thing: you don't ever seem to make these jerks history. That's the problem. I can't do this. It just burns me out, trying to fix your problems — trying to fix you. I never could."

Tessa opened her mouth to argue, and

shut it again with a seductive pout. "At least help me carry this junk to my car."

Yes. Troy had won the round, but he was sure the match wasn't over — she wouldn't be so kind as to let him off that easily — not without having a bit of sport with him first.

"Deal," Troy said, happily shouldering a box. "Let's go." Maybe he could drop off her things then outdistance her and make it back to his apartment before she followed him in.

They left the apartment in silence, boxes in hand. Troy walked behind Tessa along the dusky hall, picturing with a burning desire and disgust the total of their history together. It was a strange thing, walking so close to her, and being so far from what he had hoped to be for her. He could feel the days ticking by in his mind, taking him back to the day they had met. His mind seemed to click and whirr as the memories were dredged up, rather like a schizophrenic 8 mm film projector trying to show a horror movie and a romance at the same time.

They reached the curb, and Tessa opened the trunk of her ten-year old station wagon. Just as they set down the boxes, a car approached. It was an expensive vehicle of German make, godless rap music and greasy smoke emanating from the open windows.

"That's him. That's Andre," Tessa swore softly.

Troy wished then that he might be anywhere else. The South Pole. Done deal. He could catch seals and drink glacier water. If Shackleton could do it, so could Troy. However, for the foreseeable future (and possibly a short one at that) Troy was pinned to the spot where he stood. He decided that he had no need to die in a passion killing at the hands of some envious pseudo gangster. No furious jealousy burned in his heart, not like the first time it had happened, but neither could he simply walk away. Troy put on his best hostage negotiator face.

The car pulled up behind them, the headlights illuminating flatly the two blank expressions of those who stood behind the station wagon. The German vehicle stopped a full car-length from Troy and Tessa.

A young man got out. He wore deep blue jeans with large, white stitching and a printed shirt. Tattoos snaked down his arms to capture his knuckles.

"Hey," said the youth, "who's this, Tessa?" The young man jerked his chin at Troy.

Troy, though not desirous of engaging the cretin, had no intention of letting Tessa do so.

"I'm Troy."

"I'm not talking to you," the boy spat irritably.

"Yes," Troy insisted, stepping between Tessa and the young man, "*you are.*"

Troy had known it was a bad idea before the words were even out of his mouth. This feeling was confirmed when the butterfly knife fluttered into Andre's hand as though it were trained to do so. It caught spastically in the lamp beams, seeming a stop-motion blur of light and steel. It did an impractical dance as he opened it, and indeed it would have been comical were the situation not, at that moment, marginally life-threatening.

Two more boys, for all purposes veritable clones of Andre, exited the vehicle with similar armament and lack of taste. Troy had hitherto hoped to have phrases like "long-life" and "loving grandfather" inscribed on his tombstone. He wondered what it would read instead and then realized he would likely find out tomorrow morning. Or wouldn't, as the case may be.

"Hey loser, walk away," said one of the goons.

Troy couldn't really discern one from the other.

"This is your last chance."

Without knowing why he did so, Troy clenched both fists. "No. It's yours." He really didn't need to die for this girl. She could be over him in a week, as Troy had previously seen (a few times). He cursed himself for being such a fool.

Andre put the knife away, and before Troy knew it, he was face down on the ground.

"I'm warning you," Troy choked.

The boys around Andre laughed as their leader kicked the prone figure.

"Leave while you still can," Troy threatened.

The knife came out again. Andre knelt

over Troy, pressing the sharp blade against his cheek.

At that moment, a voice broke into the scene. "I commend your courage, young man," it called.

The three youths turned to the newcomer.

Bainan stood in the empty street, hands on his hips. His handsome face was augmented by a devilish grin.

"What do you care, old man?" spat Andre. "Leave before you get hurt," Andre said as he turned to Bainan, brandishing the knife.

"I duly appreciate your concern," Bainan returned, "yet I assure you, yond knave, it is quite unnecessary." Bainan drew the five-foot broadsword from its place at his back.

Andre paled.

Bainan, bursting with energy and suddenly finding himself once again in his element, lunged forth. Sure, it was not quite a duel worthy of song or legend, but in this strange new world, Bainan would just have to take what he could get.

The three goons left rather quickly, bearing a few very deep and very painful reminders of what could happen if they confronted Bainan ever again.

"I don't know who the heck you are," Troy said, bewildered, as he regained a standing position, "but thanks."

"Your courage was ill rewarded just now," Bainan mused. "I assure you that it is not always so." Bainan wiped the longsword on a large strip of cloth which had previously made up Andre's shirt, then hoisted Troy to his feet with one sweep of a mighty arm.

Red and blue lit the two faces. Stopping the police car, an officer stepped out of the cab. He put an instinctive hand on his sidearm at the sight of the sword.

"Greetings, good officer of the law!" Bainan called.

"Lower the sword, please," Jed called in a tone which, in a normal universe, was meant to be calming. "And place your ands in the hair." Jed was rather at a loss, for the second time that week. He looked from Troy to Bainan, expecting an answer. Troy shrugged. Jed pulled his gun from its holster.

"Have no fear," Bainan bellowed, "justice has been served here tonight. You may be sure that the house of Belan Wolfblood will permit no wrongdoing as long as Perennia is ours to rule."

"Uh, yeah. All the same," Jed continued, by now too shocked to be alarmed by this new turn of insanity, "I'll need to see you put it down." Jed drew his sidearm.

Bainan reluctantly complied, tossing his heavy sword so that it landed at Jed's feet. At least that is where he intended for it to land. In actuality, the heavy hilt hammered home directly upon Jed's foot. The primed firearm in Jed's hand let out a loud, barking protest against Bainan's imprudence. Bainan did not stagger, remaining quite still, for the tiny bullet was far too small and much too forgiving to have any real stopping power.

"That is well-nigh to causing me a small margin of discomfort!" Bainan boomed, his fearless grin morphing into a flinch. Bainan proceeded to pitch forward onto the pavement. He groaned. For the first time in his life, he was feeling very mortal.

Sunrise had some difficulty locating the *Aura Regency Hide*. Built to harvest clouds and convert them into drinking water, the ship was equipped with a vast variety of hydro-atmospheric devices. Thus she was able to glide through the morning sky under constant cover: a reverse-engineered contrivance of dense vapour cloud. As it was, a vague sunlit haze surrounded the vessel, smothering her passengers and riggings in a golden diffuse glow. The sun-deprived cold morning air was made colder still by the high altitude.

Reese wrapped herself in a heavy coat, tucking her cold hands into its deep pockets. Under the generous command of General Quercius, the apparel was on loan from the barracks of the Aura.

"You seemed nervous at the council," a voice arrested her thoughts. Quercius joined her suddenly at the railing.

"It's just—" Reese stumbled, knocked over the table, and her jigsaw-puzzle thoughts scattered about the floor. "Everything happening to you…it's my fault. Everyone here is dead because of me! This wasn't supposed to be real!" Reese' voice collapsed under the strain of tears welling up behind her eyes.

The conversation abstained briefly, and one could hear the mournful calling of a seabird—obviously lost given the land-locked location of Reese' hometown and, consequently, the current positioning of the *Aura Regency*. Quercius tapped the obsidian hilt of the longsword at his hip. He ran a hand contemplatively along his graying beard. He placed scarred hands on Reese' shoulders, looking her in the eye lest his words heedlessly pass her by.

"Nay. Everyone here has *lived* because of you."

This time Reese did not try to fight the tears as they streamed forth. Inwardly rolling his eyes and outwardly heaving a small sigh, Quercius opened his arms as the child sobbed into his cloak. At length, the moment was over.

"Thank you," Reese choked. "Any one of you could have found fault with me. Yet you didn't. I don't know why I deserve that."

Just then Perfuga approached, saluting. Quercius turned to the captain.

"Speak, Perfuga," Quercius ordained.

"I have cast a light upon a rather delicate matter. T'would be best discussed behind closed doors." Perfuga glanced about nervously.

Something in his tone and edgy manner convinced Quercius that his complaint had some serious grounds. "Right away," Quercius replied. "Come with us, Miss Richardson. I have placed myself in charge of your safekeeping on this journey."

Reese only nodded, following the two men into the General's quarters.

Quercius shut the door behind them and lit a pipe, which resembled more than a little the Aura herself.

"Speak plainly, what is the matter, Captain Perfuga?" Quercius motioned for the other two to sit, while he leaned against the desk. The desk was hard-pressed to withstand his muscular bulk but neither complained nor dared sink under the General's weight for fear of being accused of shirking its duty. It struggled in silence.

Perfuga paused perceptibly, perhaps pacing phantasmagoric, paratactic ponderings. At length, he spoke: "I have been made aware that certain factions on this ship are plotting a mutiny."

After a brief pause, "Are you certain?" The general's voice had taken on a dark hue, savouring of wakening dragons and slow-boiling wrath.

"I cannot be mistaken, my source is undoubtedly true," Perfuga closed his eyes and sighed to the floor. "We have until tonight."

"What do they want with the *Aura*?" Reese asked.

"It is not the *Aura* they seek. From what I can gather," Perfuga addressed Reese, "there are many scouts aboard who owe their true allegiance to Sven and his forces. You are not safe here."

Reese looked about, as if expecting an imminent attempt on her life. No assassins burst into the room. As Probability would have it, there were already several ninjas hidden in the room, however they were at present on other business and remained hidden. Nobody noticed.

"What do you propose we do, Perfuga?" Quercius questioned.

The other thought for a long moment. Reese briefly considered writing some sappy line about how every last body on the ship was fiercely loyal to General Quercius. However, decided the effort would be futile as she had not been able to change Azalion's behaviour on the train outside of what he would do anyway — that and it would simply be bad writing.

"General, I propose you abandon ship with Ms. Cadenza and her friends," Perfuga nodded slowly as the plan came together in his mind. "Captain Lee will aid me to quell the rebellion, with the benefit of keeping our beloved wordsmith out of harm."

"Very well, Perfuga. I agree with your plan, with one exception," Quercius acquiesced, "I will remain. It is my duty to protect crew and passengers. Yes, I must remain."

"As you say, sir. But who will protect

Cadenza?" Perfuga returned.

I WILL. The voice came from a hitherto silent suit of armour that decorated the quarters—and had presumably been empty. Perfuga noticeably jumped at the intrusion.

"Very well, Matt Ferren. You shall take charge. How did you get in here anyway?"

MATT IS ASLEEP. HE SHALL PRESENTLY JOIN ME IN OUR ENDEAVOUR—WHETHER HE WILLS IT OR NOT.

Not another person, character, soul, being, or even inanimate object was informed of the impending mutiny. Matt and Seraiah were probably the only ones who had overheard the ordeal (and a few ninjas who had no concern in the matter and did not involve themselves). Quercius seriously wondered if he ought to have all the decorative armour removed from his quarters.

The small schooner located in the cargo hold of the main vessel was fueled and swiftly made ready. Quercius gave orders, but carefully and deliberately neglected to explain them. He summoned Captain Lee and breathed in a relieved manner when he saw her stride into the cargo hold.

"Sir," she reported.

"Lee, are you armed?"

"Always, sir," the Captain replied, wondering what a strange question it was in the first place. Thinking that something was wrong,

Lee placed a hand on the hilt of her sabre.

"Henceforth you are to relinquish your arms for no reason, night or day, waking or sleeping. Surrender your sword to no one, my faithful Captain Noa Lee."

"Yes, Sir. I understand." She did not. However, she knew that such orders from her General meant trouble would soon be coming her way.

Captain Lee exited the cargo hold moments later. She was certain there were a few more weapons in her chamber that she could clean, sharpen, load and otherwise ready for their pleasant tasks of evisceration and ballistic incapacitation. It was a real pity, Reese thought, that Captain Lee had none of the modern small arms that the country possessed in such numbers. Reese laughed out loud as she pictured Captain Lee outgunning any other hotshot at a shooting range. For certainly, if the captain could accurately handle dated and unreliable dueling pistols, she would be outright lethal given any modern firearm.

Reese was summoned some hours later by Quercius himself. She followed quietly, her few belongings packed, still wearing her borrowed clothing, notebook tucked snugly in one of the deep pockets. Soon she was reunited with Earl and Charles below. To her surprise, Azalion was there as well.

"Azalion!" Reese greeted. "What are you doing here?"

"I will be accompanying you on your journey, however long it lasts." Azalion was clearly packed, and also bristling with holstered and hilted weaponry. In his new garb, less subtle (he had no longer the need to blend in among wandering city-folk) the prince looked absolutely majestic. He wore a tunic of royal caliber, a thick cloak, dark pants and a pair of knee-high leather boots. Armed he was, with dagger and a shortsword.

Captain Lee entered the hold, along with Captain Perfuga. Perfuga took a long look at Azalion, equally confused by his presence.

"General," Perfuga whispered, "I deem it most imprudent that this boy be brought into these affairs. I would not have wished to endanger him." Perfuga leveled a suspicious glare at Azalion.

"Perfuga, you forget your place. My nephew is a capable sailor and an adroit commander. You shall heed his commands from now on." Quercius could not be moved on the subject and Perfuga fell sullenly silent.

Captain Lee turned to Reese, after a moment of deliberation extending her hand. "It has been an absolute honour to meet you," Lee allowed, shaking hands with her creator.

"And a pleasure to finally, and for real, have met you Captain Lee." Reese clasped the warrior's hand, then turned to board the schooner. Earl, and Charles followed. In a moment, all were aboard. Quercius and Lee opened the bay doors themselves, as access to the hold was restricted to only those Quercius had ordered to accompany him. The schooner was soon dispatched.

Quercius sucked in a deep breath as he watched his charge sail away. He had a war to campaign, and at present his most potent weapon would be the twelve barrels of the Aura's finest ale.

The party raged late into the night; the best food and drink were on offer. Quercius posed the feast as a tribute to their creator and author, Stella Cadenza. If asked where she was and why she could not appear at a celebration in her honour, Quercius would slyly finagle his way around the question, a fox eluding the tracking hounds. He would then simply hand the person asking another stein of ale. That was generally sufficient to quell further questioning.

By midnight, the vast majority of the crew was fabulously inebriated. The remainder had gathered in Captain Lee's quarters, excused on the pretense of a night watch. Had any of the remaining company been sober enough to count, they would have realized that nearly a dozen men were missing from the feast while the night watch required a mere three. Yet nobody was and so nobody did, most of the present company being far too sloshed to count beyond the number of empty mugs in front of them — and some not even that sober. Among the revelers, Perfuga drank and ate, looking quite irritable.

"I say," he began, "ought the noble men of the Coasting Guardsmen to drink and eat like rascals on the eve of a very important, well, never mind, I'm not really supposed to mention it." Perfuga attempted to stand, righted himself, then wandered off in the direction of the fine cuisine.

A row had begun at the head of a nearby table; swords had started to appear, glimmering in the torchlight. Quercius watched the proceedings, wondering how accurate the report of Perfuga would be. Judging by the hushed conversation and the furtive glances now being tossed back and forth among those wielding weapons, the men were clearly planning to carry out the mutiny, notwithstanding their intoxicated state — or quite possibly because of it. One of them stood (sort of) and raised his sword, turning in search of the General.

Quercius chuckled, and blew a small horn hanging by his side.

Instantly the door burst open. Captain Noa Lee entered with her guards, ready to defend her general and save the ship. The men in the hall, having drawn their weapons, saw no room to retreat. Swords rang, and a few shots were fired. Musket smoke filled the room.

Perfuga, obtusely grasping the situation, rose. "See! They rebel! My general, they rebel!" With a drawn sword, Perfuga charged into the midst of the battle. Or so he thought. In actuality, they found him passed out some hours later, in the galley.

Of course, the armed and armoured men following Captain Lee were more than capable of overwhelming and disarming twenty-odd drunken sailors and guardsmen. The fighting began, and ended mortifyingly quickly. The mutineers were shortly disarmed and restrained. Only a few had been perforated with musket lead, and these were quickly tended to. Noa commanded her men from the midst of the debris, and in her battle gear she appeared a veritable goddess of war, visited upon them from the depths of long-standing lore.

Chapter 7:

Solanavis

The small schooner set a course for where, no one knew. Reese clung to the gunwales, gazing over the edge of the craft and wondering if her lunch had yet made sea level. For the first time she could see how dreadfully high they were. At this height, Reese honestly pondered the fact that a falling person would have more than enough time to consciously comprehend hitting the ground — before they actually did.

City skyline unfurled beneath the ship like an unrolling carpet. Eighty thousand feet separated the glowing spires of civilization from the keel of the small craft — hopefully gliding through the night with all lights smothered the ship would be no more than a vague black silhouette against the stars. The small vessel had outstripped the cloud cover provided by the *Aura Regency* — it was not equipped for such large scale hydrospheric operations on its own.

Azalion watched the night scene moodily — yet this was no news, Azalion did most everything moodily. What fun was existence without a little dark brooding now and then? He sometimes thought that if everyone indulged in the same habit, the world would be a much happier place. Azalion had never been to a high school, yet even he, with his noble angst, would be affronted by the black nail polish and eyeliner worn by the misfit crowd trying to affect a legitimate saturnine temperament—let alone how the girls dressed! No, Azalion preferred to cultivate an unapproachable air merely with a nigh scowl and a sharp glare—no costumed theatrics needed.

"Where are we going?" Reese' voice sounded small in the wide night sky.

"We must only remain aloft whilst my uncle quells the rebellion. When it is over, he shall fire three signal shots from the ship's guns—that is to be the signal that we two only agreed upon."

"Wonderful," said a voice. Reese turned to see Charles saunter out of his cabin, "and while we're up here, easy prey for any prying eyes, we may as well just wait for the air force to roll up and ask for our license and registration!"

"If you have a better plan," Reese returned coldly, "there is nothing preventing you from getting off the boat and following your own course."

Charles laughed incredulously, unwilling to believe his client's tone. He glanced at Reese, as if to ensure that she was joking, but her eyes glared coldly back. Charles kindled another keen remark, but it flickered out when he was suddenly interrupted.

"Just be patient, Charles," Earl coaxed

from the bridge of the ship. "We'll be able to return soon enough."

"And who is going to try to kill us then? If I thought it would help, I would jolly well—"

SILENCE, boomed a hoarse voice, the sound of which harkened to mind the noise of burning wood. Silence arrived hard on the heels of Seraiah's command, as it always did. In actuality, Silence didn't very much appreciate having been summoned and awoken from its nap—something Silence frequently did owing to the fact it could do very little else without making some sort of racket. Sighing, perhaps, was fairly quiet, and possibly a game of solitaire but one had to be careful of the cards making noise, and anything much else... well, you get the idea. At any rate, having now been disturbed, Silence set to work, wrapping itself around the individuals present, seeking to quiet them and get back to its slumber. Silence met with a very temporary success.

"That's really good, Sera," Matt jeered. "You're finally coming in useful. I think you ought to follow me around all the time and make helpful comments."

Charles stalked off to his cabin. Matt and Seraiah laughed at their own hilarity. If sarcasm had been a virtue, they both would be saints. It truly was a pity they weren't able to high five.

A glaring light blinded the occupants of the schooner, interrupting the scene. Reese shielded her eyes with her hand, only just making out the same prow and hull she had glimpsed in her apartment just before the cannon fire had begun.

The spacecraft had found them.

"What do we do?" Reese gasped.

"This ship is not equipped for battle, and I have no crew to man the guns." Azalion glanced at Charles and Earl then shook his head defeatedly.

"Tell me what to do!" Reese returned, ready for anything. In moments the massive ship would be upon them, and Reese did not wish to find out what its crew intended.

She grabbed her notebook and pen and scribbled, "the ship fell out of the sky and the pirates died". Reese looked up, anticipating the crew's demise. Nothing. The craft remained, aloft and menacing.

"It didn't work!" Reese cried. "I wrote that they fell and died, but they're still here."

"You cannot write them dead—they've already died, or else they wouldn't be here," Azalion returned.

"Oh," Reese countered weakly.

The space hulk had begun its boarding procedure. Azalion had only seconds to think of a solution.

"Now whose idea was this little boat ride?" Matt pondered rhetorically.

THAT WOULD BE PERFUGA WHO SUGGESTED WE SEQUESTER OURSELVES ON THIS SMALL CRAFT AND SAIL IN CIRCLES

UNTIL DISCOVERED.

"Exactly. I'm starting to wonder about that," Matt had activated the wings on his metal suit. Launching himself into the air, he prepared to wage a one-man war against a space freighter.

Sci-fi cannon fire broke out with a series of *spewzings*. The small schooner beneath Azalion and Reese seized violently then began to crumble and fragment into several large pieces, the vessel being slowly converted into kindling and pencil shavings. Azalion reached a desperate conclusion. Giving a low whistle and muttering something in the *Graeling* tongue (which Reese found exceedingly amusing, considering she had made up the entire language from jibberish — she had only just enough time to think she ought to write down what Azalion had said, but not enough time to actually do that), Azalion scooped Reese up in his arms, ran to what was left of the edge of the ship, and dove headlong into the air.

It was now the appropriate time, Reese concluded, for a magnificent scream. Yet it would not come. In fact, breathing at all was a difficulty while in freefall. How long they would continue to fall, Reese could not tell. Certainly, the ground would be closing the gap very rapidly. And Reese had been correct: one did, in fact, have time to ponder the disagreeable force with which they would land after falling from their current height.

It was during the course of these ponderings that Reese noticed a shadow keeping pace with their two falling bodies. As it drew closer, Reese could almost make out the lion shape, and see the large wings. The creature raced to catch them before the ground did the job.

The breath shot out of Reese' lungs. Despite the care the lion had taken in intercepting them, the impact was dreadful. She briefly wondered if hitting the ground would have been any more dramatic. Once she had recovered sufficiently, Reese realized she was fine, soaring once more through the sky on the lion's back. Azalion, however, was nowhere in sight.

"Azalion!" Reese called, but it was no use. The boy was gone. She wondered if he had fallen, then asked herself that if his own fictional death had brought him to her world—where would a mortal death send him? Reese would have a few long hours to ponder that question as she coasted through a black sky.

Quercius uncrossed his massive war-boots and rose, at long last, from his chair in the now vacant feasting hall. So complete was his trust in his captain that he had not moved from his place during the entire battle, excepting on one occasion in which he dodged a sailor's widely swinging blade. He had then severely wounded the man with a salad fork. Throughout the remainder of the battle, Quercius had continued to pick disinterestedly at a quite delectable Waldorf salad (after acquiring a clean salad fork).

Captain Lee, meanwhile, was busy interrogating one particularly ugly mutineer, a man with a scarred face known as Behrn.

"You think you won! Hah," spat the insurgent, "that's a far cry from the truth, *captain*. It serves you right to follow this fool—" his tirade was cut short by a musket ball and a loud scream. Behrn clutched his thigh as Captain Lee handed her pistol to her second for reloading. The grey-bearded sailor had served as Captain Lee's second on numerous occasions, enjoying the privilege of witnessing many of Lee's prior violent antics. He knew her routine well—more than enough to anticipate what would come next. He promptly handed her a fresh, loaded weapon and proceeded to fill the powder on the first.

"That is not the manner in which you address the General. Now pay close attention, sir; your next words will either be to indicate the party that bought you," Captain Lee commanded, "or they shall simply herald your death. Choose them wisely." Captain Lee punctuated this statement with a quiet but impactful *CLICK* of the pistol's steel cock.

"This is not your kingdom!" screamed Behrn. "We are no longer part of the Coasting Armada! Thrown from death into this living nightmare, with no hope of going home—it is no proper existence! Give up this foolish quest!"

Captain Lee proved true to her word. She always did. Quercius had chosen her for this reason—one of many.

Quercius took a moment to address the failed rebellion: "Gentlemen, gentlemen. You have made quite an error in judgment, to follow a traitor and inspire chaos in these ranks. The Coasting Guardsmen stand for order and justice—no matter the kingdom we are in. This slight against her name shall not be condoned!" None of the rebels could tell, but behind his mask of wrath Quercius was grinning widely when he said: "Captain Lee, in your opinion, do these deserters deserve to die?"

"Absolutely, general." Captain Lee had no need to ponder the manner.

"Quite so. Quite so. Captain Lee, execute them all," the General commanded.

This caused a moan and a whimper to rise from the group of men presently standing surrounded at gunpoint.

Captain Lee shouted orders. The prisoners were grouped together in the hopes of killing more than one at a time and thus save on shot. A firing squad was lined up in front of the group while the prisoners looked about anxiously.

"Ready!" Captain Lee shouted. The sailors raised their muskets and the mutineers lowered their heads. "Aim!" Muskets were brought to eye level while the prisoners shut theirs tightly. "F—"

"A moment, Captain Lee," Quercius hailed, stepping forward. The Captain turned from the business at hand to await the General's next order. She fought a smile as she waited. "I believe I've come up with a more economical use for the scoundrels," General Quercius went on.

"Have them all confined to the engineering deck, full shifts at half rations, for the remainder of this voyage. It shall do them all some good — perhaps edify their souls in preparation for their second death — while allowing this ship to function at full capacity."

"As you say, General," Lee acceded, admittedly somewhat disappointed.

The rifles were put up, and the men instead were shuffled to the engineering deck, where they would be put to demanding labour. Captain Lee smiled. Though incapable of such an act herself, Captain Lee had seen her General display outlandish mercies many times before. She admired his compassion with all her heart, even as her own broiled with wrath. Her General was proof that there were a handful of good people yet in existence, and Lee took it upon herself to personally obliterate every wicked being that would even dream to harm these few good souls. It was simply work needing to be done, and Captain Lee was a hard worker — and good at her task.

The darkness, as complete and all-consuming as the piercing loneliness, drowned out all other sensations. A distant bell tolling, heard through an ancient stone wall, seemed smothered and alien in the graveyard, the sound an intruder, juxtaposed to the milieu and having no business being there. The name graven on the lifeless stone could not be discerned, save by tracing the letters by hand. The earth still smelled of fresh soil, and the frigid autumn air sighed its falling leaves upon the yellow grass.

Had there been any moonlight whatsoever, one might have discerned a figure as it straightened from his place before the stone. One may possibly have seen the man clutch a long coat closer, and shudder minutely with rage or perhaps suppressed sobbing. But there wasn't any moonlight, and nobody to observe these things. Nor did anyone note the bloodied wound staining the back of the figure's coat a dark purplish crimson.

Dawn was slow to rise from slumber, reluctant to stir forth from behind the veil of fog heaved up in the wake of a frosty night. Horses clacked up and down the cobbled streets, carriages clattering over the grey stones. Mere mortals continued to stumble ignorantly through their lives, paying no heed to the repercussions of their hasty and reckless actions.

A young boy waited at the door to the baker's shop, pulling the threadbare shirt he wore closer about him and hunching down into its too-short sleeves. The shopkeeper eventually arrived to open for the day. The boy entered along with the few other customers and quietly waited for them to place their orders. He smelled the yeasty fragrance of bread baking in the back ovens and his mouth watered at the tantalizing aroma of cinnamon drifting to him on a warmed draft. If he closed his eyes, he could almost feel his teeth sinking into a crusty warmth and taste the sugar on his tongue.

This boy was perhaps eleven years old,

although he'd had no one to mark the date of his birth or the passage of his years. He knew these not, nor would such knowledge have changed his daily existence had he possessed it. His dark hair was in need of trimming, falling raggedly about his face and chin. His clothing, having seen far better days long ago, now hung loose about him, tattered and beyond recall of their original colours. Yet he would never be turned away from the bakery; the owner was far too proud to permit the young boy to go hungry in his own town.

"Good morning, Timothy," grumbled the baker. He was used to these morning visits, and handed out a good portion of yesterday's baking to the youth. Without a word, sparing time only for a smile and a bob of his head in recognition of the baker's generosity, the boy disappeared.

Timothy exited the shop but walked not to school, for he went not, and not to home, for he had none; instead, the boy made haste to a large building in the center of town.

This building might have been mistaken for a great stone library had such a thing existed in those times, yet all the windows were dark, stained black with char and smoke. The building had suffered a fire years ago—suffered and yet survived, but had been disused ever since, forsaken by the townspeople as irreparable and untrustworthy. Despite their ill opinion, still it stubbornly remained. Tall stone arches loomed defiantly, sentinels glaring down over the indifferent street. Whether these guards were welcoming or warning was to be judged by the person doing the entering. The boy shunned the archway. It was through a small cellar door that he entered the edifice.

Black stood the furniture; black glowered the walls. A dull amber dawn peered piteously through a shattered window as though trying to impart some life past the deadened ramparts.

Footprints and scuffs disrupted the thick carpet of soot and dust. A tall man sat down at a table, wincing as he removed his long coat and draped it over the chair on which he sat. He paused to pull in a breath then turned to Timothy as the boy scampered over to where the man sat.

Timothy held the paper-wrapped bundle, the bread not so very warm anymore, and watched. The tall man proceeded to heat a large brass spoon in a gritty bowl of coals upon the floor. Removing his bloodied shirt, the man applied the spoon in a searing hiss to first the one large wound on his back then to the other.

By the time the meager breakfast was eaten, the bleeding had stopped.

"Thank you for breakfast, Timothy. You're welcome to stay here, if only we can clear out some of these ashes," the man spoke in a voice both soft and stern, both gentle and latently forceful. Timothy had the singular thought that if a benevolent lion ever spoke, it would sound much like this man.

"What do I call you, sir?" Timothy asked.

"I suppose you can call me Adriel," the man

mused as if to himself.

The boy set about cleaning the small area of the building which was still useful, sweeping away the grime and soot and restoring a semblance of order to what furniture remained. Adriel washed his clothing as best he could, dressed himself, regretting having to wear the torn shirt. It was late in the morning when Adriel left the boy to his cleaning and set foot upon the street once again. He knew precisely where to go, and knew also that he would need several more weapons to get there.

Adriel walked the streets in silence amid the acrid smoke of industrial spires, monolithic altars to progress and industry, workers filing in to pay homage and receive their small fistful of daily bread. His first time on earth, which had been last Tuesday, Adriel had nearly retched as his newly-human lungs seized, rejecting the foul atmosphere. He remained unaccustomed to it now, breathing in halting shallow breaths and then only at need. Yes, the mortal existence was more difficult than he knew—and so full of—emotion. It rather made concentrating on his Task difficult. Let alone his shock when he first beheld a mortal woman through the very fallible eyes of his male, mortal body.

At first, Adriel had wondered why he should care about the human condition; human beings wandering about breaking commandments—that sort of thing happened all the time. As long as Adriel received his orders and carried them out faithfully (which he unwaveringly did), everything was quite all right—at least, from his own perspective. Perhaps that was where he had gone wrong. The Task was not about his own perspective, was not about orders carried out—not about the *how*—it was about the *why*. Adriel had failed to grasp this fundamental concept.

Of course it was all quite understandable. What being, watching the mankind creatures for centuries, could refrain from becoming a little frostbitten and jaded? Thus was Adriel's state. Since his arrival, he had formed a few new ideas regarding the relationship of temptation and faith. Perhaps it was not as easy as it seemed when watching from a safe distance, devoid of the one and filled with the other.

Adriel's musings were interrupted. Glancing to his left, he observed a man in dirty clothing arguing with a market vendor: a farmwife selling her garden produce. Adriel tried to ignore her female form as he observed the interchange.

"I can't give it away any cheaper! Fresh vegetables don't just grow on trees for the taking!" the woman replied.

"All I be sayin' is it be bleedin' roadside thievery, what be these prices you got," the man replied. Adriel noted the hole in his woe-begotten overalls as they floated about his chicken-bone frame, hanging by one strap, the other missing.

"Thievery or not, sir, the prices stand. You're free to take your business elsewhere if you're not likin' to pay me my due."

Adriel was busy with his Task which that day appeared to include discovering the sensation of frustration (where in the world was the street sign he was looking for?) or he should have admired the woman's steadfastness when confronted.

At the woman's curt response, the man seized not the produce he had been seeking to buy, but a handful of coins from behind the stall! The woman shouted after him as he ran—straight toward Adriel. The thief did not see the demented, demonical grin which then lit the face of the latter.

Rather, the man glanced backward to see if he were being pursued, then proceeded to propel himself directly into a wall. Or what might have been a wall. It turned out to be the unyielding form of Adriel. A bird shot from the sky by a ten-pound gun would not have been more surprised than was the would-be thief. Coins spilled from his hands and danced through the air, raining down on the cobblestone street in a cascade of cheerful wind-chime music. Several passers-by stopped to watch. The man looked down a broken nose, struggling to see his adversary through the blood that stung his eyes and the tears that had spontaneously sprung up.

"Who are you?" he croaked.

"If you had ever learned to read, you should have known thou shouldst not steal," Adriel reprimanded in a dry and emotion-void tone.

The other man made a sort of gurgly, gasping reply.

"It was only luck that you caught me," he

groaned. His next movement brought forth a dueling pistol, aimed straight at the heart of Adriel.

The man did not have time to prime the weapon; with a quick twisting movement, Adriel had the pistol by the barrel, and the not-quite-murderer had another deep bruise.

"That wasn't very nice. See that it doesn't happen again," rebuked Adriel. "Return this money and be off while I am still willing to allow it." Adriel hauled the man to his feet, thrusting the coins into his hands and dragging him roughly before the stall. The man stood, frozen. Adriel still held the weapon.

"Are you going to kill me?" shuddered the man, handing the money to the woman behind the stall.

"How could you learn, were you dead? No, you must count this a lesson," Adriel decreed, proceeding to throw the man headfirst into the street. "See you take a better path from this point forward," Adriel warned. "Next time you may face a less gracious adversary."

The man hesitated just long enough to contemplate Adriel briefly, then stumbled away.

Justice is so fulfilling, Adriel thought. He pocketed the weapon. In his mind, a shadow had lifted from the gloomy street. Little things like that made his job satisfying. If he were to put a title to the job, perhaps the next time he was hiring, it would perchance have the words "Hell" and "bouncer" in it. Not just anyone was cut out for the job; it took nerve, perseverance and quite often a keen, single-edged, silver-hilted cutlass (the silver being optional, Adriel just thought it looked nice—he had once observed a school of hunters who believed that silver would ward off the undead, but most of them were now underground—evidently their theory was unsound).

The woman had not thanked Adriel; nor had he expected her to. A wrong had been remedied, and justice had been done in time, but it had not been a beautiful thing. A few minutes later Adriel was on his way again, feeling slightly more prepared to face the room of fire and shadow. After he accomplished that Task, eternity could do what it pleased with him. Adriel knew that heaven wasn't the only place to go, and he would not be dispelled into an eternal lake of fire for lack of trying.

Chapter 8:

Livet et Mortodo

The lion descended to the rooftop of a very tall building in a graceful glide. Reese dismounted wearily, stretching stiff limbs. It was like repairing to the airport after a very long flight, only in this case the airplane had breathed and flapped its wings, offering little but a jagged spine for a seat. For hours, or so it seemed, she had flown through the sky on the back of the winged lion. After a few steps her legs worked properly again.

"Thank you," Reese said, turning to give the lion a pat on its mane. "I don't even know your name, but thank you. Now go find your master!" Reese pointed, not in any particular direction but rather in a more or less upward direction. The lion slowly padded to the edge of the rooftop and leaped, crumbling loose a few stones in the process. The beast seemed to understand her.

A nearby photographer, perusing the skyline in hopes of capturing a perfect sunrise, stared incredulously. By the time he remembered to lift his camera and push the button, the lion was well out of sight. Reese laughed. If she had bothered with film and a camera, the past two days would have yielded quite a few interesting photographs. Maybe in time Reese would come to regard those events as an uneasy dream. Some photographs would surely help assure her of their reality — and confirm her sanity.

Leaving the dumbstruck shutterbug upon the rooftop, Reese proceeded down 24 flights of stairs (the elevator had been shut down for some mechanical reason).

Reaching the street, Reese found herself breathless and quite uptown from her home. She considered returning to her apartment for food or clothing, yet it would likely be futile to do so. The building could possibly by now be simply a pile of rubble. It had, after all, been carpet bombed by a space battleship (the police were still busy cleaning up all the carpets).

An alternative course of action was suggested by a warm coffee shop window beckoning from across the street with its breakfast specials splattered in large letters across its windowpane and the tantalizing aroma of bacon spewing from its overhead exhaust fan.

Reese unreservedly sat down to a greasy sausage sandwich and a cup of steaming coffee. Not black, goodness no. Reese was not such a hardy nine-to-fiver that she could take raw caffeine without a buffer of cream and sugar. Despite being quite well fed on the flying craft, Reese was really very ravenous by the time she alighted upon the rooftop. At this point, the slimy, overcooked, hastily prepared sandwich (the cheese had nearly missed the bun altogether) looked absolutely delicious. For the next several minutes all thought ceased aside from the singular idea of the challenge before her: consuming the unwholesome breakfast before her conscience smote her for it or her stomach reprimanded her. Reese dove in enthusiastically, avoiding the parry and thrust of her conscience with a quick side-step and mental pivot, countering the move with the idea that today of all days was no time to be worrying about such menial things as dietetically balanced meals. Reese soon popped the last bite of sandwich into her mouth, effectively ending the match. She then turned to her coffee.

A television flickered silently in one corner. Sports updates flashed by, for any who bothered to care. Reese certainly did not. Her coffee held far more interest for her than did the sports announcements. She also wondered exactly how she would be paying for her meal...

Reese wondered then what she was to do, where to find any help to deal with the colossal catastrophe that she had unwittingly managed to unleash on society — the entire world may be impacted for all she knew. Reese had no idea what her villains had been planning, but given their penchant for evil, their malicious intent ensured that it would be nothing good (after all, what else would villains be doing?). It was not written in their characters to do anything beneficial, at least without planning it as part of a grander sinister plot, and Reese could do nothing to change that at this point.

She wondered if Azalion had survived — once she had begun falling, he had been nowhere in sight. She sincerely hoped that he had not plummeted to the ground below. Then an idea struck her. She pulled the battered notebook from her pocket and scrawled the phrase "Despite the fall, Azalion was fine". So he ought to be, wherever he was. Returning the notebook to the pocket of the borrowed coat, Reese heard a slight jingle. She rummaged around in the pocket, withdrawing several gold coins. Well, that should certainly cover her tab.

Feeling much better about the situation, Reese returned to the counter for a doughnut — the sandwich had not been sufficient and she was superiorly positioned against her conscience with respect to nutrition. But now that she had eaten, it was time for a plan. Reese returned to her booth and got down to work on the iced vanilla, rainbow sprinkled doughnut. She had not the time to really think a hole in her seat, for she noticed just then that the television sportscast had been replaced by a news program.

Images of the spaceship firing upon the apartment building appeared on the television. *Ah, so I haven't dreamed the entire thing up! No — wait — I did actually, when I wrote it.* Reese did not know if that thought was comforting or not. The caption beneath the video attempted to explain the situation, and quite failed to do an adequate job. Due to the muted state of the television set, Reese had to read the news anchor's lips. However, being normally dependent on listening to words, had some difficulties.

"*Goldilocks' lumberjacks go strictly gangster, snowboard fusion slippers may prove hazardous,*" mouthed the moderately handsome anchor. All right, that approach was useless. Reese approached the television and pressed the subtitle button. A black strip filled with choppy white letters began scrolling across the bottom of the screen:

Man arrested for drunkenness and dangerous behaviour involving an archaic weapon.

A mug-shot flashed onto the screen. Though Reese had never actually seen Bainan's face, she knew him instantly, for he was exactly as he had appeared in her mind. She was utterly shocked for a moment. To think that she had gotten to meet, in the past few days, many people who should not exist at all, mere actors in the fantastical theatre of her imagination. Now why had she not written a handsome and rich bachelor who died tragically young? The closest she had come was Bainan.

Instantly Reese had a plan. She wrote down the name of the police station Bainan was being held at, and started on her way there.

She would soon find out that liberating

him was no easy task.

Chapter 9:

Duplei Falsierun

Jed escorted the large, brutish sword slinger to the police station lobby, trying not to limp from the dreadful pain that seized the middle of his foot with every other step. He did not think the man should be released (someone who ran around with a sword all day shouting about mystic quests and rescuing princesses clearly needed some sort of help) but all the paperwork had been put in order — evidently Jed's concern was not shared by all parties involved. The gunshot wound in the barbarian's shoulder had been looked at in preparation for his release. After it had been assessed, it was also cleaned and bandaged. The nursing staff was good at that sort of thing.

Jed reached the lobby, and unshackled the unnervingly large man he was escorting. Jed then noticed that something was terribly wrong. It was not the young woman waiting for the prisoner's release that caught his attention, nor was it the fact that the entire room was vacant of all other officers. What immediately struck Jed as being out of place was the fact that every chair in the lobby was occupied by a grimy, unshaven man in weathered clothes wearing a wide-brimmed hat. Even more disturbing was the stockpile of firepower they collectively sported: each bore a Bronco six-shooter. A few held vintage Manchester lever-action rifles.

Jed did not have time to address Reese, to suggest she would perhaps wish to take her delusional boyfriend home (or, alternately, to the psych ward) and in the future discourage him from donning leather outfits and running about with a claymore. He did not have time to give Bainan a disapproving frown nor the stern warning he had rehearsed.

One tall chap proceeded to rise, and if Jed hadn't known better, he would have sworn the man stirred up a swirl of dust as he stood. The man wore a long, waxed-cotton greatcoat, a wide hat similar in fashion to that owned by Glint Westwood, and a shirt that should likely have been white if washed, vigorously, for ten years or so.

"I reckon this must be Bainan. Say hello t'the boys." The wrangler addressed Bainan, who was about to reply until the conversation was interrupted.

"What's going on here? Those firearms are not permitted in here." Jed was getting jumpy, afraid to reach for his sidearm lest there be one in the room that could prove a faster draw. He thought this was highly likely.

"Name's ... *Al*. Now deputy, we're just a'collectin' our fri'nd.... *Bainan* here, and escorting the lovely Mizz Cadenza... *home,"* fibbed the cowboy, massaging the butt of his holstered weapon, as if it helped him think.

Jed looked at the young woman. Her eyes were already wide with terror. Jed correctly deduced that in all likeliness these men were no friends of hers, or Bainan's. Jed was about to open his mouth to negotiate, protest, or perhaps laugh hysterically, but could not decide which one he ought to do.

Before Jed could decide on a response, Al drew his pistol. Acting on instinct, Jed responded in kind. One shot rang out, and Reese ducked in terror. Bainan calmly watched as Al fell screaming to the floor, his left leg caving in under him. None of the other wranglers moved.

Just then a small party of police officers walked into the waiting room as one body, flocking around a box of pastries carried by the man front and centre of the group.

"Time's up, amigos, grab 'em an' run!" Al shouted from the floor. Every gun in the room was simultaneously drawn. The half-empty box of confections hit the floor with a comparatively thunderous smack, seemingly unleashing a torrent of gunfire.

Bainan instinctively ran toward Reese — the only female in the room and the closest thing to a princess in distress. Without the requesting or giving of consent, she was hoisted over Bainan's shoulder and borne out of the building where the wranglers were facing off against the police.

Plaster and cheap laminate flew about the room in small blasted fragments of plastic and powder shrapnel; the roar of the firearms was deafening in the echoing concrete room. Every table was upturned and provided very safe, bulletproof cover, as wooden tables often do in movies and on television. While this situation was rendered entirely in print, it proved no exception to the rule.

Six rounds later, most of which had maimed and wounded only the walls, all the westerners were forced to reload. The surviving police officers, using that moment to their advantage, fired off their remaining eight bullets, thinning the crowd of wranglers.

A silence descended on the room, punctuated only by the hollow, metallic *tinkling* of expended ammunition and the *clackity clicking* of firearms being primed for action.

The two factions faced each other silently from little wooden-table fortresses twenty feet apart. By that time, the lobby looked like the inside of a cheese grater; every flat surface (though surprisingly few combatants) had been thoroughly perforated. A few rounds had even passed through the holes in the fallen doughnuts, although most of the delectable pastries had been pulverized.

Jed hoped that someone had heard the commotion and dialed 9-1-1, then realized that the undertaking would be somewhat remedial.

Who would respond — the police?

Reese and Bainan had, by now, reached the street, first checking for more wranglers before fleeing into the neighbouring area. Of course they felt badly about leaving Jed to deal with a horde of dirty cowboys on his own, but Bainan seemed to think that the safety of the Author was the prime objective. Jed would be just fine with himself and the woman out of the picture, though he knew nothing of their literary ties to Reese Richardson.

The *clickety clacking* of firearms had mostly ceased. Everyone waited, a loaded weapon in hand, a racing heart jumping to the throat, for a chance to resume the fighting.

"Hand over the writer lady!" challenged Al from where he still lay on the floor. Remarkably, despite lying openly on the floor between the two makeshift battlements, the cowpuncher had sustained no additional injuries, although he was covered in candy sprinkles and powdered sugar.

"Won't happen," Jed replied, looking about at the few surviving police officers. They seemed to agree. Jed glanced at Tim.

"Tim," Jed said dubiously, "what are you doing?"

"Just a bit of frosting, sir. Chocolate glaze," Tim explained, licking two more fingers.

"Got any suggestions on how to end this nightmare?" Jed asked, without any real hope of a useful answer.

"Well, they might stop shooting if we just directed them to the nearest—" a shot loudly *ka-pwinged* past Tim's head. Alarmed, he fired back angrily.

The wranglers at this point seemed to realize that Reese and Bainan had vanished, and started to feel that their time would be better misused elsewhere. A heavily armed tactical unit (down the hall and to the left) knocked politely on the door.

Darn it, Jed thought, I bet them a pizza on this.

An awkward silence followed.

"Place the revolvers on the ground," boomed an emotionless, robotic-sounding trooper over a tinny intercom. Many complied, and waited to be cuffed.

Al had regained his feet, and now stood bleeding dejectedly, a sour twist to his mouth. Jed approached to handcuff him, feeling slightly more secure now that a row of friendly assault rifles pinned the transgressors against the far wall.

A mad light came suddenly to Al's eyes. He ran at Jed, drawing a very large, single-edged, forged-from-an-entire-ploughshare knife. Jed had little time to react, and grabbed the first object he found on his belt.

The knife cut the air. Unfazed, Jed stepped to one side then tazed the crazed cowboy, leaving him dazed on the floor, eyes glazed. Only then did Jed feel the warmth running down his hand,

and see the knife protruding from both sides of his arm.

Crap, he thought, that was my television-remote arm. Jed looked sadly about the floor, not to count the bodies, but to see if there were any edible doughnuts left—he had to prevent shock after all.

Somewhere far away from gun-slinging cowboys, several spinal discs rearranged themselves, making sickening crunchy noises, not unlike broken porcelain rubbing together. A shuddering, fluid-saturated breath was sucked into shaky lungs followed by several seconds of washboard wheezing. Fifty-three bones un-broke all at once, hurting no less in their re-joining than when they had first shattered. Blood seeped viscously from the pavement and back into its respective veins, filling the prone human form slowly like a water balloon, and saturating it with a pink hue—much more pleasant than its recently acquired ash-grey. Lastly, the lacerations and ruptures closed in on themselves with a not-so-vague burning sensation. Azalion rose with a mad, electrified leap, screaming out in agony. A few breaths and a fit of sea lion coughing later, he was calm. The pain was gone. And Azalion was fine.

He would, however, very much have wished Reese had written more quickly so that he might have been spared his rather disagreeable landing and thus prevented his resulting fear of heights.

The Prince looked around. He had landed, he supposed, a few kilometers outside of the city. The sky ship was nowhere to be seen. His clothing in tatters and covered in vestiges of blood (Reese had failed to renegotiate Azalion's clothing in her journal), Azalion decided it would be best to seek shelter, and pants, forthwith.

Azalion knew exactly how he had come to once again be walking, or breathing, or cognizant for that matter. He resolved to help Reese as best he could, in order to repay her for preserving his life. He stumbled over this thought exactly once — it had been Reese who had killed him in the first place — but quickly righted himself as his uncle Quercius would have had him do. When back on solid mental footing, Azalion found himself walking alone and nearly naked through a field clad in a warmth-leeching evening fog.

Coming at length to a farmhouse, Azalion could feel, but not quite hear a television broadcast, its canned laugh-track just on the edge of hearing. Pressing onward, Azalion soon found himself in a very large, if rather poorly tended, garden, the plants vying for dominance in an age-old fight of survival. Grotesques were strewn about, broken and with pieces scattered amongst the greenery. Water trickled indolently in the dimming twilight — the dribbling of a hose that would not shut off. Despite the area's appearance of a fallen garden, Azalion was glad to have found somewhere, even if he knew not where that might be. Rather, he was closer to anywhere than he was to nowhere.

Casting about, Azalion spied a clothesline, sparsely populated with a few items of clothing. He hurried to it and picked off a shirt and pair of pants as they fluttered cheerfully on the chilly evening air (the pants put up a brief struggle, intent on not being kidnapped). Azalion had subdued and donned the pants and was just pulling on the shirt he had pilfered when the stillness of the evening was shattered by a tinkle of broken-glass laughter. Azalion spun around, finding himself presently being scrutinized by a small urchin of a girl, her mop of spun-gold hair hovering around her face in disarray.

"Who are you?" twittered the girl.

"So sorry to intrude," Azalion began. "I am one who is very lost. I am Prince—"

"Wait," the girl squeaked. "I know who you are! You're the prince from my story-book!"

"Perhaps..." Azalion replied, wondering if that were true. "And who might you be?"

"I'm Katie," the girl chirped. "You're here—really here!" she squealed, doing a little hop-step.

"Yes, but I'm afraid I am in need of some clothing. Would it be all right if I borrowed these?"

Katie twisted her face as she pondered. "I don't know...they're my Dad's..."

"Well, I would be most grateful and would make restitution as soon as I am able."

"Maybe... I'll ask my sister if it's OK," Katie determined, seeming to confirm her own plan with herself. "C'mon," she said. Katie turned and waved Azalion forward.

The two walked toward the house.

Sitting on the porch, sideways on a dilapidated wicker lawn chair was a youth — not much more than a girl herself. Her face was hidden behind the book she held, her hair curling recklessly out the sides.

"Emily," Katie called as she skipped up the porch steps.

"Mmm?" Emily responded absently, face still anchored in the book.

"Can the Prince borrow Dad's clothes?" Katie asked.

"Huh?" Emily replied, not looking up.

"The Prince from my book is here and needs to borrow Dad's clothes. Is that all right?"

"From your book?" Emily asked, turning a page. "Yeah. Sure, whatever."

"Okay, thanks," Katie lilted. She turned and hurried back to where Azalion stood, prudently out of sight of Emily.

"Emily said it's OK," Katie offered. "You can borrow the clothes."

"Thank you," Azalion said, as he supposed that one must be grateful even for red plaid. He turned and started off across the field.

"Bring the Princess with you when you come back!" Katie called after him.

Azalion stopped and looked back at Katie.

"I shall certainly do my best," he replied.

Katie watched as the Prince left. She looked back to the cover of the book in her sister's hands. It was him all right; he was the prince she had been reading about all her life—the prince her sister wouldn't stop talking about.

Azalion looked back briefly, smiling at the girl who had helped him. To Katie, he looked strangely ordinary in plaid and faded denim, but he had lost none of his boyish good looks. Katie smiled broadly and waved. Her prince waved back, but kept walking, disappearing in the drifting fog taking up residence in the cooling field.

Katie would spend the rest of the summer searching for fairy tale creatures throughout the entirety of the farm, trying to explain the missing plaid shirt to her father numerous times over (eventually satisfying him with a fabricated story involving a stray dog and a ham bone), and desperately calling the names of fictional characters into the evening. She would be largely unsuccessful, though she came to believe that the woman residing in the neighbouring farmhouse (some twenty minutes away) was a genuine, classical witch. Having a serious aversion to being cooked alive and eaten, Katie never again strayed in that direction.

Eventually, Katie would grow up, admit she had been a very fanciful child, and quit searching the farmyard for griffins, secret treasures, fairies, gnomes, talking trees, and elves.

She would instead begin a search of the neighbouring towns for her very own prince charming, and having grown into an enchanting and optimistic young woman, would have every chance in the world for success. She would, however, upon meeting the son of the neighbouring rancher who returned home after completing an agricultural degree, come to the halting discovery that the evening encounter with a prince in plaid and jeans would be far closer to her version of reality.

Bainan and Reese stopped in an empty street, gasping for breath. Rather, Reese gasped while Bainan breathed with perfect ease, head high and hands on hips. Gym classes were fairly useless, Reese generally believed, until one had occasion to run for their life from gun slinging bandits. At that moment, she wished she were as crazy as her friend Macy, who got up while the sun slowly dawned to run a few kilometers, yet cover no distance at all, on a treadmill at the gym. Bainan, who would be unaffected by anything, watched her with vague concern — or rather, contemplating whether he ought to feel concern for her. The man was probably a machine of some kind.

The two got in line for a subway ticket. The dingy fluorescent bulbs flickered piteously, pale specters of light after the noonday glare. A few curious glances were directed at the man with the broadsword, but whether not wanting to become entangled with the situation or discounting him for a B-level thespian, anyone noticing simply passed by, continuing on their way. Security looked like they were going to make a move, but then appeared to have decided they would likely all die before wrestling a swordsman of that bulk to the ground—they had heard the recent news stories after all. Rather than tackling the situation, they simply busied themselves conveniently as Bainan and Reese passed, ostensibly re-wrapping a roll of police tape.

Reese and Bainan boarded the train in peace. A kind man even gave up his seat for them. As did a woman with a small child. And a guy with a backpack. A few people did, actually, Reese noticed—all seats surrounding them were vacated in relatively short order. Reese, even on her best days, had only been offered a train seat a handful of times—and then only if she carried a great deal of baggage. She kind of liked having a burly warrior as a bodyguard. Bainan stroked a scruffy chin thoughtfully as he sat in the seat next to her.

Reese was suddenly reminded of the long nights before the computer during which she had written Bainan's story. It had been a dark and depressing time for Reese, a lonely time, thus all of this emotion fell to Bainan's stern character. Nasty things tend to roll downhill, Reese knew, and so it had occurred with more than a few of her characters. She had in fact, been very close to writing, just after THE END, a post-script that read: "and you better have enjoyed this book because I listened to way too many depressing metal albums during its creation for you not to appreciate my efforts".

Reese wondered if her story should have turned out differently if she had quit her oppressive (at the time) day job. She had been waitressing in a second-rate restaurant. Her co-workers were petty, and there were few she felt comfortable talking with. There was one in particular—her name was Cathy—with whom even the briefest of conversations made Reese want to stick sharp pencils in her eyes if only to counter the pain of the interaction. Cathy would (hopefully) never know it (unless she is one of those braving the reading of this very book), but Reese had at the time based one of her least favourite characters on Cathy's real-life exploits. Reese was very grateful she no longer worked that job. Writing suited her much better, but of late she was being forced to re-evaluate her career choice—though at this point any decisions on her part may well prove moot. Reese's musings were interrupted by the thrumming voice of Bainan.

"Who wert those uncouth marauders?" Bainan asked, fidgeting with his sword. He was having a little trouble coping with a five-foot sword in the confines of the train car and tried another angle with it.

"They're outlaws from a western story I wrote. Their band was slaughtered by a desert tribe after they were caught robbing a bank and got lost making their escape. Their leader is Al Gunnar, *Th'Nameless*," Reese replied. After a long pause, she added, "Every character that died in one of my novels has been brought here—and I always make sure to kill all the villains!"

"I suppose an offer to lay down my life to protect you is slightly remedial at this point," Bainan mused.

"I suppose so," Reese agreed gloomily, "in a sense you already have."

"This situation is dire indeed," Bainan declared. "Is there anyone who might be able to help us negotiate this conundrum? How many other heroes have died in thy writings?"

Reese looked at Bainan quizzically, wondering if she had ever written it in his person to use words with more than three syllables. Probably not. It was odd that he should begin to do so now.

"Um, I don't know," Reese replied. She tried to think of any. Aside from Azalion, his uncle, and the crew of the ship that was gunned down, all of her heroes were present or accounted for. Reese had a very difficult time killing her favourite characters. She loved them too much— she usually just had them live happily ever after. Sure, she let them suffer a lot so they built character and were refined into better people (something she thought more real people ought to do), but she could rarely bring herself to kill them. She was well aware that it had to happen if she was to write any convincing narrative, so she had on occasion bent to the task with a heavy heart. She had a less heavy heart in the killing of Bainan—he had been her allegorical sacrificial lamb representing all of the macho jerks she'd had the misfortune of dating.

As for Azalion, *et al*, Reese had only killed them in an effort to still the unending demand for her to continually write essentially the same book over and over again—she might just as well have put the characters into a computer model and had it write the stories. The upshot was: Reese' list of downed heroes was likely to be short. She never thought she would consciously wish death upon her best protagonists, but if ever it were to happen, the time would be now.

Reese looked at the small notebook before her, contemplating writing the words that would transport any of her lead characters from death to a new life in the real world (or was this the real world anymore? Reese hardly knew). However, those books were already published. Reese couldn't change what had happened in those stories. Reese mentally sifted through about a half-dozen partly-finished and almost-started manuscripts piled up in her closet at her apartment—if it had survived the cannon fire. Were there any heroes in there that might help?

Reese and Bainan sat like that, deliberating, while the plot progressed, much like the train, in its predetermined direction. And again, like the train, nothing would be able to stop it or alter its course. Except perhaps the brakes, but we all know that the best stories have no brakes and therefore stop for nothing.

Quercius returned to his quarters. He hung up his cloak and his sword, sitting down in a large wood-and-leather chair. The sword and cloak seemed to grow heavier each day.

Diffuse lamplight cloaked the room in a glow that, in one forlorn existence, could be mistaken for romantic. Sighing now, he could only think of his darling wife, lost to him beyond veils terrestrial and dimensional.

Quercius had first met Anadesta in the court of Count Frigalis, at a ball thrown in the honour of a recent naval victory. Quercius had been but a Lieutenant at the time, and Anadesta the daughter of a demi-prominent duke. It had been an unpleasant and cloudy day, so the naval parade had been unfortunately canceled. Only once the dancing began did the moon condescend to grace the company, favouring party-forsaking nobility with her weak rays. The cancelation of the parade meant that Quercius, among many others of the lieutenant rank, chanced to enter the ballroom.

The moment Quercius saw Anadesta, he knew that he was doomed. Doomed to lay the remainder of his life at her feet, doomed to wait to see if she would cherish this gift and hold it close, or spurn him for a despicable rogue. Yet was it so awful an end? To once know what love is, Quercius was certain, would be worth staking everything to come against a bid for either joy or endless anguish.

Quercius crossed the shining ballroom in a trance. Every pulse faster than the last, and every step sounding more sure and direct, he caught her eye from a distance. He immediately offered his best smile, as did she. Or, were it not her best, it was only calculated to the potency necessary to irrevocably bind the heart of the young sailor in the staunchness of admiration's chains.

"Good evening, my Lady," Quercius began, "it is my great fortune that I am in attendance on official business. My name is Lieutenant Quercius."

"The business of the night is dancing, kind sir. My name is Anadesta."

"Indeed, you are correct, my Lady," Quercius flashed a (he imagined) charming grin and offered Anadesta his arm, motioning one sweeping and only slightly shaking hand to the dance floor. To his great surprise and delight, she placed her hand on his arm and deigned to allow him to lead her onto the dance floor.

Quercius had conducted the necessary, yet enjoyable, introductions. Depending on the company, introductions are either an enchantment or a burden. Conversation with Miss Anadesta, it turned out, was no burden in the slightest. The two had danced together (four dances in a row) then repaired to a moonlit balcony adjacent the ballroom.

It had taken the pair scarce several months

to determine that neither could continue to exist without the other. The marriage took place on a clear spring day, on the deck of the *Aura Regency Hide* and officiated by Quercius' commodore himself.

Quercius sighed, took out a large pipe and began to light it. He wondered if his wife had received news of his death, and the accompanying destruction of the *Aura*, which had spurred his transition into this new existence. His one regret, that she should lose the right to their estate — Quercius had no sons — tore at his breast. Only through a remarriage would their property remain in the family. This thought comforted Quercius, needless to say, not at all. If only he were able to reach back, to either return to her or merely see her once more before she would be forced to move on and forget him forever.

Quercius sat, boring a hole in the deck with the fire in his eyes. Pipe smoke had cloaked the entire room in a dense haze. For a time not a soul dared to break the brooding, melancholy silence. The only sound to be heard came from the single lamp, flickering dimly. Quercius was at length interrupted by a loud and urgent knock at the door.

"Come in, if you must," he grunted. The door swung back, and entered Captain Perfuga. He seemed quite out of breath.

"Speak," Quercius granted. He would have been otherwise happy to dwell upon the past, allowing the memory of his love to burn a hole in his heart. For in his mind, it was better to burn eternally for a love that has been lost, than to feel nothing at all for the space of a lifetime.

"Sir, I see strange lights on the horizon," Perfuga panted, "I think it may be a hostile vessel."

"By all means, show me," Quercius rumbled unenthusiastically, rising reluctantly. He followed the Captain onto the quarterdeck, where they were quite alone. Not one sailor could be seen on deck. Quercius resolved to find and reprimand the watchman who ought to be on duty.

"Yonder," Captain Perfuga pointed pensively.

"I see nothing," Quercius replied, "are you sure it is an enemy vessel?"

"Quite certain, sir," a vague white pinhole of light was now apparent, "it is the vessel from beyond the sky, bearing countless armed brigands, the words "spare none" painted crudely on the hull. She is captained by a fellow named Umbrage, who answers only to the one known as Ignes."

"How do you know all this?" Quercius demanded.

Captain Perfuga only smiled, thrusting a somewhat blunt dagger swiftly into the abdomen of Quercius.

"Oh, I can only speculate — to within a negligible margin of certainty," Perfuga returned.

"I know the ship and its crew well. It is such a pity that your soft-hearted, nostalgic sentiments of honour and duty has numbed you to the formidable ideas of progress and power."

"And a shame that pride and deceit have blinded you. Memory and Mercy are all we truly possess," Quercius gasped.

Perfuga only laughed, walking away with a hurried nonchalance.

Quercius clutched the fresh wound, collapsing to the deck.

The enemy ship now approached with a marked increase in speed. A sailor raised the alarm, and Captain Lee immediately appeared on deck.

"Hark! All hands, prepare to engage the enemy!" Captain Lee made full use of her distinguished commanding voice. "Captain Perfuga! Where is the General? Do not merely stand there, command the crew!"

"What crew, my noble captain? I am afraid there are a pitiful few remaining," hissed the snake. He tucked the reddened dagger momentarily behind his back.

Captain Lee, for the first time in her life, was quite at a loss. Her crew no longer sufficient to man the guns, or even repel an attack, she tried to decide which course of action was best.

"Don't be alarmed," Perfuga went on, "it was always going to be this way."

A sudden blast of science-fictioney cannon fire reminiscent of a slinky in a cardboard tube silhouetted the dagger, raised to strike. Perfuga displayed a mad glint in his eye and too many dreadfully white teeth as he brought the dagger down.

His wrist suddenly clamped in an iron fist, Perfuga hissed venomously. Captain Lee spun Perfuga round by the arm, and he cried out in pain, dropping the dagger.

"Who are you, really?" Lee demanded. Perfuga only laughed as one who is threatened by a child. He made no other reply. "If you will not say, then I will tell you who you are, *captain*," Captain Lee continued, disregarding the flames all about her, the inferno consuming the better portion of the deck, "you are the idiot fool about to die by my side."

Moments later the vessel was naught but shattered timber and ash. Wicked cries pierced the night sky, mingling with the screams of the sailors trapped in the descending wreckage.

Chapter 10:

Timeo Frigalis

The train stopped with a recalcitrant lurch, as though unimpressed that its progress was suddenly impeded. A man and a woman exited the car, weaving among the large crowd. She wore grey pants, a dark top, and a coat that looked in need of laundering. Her shoulder-length auburn hair hung loose, framing a handsome yet troubled face. He wore little — mainly leather and furs, with a goodly number of belts loaded down with an even goodlier number of daggers, a single bow, a full quiver, and several swords. His golden hair flew freely in the apparently rather drafty tunnel. His beard was plaited and braided among gold ringlets. This only the two held in common: they both wore the same worry and urgency projected readily on their faces.

The woman led, seeming to know best the way from the underground rail labyrinth, and the large man followed. He appeared really more a bodyguard than a companion, and indeed moved with a lithe but wary confidence through the crowd, scanning left and right as if for hidden enemies. Upon first spying the couple, the terminal security guard dismissed himself for an early break, or perhaps for a hallucinating moron. He did not return to his station for the remainder of the day.

Thus, Bainan and Reese repaired to the street-level platform amidst a host of weary, sorry-looking nine-to-fivers, each carrying an empty lunchbox and a full briefcase. One thing could be said of the ragged workforce: it is a well-known fact that a worker on his way home weighs significantly more than he did when he took the very same train to work that morning. This is because after eight hours of continual work, he has found that his heart has become heavy — that and the various confections he consumed to make his miserable existence more tolerable for the day have added to his mass.

None of the dogged workers took any notice of Reese or Bainan, the workers lost in their own mental morass. In their dreary, routine worlds, the concept of a six-and-a-half foot warrior with a claymore was completely unthinkable, and since none of them could think Bainan, they could certainly not see him. In addition, none had enough energy to contemplate him even could they have seen him. Bainan weaved nigh undetected and ghost-like through the crowd, following his charge as her self-appointed personal militia.

It had been decided that the best course of action would be to collect Bainan's men-at-arms. The men would likely prove to be an essential component in any plan that involved, for example, singing drinking songs, or winning a contest for "most impressive beard". They could also be instrumental in disposing of large quantities of alcohol and foemen, and indeed, preferred to do both at the same time — the latter of which made up Reese' primary objective in locating them.

Thus, the pair set off to walk the remaining few blocks to the place Bainan had last seen his men-at-arms. For this band of men, loyal as they were, would surely await their captain like a well-trained dog at "stay".

"Um... Bainan, there is something I wanted to ask," Reese began, wondering if this would be a good time or not, but then she had positively no idea if any other time might arrive.

"Verily, my lady. Say on," he responded coherently, but continued to look straight ahead as they walked side by side.

"It's my fault that you couldn't save Tsarmina. And I'm sorry. But why are you helping me?" Reese was puzzled by the worthy warrior's trueheartedness when his loss had come at her own hands.

Bainan appeared to think for a moment, but Reese knew better. It was only a fair approximation of thinking that he portrayed; Bainan was a creature of instinct and barbaric conviction.

"My fate is not my own to decide," began the bearded warrior. "I am glad of the time I have lived and the love that Tsarmina and I shared, yet even I must accede to my maker. My will matters little when faced with such a planned and detailed destiny. I am but a small part of the story, I feel. And verily, you gave me a fine warrior's end."

Reese was speechless. For the second time, she tried to get through without choking up. It was proving difficult.

"Thank you, Bainan," was all she could manage. Despite his staunch and stoic composure, Reese knew he was capable of delving deeper than any into his infinite stratum of dedication and devotion—she had given him that to promote the bromance component of his story—a theme that appealed to male and female readers alike for some unknown reason. She prayed silently that Bainan's courage would be enough to see them through whatever events the new day would bring.

Earl, Charles and Matt had each found a very comfortable spot on the concrete floor of the brig. Their tour of the space frigate had been brief, with too few friendly expository narratives, and much more handcuffing, and also a great deal of regular cuffing. Earl nursed a large bruise to the back of his head. His one shot at diplomacy ("I say, can't we simply discuss this over coffee—and perhaps a cheesecake?") had not been appreciated by his guard.

"Have you still got the manuscript?" Earl asked.

Charles, looking quite miserable, nodded. He withdrew the battered, wrinkled, but still solidly stapled packet of papers. If there was one thing Charles was good at—besides seeing punctuation over plot—it was ensuring the pages of documents stayed together. He had learned that little lesson when the pages of a horror story he had been editing became entangled with an autobiography that was next in line. Charles still asserted both stories had been improved by the error, but others had not shared his opinion.

"I've given it a once-over," Charles put in. "I still don't understand why she killed off her best-selling character, but it appears that Azalion's death is the key issue at hand."

"That document is somehow responsible for all this rampaging and kidnapping," Matt stated. "It's probably in our best interest not to give it up."

"What can we do? They will surely find it on us," Charles grumbled.

The trio cast about despondently, yet the forbidding steel and concrete chamber yielded no convenient hiding places.

Charles heaved a frustrated sigh.

THOU FOOLS DESPAIR TOO EASILY. Seraiah chose that moment to speak up, and the three were soon to be grateful that he had.

"If you aren't going to be of any help, you may as well give us some quiet," Matt groaned. The suit of metal began to click and creak. "Hey! Hold on, what are you doing?"

AND WHAT MAKES YOU THINK, Seraiah chuckled dryly, THAT I AM UNABLE TO ASSIST?

A small compartment in the side of the suit clicked open, revealing Matt's torn and stained security fatigues. By now, the clothing he wore beneath the armour consisted of 96% sweat and 4% itchy and the proportions were changing by the hour. Matt would have gladly sold his soul at that point for a shower and a thrift store tee. As for blue jeans: for Matt, they were only a distant memory. He had been trapped in the EVA suit for some days now, and to say he was growing weary of it would have been a gross understatement.

"Neat trick," Matt remarked, "any chance you can open the REST of this thing?"

NO CHANCE WHATSOEVER, came the resonant, steely voice.

"Some friend! Come on, can't you get me out of this thing already?"

IT IS FAR MORE PRACTICAL THAT YOU REMAIN AS YOU ARE, Seraiah explained.

"Perfect, I always wanted to be a tin of meat," Matt groaned.

AN AMUSING ANALOGY, Seraiah mused, SINCE ONCE A CAN OF MEAT IS OPENED, IT IS GENERALLY IMMEDIATELY DEVOURED.

Matt fell silent for some moments, pondering this portentious prophecy. He wasn't sure he liked Seraiah's implications.

Charles approached Matt, who turned to

allow the papers to be placed inside his suit. Charles rolled up the manuscript and tucked it into the holster which had formerly held Matt's flashlight. Seraiah then electronically closed the hatch in the suit.

"I suppose you're not completely useless," Matt conceded.

BY THE WAY, Seraiah continued, SINCE THIS SHIP IS, TO USE A HUMAN TERM, MY HOME SHIP, MIGHT I UNLOCK OUR CELL?

The suggestion seemed a great idea for approximately 18 seconds as the trio contemplated it.

"Wait," Earl cautioned. "We have no way off this ship, even if we do get out. The fact that we can get out of here is our only weapon right now, so we should wait for a better opportunity. Let's see what they want first," Earl stated sagely.

"And pass up a chance to escape?" Charles whined. The argument would have continued, but was interrupted.

The iron slats withdrew from the doorframe with a rather loud CLNK. The reciprocal 270 degree bolts retracted with a SLAM of ominous finality. Earl, Charles, and Matt looked on in suspense. (Seraiah did not "look" as such, since he is a computer simulation of a personality, who can only perceive electrical impulses and more often, accidental user input, but he nevertheless silently observed the proceedings.) Four bolts retracted as the guards unlocked them. CLCK. KLCK. THNK. HERBERT.

(The last lock was voice activated.) Finally, the door's infrared proximity sensor visibly deactivated because, as everyone knows from watching any decent film, lasers are entirely visible to the naked eye. The large cell doors swung inward mechanically on several dozen unnecessarily intimidating sprockets and gears.

Into the cell strode a tall, thin, completely bald man, looking rather like a billiard ball balanced atop a pool cue. He wore a leather greatcoat, high boots, and what appeared to be body armour, in addition to (we must assume) pants and presumably socks. The remainder of his clothing (specifically underpants), though not noteworthy or warranting any documentation, was nonetheless present. He wore, holstered at his hip, a large and advanced-looking firearm. Three guards attended him, similarly dressed, hauling in their midst a protesting Perfuga. The guards threw the capitulating captain cruelly upon the concrete floor, where he lay much like a chicken with its bones removed.

"Icgk Schwign hirrr Illi Umbrage" said the tall man in his native language, the only vowel in which was the letter "I".

"I am captain Umbrage," his guardsman, acting as translator, repeated.

The four prisoners stared for a moment.

"Really?" Matt jibed, "I can't make it out very well, but I thought this bald guy just said he was the captain!" Matt laughed. Another guard kicked Matt in the abdomen with a loud clang, then instantly regretted the decision.

"Ing ittin iyn miniscript," the bald man continued.

"I require you to immediately hand over the manuscript, or you shall be subject to extreme punishment and fed to a domesticated Glirynx," the translator repeated.

MY UNFORTUNATE INTIMACY WITH THE HIPERBOLIC TONGUE INDICATES THAT YOU MADE UP THAT LAST BIT. Seraiah taunted mercilessly, safe within the steel suit, and certainly not intimidated by threats of alien predators.

The guard glared menacingly at Matt, yet made no move to physically abuse him this time, still standing on one foot and wincing.

"If yii di niit pridice thi miniscript within thrii hiirs, I will kill ine if yii," the bald Umbrage, it seemed, could speak nigh perfect English when he was not intent on implementing his intimidation tactics. Indeed, a Hiperbolian accent is one of the hardest to overcome.

"If you do not produce the manuscript within three hours, I will—" the translator stopped short, somewhat embarrassed as Umbrage shot him a look.

The guards retreated, following their captain, and leaving Perfuga attempting to peel himself off the cement floor.

"Those brutes," Captain Perfuga complained, "they have destroyed the *Aura Regency*. Quercius and Captain Lee are most likely dead." He lifted himself from the floor with a deflating sigh.

"How do you know all this?" Matt demanded.

"I was captured fleeing from the wreck of the *Aura*. Goodness knows if anyone else survived," the captain certainly had the appearance of one who has survived a fire: his clothing was singed and he smelled of burnt hair — that and one eyebrow was singed into a melted mess that made his co-prisoners twist their mouths when they looked at it.

The four sat for some time, each mutually despondent in his own defeat.

"Does anybody have any idea what they want from us?" Perfuga voiced.

"They want the manuscript Reese was working on," Charles mumbled. "The one where she kills Azalion." He had scarcely said a word since they had been captured. His only thoughts were that they would soon be forced to endure unspeakable tortures like badly syntaxed run-on sentences, wet socks in sandals, and free verse poetry readings — they may even resort to abstract art critiques. Charles most fervently feared the latter.

"At least the document is safe with Prince Azalion, no doubt. He must have escaped with it," mused the captain.

The other three looked about sordidly.

"Surely you do not still have it?" pressed Perfuga. "We mustn't let them get to it! Might we hide it somewhere?" Perfuga, now establishing a conclusion reached two pages ago, was eager to see the manuscript in a secure place.

"It is quite safe enough," Earl concluded the conversation, nodding to Matt.

QUITE RIGHT.

Perfuga scanned the metal suit, appearing satisfied that the manuscript was safe within. He thought for a moment, then rose.

"Guards!" he called.

"What are you doing, Captain?" Earl inquired. He was sincerely ignored.

The guards entered then, carrying a long black cloak.

Perfuga doffed his tattered and burnt captain's greatcoat, and the guards draped him in black. Earl and Charles looked on in shock, but Matt had not moved to indicate either surprise or anger.

"Guards, leave these two to rot here. Bring the metal man to the repair deck and cut him apart. I will have that document," Perfuga commanded with an authority none of the others had seen in him, "even if I must cut it from his congealed corpse." This last comment was directed at Matt.

"At least he's charming about it," Matt acceded.

"You traitor!" Earl spat.

"Not so! You see, for me to be a traitor, I must have been removed from my purchase at your side. That never happened. I never was your ally. That makes me not an opportunistic traitor, but a very thoughtful and successful spy. A much more ambitious thing, don't you agree?"

"And a fool through and through," Matt said in a neutral tone.

"Pardon me for failing to give my real name, gentlemen," Pseudo-Perfuga continued, "for I am Count Ignes, and the horrible power of the Artifact is mine to wield since having liberated it in Bainan's last story. Now that I have the manuscript, I also have the means to subject the people of this world to my just and merciful rule," he formed the adjectives with a malicious, straight-faced sarcasm, indicating that any rule he carried out would be, in fact, neither just nor merciful. [The editors would like to add a note at this point to say that a sarcasm font is desperately needed and we appeal to the writer's guild to coordinate discussions to devise the same in order to spare readers such expository explanations.]

Charles remained quite confused, missing the tone of Ignes' voice entirely, and certainly would have been aided by the presence of a sarcasm font.

The count whirled, a motion made more dramatic by the theatrically loud *swoosh* and flaring of his cloak, and exited the room. Matt, bound and chained, was led away. Charles and Earl were left to mope, which they did extremely well—Charles for their predicament and Earl for the lack of lunch. Both had much experience in the field of moping and were equally well-versed in its other variants: languishing, lollygagging, and loafing about. Earl had once won the "most-laziest-person-this-week" award, he simply never bothered collecting the prize.

The doorbell rang, though its affect was barely audible. Troy had returned home after the broadsword incident, and found himself followed by several swarthy and sturdy men, all wearing unwarranted amounts of fur and leather; their hair was long, their faces unshaven, and each was armed from boots up. They sported daggers, axes, maces, flails, longswords, shortswords, smallswords, and every variation of knife ever invented. In absence of their leader, they followed Troy home to celebrate his act of courage. This they did by draining his apartment slowly of all drink (alcoholic or otherwise), emptying his fridge swiftly of anything edible (and things not so edible), and scattering Troy's plates, cups, and utensils freely about the apartment, all done to the playing of various piped instruments they produced from within the furs they wore. A chorus of doughty, deep voices belched forth raucous songs in a language Troy (nor any other member of humanity) could not comprehend. And this is precisely why, when the doorbell rang, nobody answered it. Reese and Bainan stood in the hall, and could hear clearly (as could the other 53 tenants) the reveling within.

"Do you think they're in there?" Reese

asked, part chuckling.

"I do believe it, as verily as I believe that on the Northern Shore of the Great Maranian Sea—"

"Um, Bainan? I would love to hear more about the Maranian Sea, but perhaps inside," Reese suggested. Bainan, who had never before been interrupted in such a manner, struggled in the vague haze of his mind to perceive why she would not be utterly enthralled at the prospect of his story—perhaps she was, he thought, in a hurry. Or insane.

"Of course, my lady. Or would you prefer 'Your Highness'?"

Reese could tell that Bainan was completely serious (despite the previously mentioned lack of sarcasm font), and not making fun—she had not given him sarcasm or even levity as a trait, although certainly some of her critics had thought so. Her characters—the heroes, at any rate—seemed to be developing some sort of devout admiration for Reese.

"Just call me Reese—oh!" Reese gasped as Bainan shouldered his way through the flimsy door. It disintegrated before only the slightest shove of his mountainous shoulder. A chorus of rough voices chanted his name, and moments later Troy dove from the apartment. He dusted the wood-dust of his late doorway from a faded IC BC t-shirt. (The band had originally planned to title themselves "IC BS", but deemed it too inappropriate for an immature audience.)

Reese and Troy stood just outside of contact range and watched the active destruction progress within Troy's apartment.

"Um. I'm Troy. Do you know these guys?" Troy addressed Reese.

"Yeah, they're with me. I'm Reese Richardson." Reese shook the young man's hand.

"You're an author, right?" Troy wondered.

"Oh no, you're not a fan, are you?" Reese expected the usual response.

"Sort of, but only by acquaintance. A friend told me about your work," the two squeezed back into the crowded apartment.

"My lady," Bainan began, "we are ready to march at your command. May my diminished yet worthy band be a scourge upon thine enemies until every copy of your writings is recovered! Whither shall we journey?"

"Oh no! There was another copy! I forgot. I left it with Macy. We have to hurry!" Reese was growing more and more frantic.

"Macy's in trouble?" Troy asked, yet nobody heard.

Some moments later, it was decided that all would make the journey to Macy's in Troy's diminutive sedan. The chassis ground the concrete under the weight of Bainan's men as the small engine groaned pitifully, trying to haul its load. The roof rack bristled with bladed weaponry, and one extra bearded ruffian who didn't quite fit in the small trunk. Troy fervently hoped they would not get pulled over.

A shrub near the house cursed softly. Even across the small front garden, it was apparent that the doors were locked and the windows barred. The shrub stayed stock still, as if trying to concoct another plan. Shrubs are generally quite still while they are plotting. It is when they take sudden leave you must be concerned.

Jack Grendel sighed and stroked a sharp blade, deciding that patience was the best course of action. Soon enough, he would enter the house and kill the only occupant. It would then be a few more minutes before Jack would find the manuscript and disappear like a shadow in a dark room. It would be simple, and hopefully, silent. Jack was grateful then that his adversary, a stubborn and unlawfully plucky detective, had survived the novel in which Jack had died. Jack had met nobody since who could stand toe-to-toe with his murderous self and survive. It would be quite different had his nemesis appeared in this life to stymie him. The only other character able to do that now was that insipid prince. Jack grinned darkly. Soon he would have killed all real people who knew of Azalion's death. He would have the writer put Azalion back into his book, and Jack would be free to run things as they ought to be run.

Jack Grendel walked from his station behind the shrub to the back garden, seeking entrance. He would soon grow desperate enough to put a fist through one of the windows, or impersonate a pizza delivery man, were he in a position to know what that was. It was fortunate he did not. His customers would likely not appreciate paying by the slice.

Aha! Jack had found his opportunity. The back window was a jar. Jack pushed the jar aside and entered stealthily, scarcely breathing. He found himself in a bedroom, the style difficult to make out in the dark. But not for Jack. He took in every detail of the small room, and could hear someone moving about in the kitchen. Jack grinned involuntarily, clutching the knife and flitting like a deep shadow into the hall.

To everyone's amazement (the warriors were all still enraptured with the concept of mechanized locomotion) the car made it across town without collapsing. Bainan surveyed the front garden and took in a deep breath, tasting the air.

"He is here," Bainan muttered, crouching.

"Who is? What?!?" Troy was evidently struggling to keep up.

"Jack Grendel," Reese whispered.

"Oh," Troy tried to decipher the information. "Who?"

"A dangerous killer lurks within," Bainan narrated in exposition. Bainan had difficulty with the flow of dialogue at times.

"We have to do something!" Troy spluttered, ineptly clenching his fists.

"*We*," Reese shot back, "will keep the car

company. Let's just hope Macy isn't in the shower or something as equally cliché."

Macy was not in the shower, nor was she in fact in anything cliché. The thing in which she was could be vaguely described as a living room, if only a very small one. An old couch, a dim reading lamp, and an end table occupied the vast majority of the confined space, all sporting clashing pastel colours in horrific, deplorable and immoral floral patterns of the circa 1970s variety.

In Macy's hands was the new bestseller, *Fifty Blades a Day*. Macy set the book down with some measure of finality, only three pages in and thoroughly disgusted. She had anticipated a fiction-fantasy questing adventure, but that was not what she found within its pages at all. Why on earth had all her friends read that thing? It was going straight back to the library—after she had finished her cup of tea—the only saving grace of the rather disappointing situation in which Macy presently found herself. She sipped her tea, recalling the past 24 hours.

Macy had enjoyed her first real date with Troy. The two had gone to a downtown restaurant serving fast food, Mexican-style. Macy contemplated the fact that Troy needed a few lessons in culture. Oh, and fashion too—Troy had appeared at Macy's door, ready for their evening in a completely tattered metal band print t-shirt (Von Hell Sing to be precise, complete with art-deco skulls sporting flowers in place of eye sockets). The shirt appeared to be the rugged sole survivor of several metal concerts, or perhaps a civil war, or maybe multiple knife fights. It was hard to tell which. Macy had invited Troy into her very small house long enough to throw a plaid shirt over his tattered tee, buttoning several of the buttons just for good measure.

Rather than being embarrassed, Troy had been quite amused that she would take the time to dress him properly. He made a somewhat inept but heartfelt compliment on the interior of the house, whereupon Macy retorted that he ought to get better at lying. Troy had rather no idea what she meant and Macy was only left to guess what kind of hole Troy had crawled out of — evidently the sort of hole where fashion and home décor were foreign concepts. That, however, could be remedied.

They had proceeded downtown in Troy's car — a thing that could almost be described as luxurious and sporty — thirty years prior, perhaps. Macy offered to buy dinner, Troy having saved her life and whatnot.

It was a cool night, and Macy thanked Troy for turning the car heater on. He replied that it was the only setting that worked, don't ask what happened to the air conditioning.

They reached the restaurant and found a table, seating themselves. In a short while their food was brought: a spicy variety of tacos and sopes. The two found the evening quite agreeable. Troy had got salsa on his chin, and they both laughed when Macy tried casually to point it out, but failed dismally in her attempted subtleties. In the end, she wiped his chin for him.

While Troy lacked grace, and fashion, and taste, he seemed quite amiable—charming, in fact, Macy had thought. They had agreed on a second date in the near future, and with that established, Troy dropped her off at her home.

Macy mused that had their date been a job interview, Troy certainly would have failed, and would have done so rather convincingly at that. She could picture herself asking, "What makes you qualified for this role?" and many such questions. He would squirm in his uncomfortable plastic chair, fiddle with the chain about his neck, then mumble something incoherent to the nature and effect of this-and-that, or something-or-other.

"And what skills are you bringing to the team?" Macy would ask jokingly with a subtle smile.

"Uh… team? What? I thought I was the sole applicant."

And yet, Macy thought, his efforts had been sincere.

25 unstimulating hours later, Macy sat on her couch and sipped her tea. She glanced out the window to see if it was too dark to walk to the library. She was suddenly surprised to see Reese standing in her front garden and waving frantically. Reese gestured violently to the front door, then held one finger to her lips to indicate silence. Macy got up, wondering why her friend did not simply knock. Macy opened the door.

"Why didn't you just-eeemmmfhp!" This last utterance was Macy's stifled cry as she was silenced by the large hand of Bainan who then deftly picked her up and swept her off to stand next to Reese.

Jack Grendel waited in the hall. He tossed the knife in the air, caught it again, and waited some more. He had heard something that sounded like a door opening, then some dialogue he could not make out. At last the door could be heard to close again. Footsteps were then heard, making their way to the sofa. With a soft creak, Jack knew then that the sofa was once more occupied. He dashed around the corner, and 3.5 steps later stopped suddenly.

There was no young woman on the couch. Seated where she ought to have been was a large, grinning, brutish looking man, dressed (almost) in fur and leather. One muscled leg crossed, he appeared to be reading the book Macy had left on the coffee table. The book was upside-down.

"I have no idea who you are," Jack Grendel pondered to himself, rather surprised that there was an unknown detail in the present circus in which he found himself.

"Indeed," Bainan glared at the book, as if mere concentration could make the squiggles on the page form plain sense. "We have not been acquainted prior. But that is quite enough of words for me." Bainan replaced the book on the table and rose. Rounding the sofa, Bainan drew a shortsword. Yet even a shortsword could outreach Grendel's dagger; Grendel surmised with a keen, survival-like instinct that he ought to leave, and soon. But the burly barbarian barreled blithely toward Grendel.

Bainan slashed more than air with the keen shortsword; Grendel cried in pain, his clothing rent. Though the wounds had been shallow, Grendel was now bleeding profusely.

Jack Grendel, with the instinct of an animal that must kill or be killed, lunged for Bainan's throat with his dagger. Bainan brought both arms down, violently knocking the dagger from Grendel's grasp with the heels of his hands.

The lunge had been a feint; Grendel now had hold of the doorknob, pulling the kitchen door closed between them.

With Bainan on the other side of the door, Jack made to exit the house but found his progress inhibited by a glass door. He fumbled with the latch. It came off in his hand.

Bainan had, by this time, shouldered his way through his second door of the day—he appeared to have quite a talent for it, having practiced on the much sturdier doors found in his own story. Splinters and wood-dust showered from his shoulders.

Bainan lunged—it was his turn to aim a keen stab at his opponent. Jack swiftly turned up the narrow table between them; the sword impaled the inexpensive woodwork flawlessly. Before Bainan could retract the sword, Grendel twisted the table and it cartwheeled out of the way, taking the sword with it.

Grendel had by now drawn a small and especially nasty push dagger from somewhere about his person; he drove it deeply into Bainan's shoulder and let go.

Bainan glanced unapprovingly at the knife handle protruding from his shoulder. He drove his right foot into Jack Grendel's chest and propelled Jack forcibly through the glass door. The fight was over before it truly had begun. Grendel slunk into the trees, and Bainan returned to find Reese and Macy. Macy's agitation was not at all improved by the night air—or perhaps it was stirred by the way Bainan succinctly pulled the knife from his own shoulder then neatly snapped the blade in two with a determined grin.

"Who are these guys? Reese, what's going on? And why is Troy here?" Macy spoke faster than some of her companions were capable of thinking.

Bainan's men had long since given up, content to simply watch the young woman's hand gestures, mouth movements, and the twisted set of her face as it morphed into various comic strip expressions, thinking to themselves how beautiful and serene she might look if only she would stop talking.

"Calm down, Macy. There's a lot to explain," Reese explained while managing to explain nothing at all.

"That's not an answer, Reese! Is it really so much to explain?"

"Okay, so... All the characters from my books — but only the ones who died — have come to life here, and all the villains are trying to kill us, so we have to recover my manuscript and find a way to stop them from using it to take over the world, only I just realized you had a second copy and they might come after this one too, so we came to get you and the manuscript." Reese gasped after the torrent of words.

"There, now. That wasn't so hard. The manuscript is on my desk."

Bainan departed, using the door properly this time (or at least what was left of it), and was shortly returned with a shoddy off-centered binder, its spine worn, the cover scribbled dozens of times over with the kind of permanent marker that was found to be responsible for major brain damage in school age children (that, and mimeograph ink).

"The acquisition of this manuscript has proven most fortuitous," Bainan seemed to have gained access to his vocabulocampus, the (for Bainan at least) very small portion of the brain responsible for vocabularian development. "However, this house is no longer safe for you, my lady." Bainan addressed this comment to Macy.

"He's right," Reese agreed, "you'll have to stay with us until we sort this all out."

"Then I'm coming too," Troy insisted.

All then paused to wonder what possible use Troy could be on their quest. Not much, they each decided, silently. All present, save Bainan, had the ability to think silently, and it was he who reflexively spoke the group's collective thoughts out loud. The group had by now become accustomed to this and allowed Bainan a degree of privacy by ignoring him utterly. Troy, however, was the only person present not familiar with this unspoken rule and was mildly irritated.

"We ought to find that spaceship," Reese suggested, easily overriding the faux pas.

"There's a spaceship?" Troy blurted, again ruining the flow of the narrative with repetition and exposition.

"Yon craft of metal sleek needs must have sought a hiding place," Bainan was becoming more and more enraptured with his newfound powers of articulation.

Just then a tremendous whoosh was heard, the gust of which ruffled clothing and tousled hair. With a fantastic roar, a great winged lion descended among them. Azalion, clearly in one piece (though for some reason dressed like a farmer) swung lightly off the lion's back.

"Azalion! My notebook worked!" Reese wrapped the boy in her arms.

"Yes. I owe you more than I can ever repay," Azalion replied.

"For now, let's just try to fix this mess I've made," Reese decided.

"Of course. While aloft I could see a great distance. The steel battleship has landed at the top of a mountain to the East. The wreck of the *Aura Regency* is located in a valley many hour's walk from that place."

"Excellent," Reese said. "Bainan, we must take your men and locate the spaceship."

"I, however, must seek my uncle," Azalion offered, declining to join them.

"Then I'll come with you," Reese directed. Azalion made no objection. "By the way, Azalion, this is Bainan. You two would probably get along. Please do keep Macy safe, Bainan."

"Fear not, my lady," Bainan replied. "If I can, by life or death safeguard thy lady in waiting, I shall not fail to do so, even should I have to walk the path to the underworld backstepping, or face the thirteen Improbable Tasks of Harkanese."

The lion was by far gone by the time Bainan's declaration was finished, taking Azalion and Reese with it, yet Bainan was no longer speaking solely for the benefit of others present.

The large group before Macy's house once more contemplated Troy's tiny sedan. It would surely be a long drive.

Chapter 11:

Valorium Ascentii

The yet predawn sun peered over the trees upon the fecund earth, promising much but yielding little. As the sun rose, it lay bare every good deed and each ill act transacted among men—all save one, presently unfolding in a shady grove just outside the small village.

It was a clear morning, with little mist to obscure vision. Though it was bright, the light was deathly chill; the sun deigned not grace the earth with its warmth. A faint smell of predawn rain lingered in the air, and a calm breeze swept the grassy plain with it.

The spot had been chosen for its isolation. Here, at a great distance from the closest village, were those present who were loth to have their business witnessed; the sheltered glade was ideal protection against discovery or interference. Even the sun spurned their intent, covering its face momentarily with cloudy hands.

Upon this glade four men were gathered, two facing two. All were silent, their faces grave and grim. One man from each opposing faction bore a small wooden box, which was presented to each master. Each box was elaborately decorated, of a dark wood, carved with scripture and figures of men and beasts.

The lid could be opened only by means of a brass latch and a key. Two men opened two boxes with two keys.

At one end of the small field was a thin, trim looking man, well dressed. He appeared younger than the rest, but very cold, and cruel. Reaching into the proffered box, he withdrew a weighty dueling pistol. It was loaded, he assumed, with powder and shot. The man before him was a trusted friend; one he knew would never let him down. Yes, the pistol would be adequately prepared. He contemplated the precise manner with which he might project the small steel ball into his opponent.

At the other end of the field was a burly man, grimy and bearded. He regarded his opponent with remorse and refused to take the proffered pistol for some minutes. He knew this kind of man, and knew him to be both young and ambitious—a quarrelsome youth. His name, the blacksmith struggled to remember, might have been Andrews. The duel had been insisted upon by the younger man, who was evidently dissatisfied with the workmanship of the metalwork the blacksmith had undertaken for him.

The large man reluctantly picked up the pistol. He had no desire to fight this man, and his marksmanship was in disrepair. He took several paces toward his opponent, and his second backed away, ready to aid him should he require a fresh weapon, or worse, needle and thread.

Andrews' second strode to the middle of the field. At this cue, Andrews and the smith stepped forward to the smallswords protruding from the ground, set at the agreed-upon distance.

The second stood between the two men. He raised one arm, and let his handkerchief fall.

Both men raised pistols and fired.

For a moment there was naught discernible but smoke between the two. The two shots echoed back from a distant line of trees. The two men, holding the wooden boxes, strained to see whether their man had succeeded or fallen. None could tell for some moments. Gradually the smoke lifted.

The blacksmith stood unscathed; perhaps his opponent had missed. A tentative breeze swept through the clearing, driving away the lingering haze and revealing a blood-soaked Andrews lying upon the ground. The smith sighed, returning the smoking pistol to his second, who packed the box and moved off. The smith was left scratching his beard and wondering if he would have to shoot all his disgruntled clients from then on. It might be bad for business, he decided. Yet mercenaries made quite a lot of money shooting their clients. He would have to consider a career change.

The smith noticed then a shadowy silhouette of a man standing somewhere in the vague corners of his pre-dawn peripheral vision. He turned to verify the vision, only just making out the dark cloaked figure aligned with the trees.

"Quite well-aimed, considering your lack of practice," came the full-toned voice of the stranger.

The blacksmith grunted sullenly, imagining that the newcomer had witnessed the entire ordeal.

The smith contemplated the man, tall and handsome with black hair and blacker clothing. The stranger was positioned nonchalantly on the edge of the field, perilously in reach of the flying balls of steel that had certainly presented a hazard a moment earlier. The smith wondered if this man had been standing within the range of fire all along. Must have been, he decided, the man hadn't just walked up.

"Who are you?" asked the smith.

"A friend," Adriel replied.

"You are lucky Andrews missed us both."

"His aim was not faulty," mused the stranger casually, "his pistol failed to fire. I saw it quite plainly. Perhaps the powder had been wet." Adriel met the blacksmith's level gaze with two dark, glinting eyes. There was something in his physique and posture that chilled the smith, for to him, the man seemed blessed with an otherworldly grace and eloquence that laboured within the confines of his massive form and hinted at something powerful—a power that, if once released, might be more terrifying than eloquent.

"It hasn't rained for two days," the smith replied. He was curious to see how deeply he could probe the conversation, and what it might reveal.

"Then it seems," said the stranger with a roguish grin, "that the weapons have been tampered with. It would have been quite simple to open the box, wet the powder using a small flask, and replace the lid."

"Provided you have the key... What gave you the right to interfere?" asked the smith.

The stranger's smile sobered.

"Merely this," said Adriel with a graceful bow, "there are some with the power and desire to tilt the balance of the Eternal War from the favour of wickedness—to cheat the loaded die cast by the hand of the Devil. The imagined slight he received did not warrant death, particularly not yours. Also, you have other work yet to do before your end. I have need of a sword—a special sword—and you only have the skill to make it to my purpose."

The smith made no reply.

"You ought to thank me, you know. Your pistol was in pitiable condition. Come now, I need your help."

"Supposing I do help. I still won't thank you for killing Andrews."

"I expect no less from so worthy a man. Have you got a name?"

"My name," said the smith, "is Zalel—people around here call me Zak."

Adriel handed the smith a folded piece of paper, on which was written a time and an address. The smith agreed to help him, whatever he might want, whereupon Adriel turned and entered the deep grove of trees from whence he had presumably appeared. The smith was left trying to decipher both what the stranger could possibly want of him, as well as the inky scrawls on the paper. The man could read neither.

Adriel entered the woods, seeking the horse he had tethered there.

It was dark between the trees; dawn had not yet sought to pierce the canopy of green with its omniscient eye. The breath of the forest was chill and musty. A sudden rush of cold air caught Adriel's mortal frame sharply, and in the throes of a heavy shiver, he could feel his wounds split. The blood soaked fresh clothing, warming a gently tracing finger-line down his back. Adriel saw her then, leaning forward between two close-growing trees, looking keenly back at him. Her grey eyes pierced him with a fiery passion, and his breath came as a sudden vapour.

"When did such a faithful servant see fit to tamper in the business of mere men? When did the great Adriel stoop to fixing a trifling duel?" she asked him hotly, her gaze unrelenting. Her pale lips gave forth no warmth; no vapour escaped her mouth as she spoke.

Adriel could find no response for a moment, incapacitated by her presence.

"You are dead, my lady," was all he could say. "What do you mean by lingering in this place? I left you properly in the ground, and the earth welcomed your broken body. What more can you possibly take from me?"

The woman moved closer, forsaking her doughty, branched guardians. Yet her feet made no noise, and the very forest gave no notice of her presence. Her gaze flickered from challenge to pity then back again. Yet in that brief moment of remorse, her softened face appeared changed to a perfect visage of grace, compassion and gentleness. She seemed to regard Adriel, if only for a moment, lovingly.

The girl's dark hair was nearly black, flowing in a series of tresses and braids to her pale shoulders. Her gown was green, greener than the forest around her. Her grey eyes took him in with their silver sparkle, gleaming brightly from her fair face. Her bare arms hung heavily by her side and seemed unable to reach for him.

Adriel stood before her as one turned to stone; He feared to move, lest the vision before him fade into the trees. The blood could be seen seeping, soaking the back of his dark coat and he could feel the heat of it, yet he made no move to staunch the flow.

"You are alone, Adriel. There are none who can help you here. Yet the Task that can be accomplished by you alone—the path before your feet that only you may walk—is far too important for me to allow you to fail now."

"I have already failed, Isabel," said Adriel heavily, the weight of his failing dropping him to his knees. "You are evidence of that. You deserved better in life. I do not ask you to forgive me."

Isabel stepped forward, raising Adriel from his knees. His eyes lifted to hers slowly, his own expression pained. Isabel soothed his fevered brow with a cool hand. He closed his eyes, leaning in to the softness of her skin.

"Find strength!" she whispered fiercely. "Even the stars have their number, and each its own name!

Surely so much more you."

Adriel's eyes were still closed as she leaned forward, kissing his forehead softly with cool, soft lips. When Adriel opened his eyes again, he found only a gentle breeze caressing his cheek. Her kiss, perhaps, had been merely a drop of rain on his face. Isabel, or whatever remained of her, had vanished. Adriel sank once more to his knees, alone and bleeding, in the darkest part of the forest.

It was some time later when Adriel found the strength to stand, leaning heavily against a tree. After some minutes, he resumed his walk along the disused forest path. The richness of the forest around him, the vibrant greens and browns, even the birds' sweet music was lost on him. Adriel could do naught but think over his conversation with the spectre of Isabel. Was it real, or had he dreamed the whole affair? He had no way to tell. He untied his horse, or rather, he untied someone else's horse and mounted up for the ride back into the village.

Adriel rode through the glade; the body of Andrews lay there still, a perch for a large and ominous raven. Adriel wondered to whom the raven would make its report; birds are distrusted as spies wherever folk spin tales—stories by which the old sway the young with fairy stories. Nevertheless, Adriel had done as he saw best. There was no way to stop the events he had now set in motion.

The ride was less than smooth; Adriel felt the sticky cold clinging of the remainder of his garments. He had no way to mend wounds he could not reach;

he knew not where he ought to turn for help. There would be no time for such until he had accomplished his business in town. Adriel pressed the horse forward; for centuries he had watched men rushing about, frantically racing against time—an abstraction he had not understood clearly before. He was quickly coming to comprehend its powerful and heavy hand now he had so little time himself. Another lesson learned.

The sun was soaring high overhead by the time Adriel reached the village, marking his second morning among men. For the next two hours, he searched until he found the small shop; Adriel asked many for directions and received less in the way of helpful information. The sun beating down, he fought not to faint, his steps growing heavy. He must pull through yet. Isabel had bid him to do no less. At last he found the tiny shop; it sat hidden in the crook of a small street, as if it knew it ought to remain hidden. Adriel took one step from the horse and pitched forward. He lay, unconscious.

The cobbler proceeded to case a leather shoulder with water. As the water softened the leather, it became suitable for working. First the old man set to work with his shears, cutting the leather to pattern with incredible skill. Next, he moved to a very small anvil. Setting down the damp leather, he selected a set of punches and a mallet. With these tools, the cobbler began to punch designs in the leather pieces. Soon they would be dry; after dinner, he could punch the holes and stitch them together.

His wife had always remarked that, to her, it seemed his efforts strayed in every direction of madness. She was constantly astounded to watch his projects come together through small pieces and minute details.

The cobbler called to his daughter; she would remain the only trace his wife had left in the home. He could see her every time he looked upon his daughter.

The girl entered. "What is it, papa?" she asked cheerfully.

"Make sure you take some dinner to our guest," the cobbler said in a quiet voice.

"Of course, papa. It's nearly dinnertime. Wash your hands!" the girl embraced her father then left the room.

Adriel awoke in a dark room, prone on a bed of soft down and cotton, his heavy limbs welcoming their relief.

Hearing movement behind him, Adriel struggled to turn. His back burned, but no longer seemed to stream freely with blood.

"Isabel? Is it you? Have you returned?" he asked the darkness, wondering if—hoping—the phantom had returned to torment him yet again.

"Be still, sir," came the young, female voice. "I am Lila, the cobbler's daughter and you are in our care. Dinner shall be ready shortly. You must be hungry."

"Let me lie for a minute or two, then I shall join you for dinner," Adriel replied.

"It won't be ready for a bit," Lila said. "Rest as you have need."

Adriel could hear the door shut as the girl left the room. He remained as he was, trying to garner the strength to get up.

A short while later, Adriel made his way, mostly dressed, to the table of the small house, finding his way by following the aroma of simmering meat and herbs. There, an old man waited with his daughter. The elder gestured to a third place at the table.

The meal was a humble stew, yet in his famished state, Adriel could not help but eat ravenously.

"Thank you for your help, and for the meal," Adriel mumbled between mouthfuls.

"It is no trouble. Those that can must do what they may to help the less fortunate," the old man said.

"You never know when someone might be an angel or a fairy, in disguise," the girl whispered with a crooked smile. "They come to test one's charity," she added with a nod of certainty.

"How fascinating," Adriel mused. "Have you ever seen one?" Adriel grinned.

"To be sure, I have," the girl replied soberly, casting Adriel a knowing look.

Adriel met her gaze briefly then turned back to his stew.

The three had soon finished the meal.

"Thank you again," Adriel said, "but I must now be on my way."

"It was lucky you found us," said the old cobbler. "Flesh and leather stitch the same, when one has skill and a needle."

"It was not luck that led me here," returned Adriel, "and, again, I thank you."

The dingy shop was lit by a single, sputtering lantern. A dusky light whispered murderously through the chipped wooden slats obscuring the window. The dismal shop was adorned at every point with rare and strange looking artifacts—the kind that glared down from shelves with disconcertingly aware gazes, imparting fear and apprehension on those who passed by. But few found the need nor the desire to pass by, and the building had not seen a single patron throughout the entirety of the day. It was close, cluttered and crowded inside, the atmosphere warm, dust-laden, and pressing. The very air in the shop was thick with an acrid incense, and something else... something far darker.

Tribal masks and trinkets were scattered among disorderly piles of things antique and rotten. Three suits of gothic armour stood empty, the backs of their helms glinting through their visors. Each held a long sword, as if expecting a sudden call to arms.

The door swung slowly inward, uttering a hideous creak that might have chilled the spine and grated the teeth of lesser men. A heavy boot *thunked* resoundingly on the floor, a portentous herald of the man to which it belonged. The echoes of his own steps proclaimed his arrival throughout the silent shop.

He had been thirty-six hours with the searing wound, and Adriel had learned that one could become accustomed to pain—could wear it heavily but steadily. However, the one thing he knew he would never get used to was the sweetly acrid smell of a demon's flesh as experienced through the human senses—a scent that he now had to endure.

Adriel paused, a daunting figure filling the doorway. His long shadow crept across the floor, as if trying to penetrate the stygian gloom of the small shop. He entered the shop against every instinct.

Adriel knew he was vulnerable here. On this bacteria-ridden spit of rock hurtling through the finite infinite of space, Adriel stood imprisoned in a decaying and insufficient piece of earth that now formed his body. He felt for the first time in centuries very... exposed.

The day had passed in gloom and misery. And pain. Lots of pain. Adriel thought again of the shattered gravestone he had visited that morning, and the lust for revenge burned hotter within him. He would find the head of the Vermes Deformis—a powerful cult headed by one notorious demon—and bring the order crashing down before his miserable human body succumbed to the pull of decay.

Adriel had watched for decades as the Vermes Deformis had eaten to the core of a small town—a town that had grown into a city, one terminally infected. The Vermes Deformis would never stop until they had destroyed the city. Chaos was their light, their bread, and their sweet wine in the evening.

Then, combating them from his superior vantage point had been easy, but Adriel now found himself under a new set of rules, with limited options and imposed confines. The game was no longer tilted in his favour. He had little time and few friends. Enemies would have to do for the moment.

Adriel attempted again to survey the dark room, however his dim human vision was unable to aid him.

A voice reached him from the bowels of the shop. It had the disposition of a graveyard and projected all the welcome one might expect in a pit of lions. "I know who you are. What brings a man of your... *standing*... into my shop?"

Adriel looked around with distrust, trying to determine if they were alone. There was absolutely no way to tell. The thin walls provided little privacy, and the masks hung thereon watched like twisted spies. The door clicked shut behind him.

The shopkeeper's sparse hair revealed much of his scalp, greying skin stretched taught across his cheekbones, his eyes sunken, and his gaze keen. His manner was as sharp as his gaze and his movements shrewd. The spectacles pushed to the end of his bony nose glinted in the lantern light, reflecting a menacing red glow.

"I have come to make a trade," Adriel began. He walked to the counter, feeling not one but several pairs of eyes boring into his skin. The canvas sack in his hand began to grow heavier.

"What is it you have for me?" asked the

spectral old man.

Adriel advanced the remaining three steps to the counter. He swung the sack to the counter with one hand. The canvas bag landed with a thud and whimpered in protest.

"Your assistant ran afoul of the Dragon. Be sure he does so no more." Adriel released the bag, and out crawled a bearded and extremely terse-looking dwarf. The dwarf greeted its master with a light head-butt and then stood glaring at Adriel.

"That's a rather raw deal. It was quite the task getting rid of this mongrel in the first place." The old man frowned then seemed to address the room itself. "Kill him."

For a moment nothing happened. Adriel thought briefly that the old man had issued the order to the dwarf, but the latter did not move. Adriel stood quite still then heard a hollow metallic clamour.

The suits of armour rattled, shaking off layers of dust. Weapons in hand, they advanced. Adriel had the small dagger, but knew it would serve him little against broadswords. He left the knife sheathed. Keeping his enemies in sight, Adriel backed into a narrow aisle between two bookshelves.

The false knights were forced single file as they followed. The first one attacked, swinging its longsword high. Adriel quickly advanced. He caught the dummy's gauntlet mid-descent, stopping the sword. Next, he aimed a low, stomping kick to the knee joint of the armour. The lower leg came off completely, and the suit of armour fell. Adriel scooped up the sword.

The second dummy was more difficult. Adriel lopped the empty helmet to the floor then quickly realized that the golem needed no head to function. Adriel was left to knock the armour limb from limb; it seemed to lie still once it was in pieces. Within three minutes Adriel had scattered the floor with pieces of armour.

Adriel leaped upon the counter next to the old man. He swung his hefty sword, embedding it in the counter between the old man's hand and the pistol for which he reached.

"I shall make you a new offer," Adriel said. "Find what I need, and I let you live, demon. Fail to do so, and you will shortly begin your eternity in the lake of fire."

"What is it you want of me?" asked the serpent-like man. The fire reflecting in his glasses took on a spectral menace.

"I need weapons. Some very special weapons."

Chapter 12:

Aurum Argentum

Captain Noa Lee was lying upon something that had once been and still partially resembled the quarterdeck of the *Aura Regency Hide* if, perhaps, it had been the main event in a lumberjack hatchet and chainsaw expo. The ship herself could not in point of fact, look worse had the logging industry run out of forest and sought to make its business from the ship itself. There were few timbers still attached to one another. The first thing Noa wanted: her sword. She could feel something crushing into her side. That might be it.

Unsure how many of her bones were possibly broken, Noa Lee struggled to cautiously rise. A large plank impeded her efforts, pinning her to the fragmented deck of the ship. Reduced from a proud captain to a clawing victim, Noa Lee struggled with the obstinate piece of wood that sought to slowly crush the life from her chest. This strategy failed entirely, and the beam renewed, with hardened vigour, its efforts to kill her.

"Guardsmen! Sound off!" Captain Lee choked through a haze of ash and dust, pitch and sulfur. Her voice was faint and weak, dust coating her throat and impeding any attempt to shout. Her cry went unanswered for several minutes. Captain Lee struggled to see through the smoke, but could not make out a single human form.

"Guardsmen! I command you to sound off!" she cried out again.

From her left a suffocated murmur reached her ears. She waited for several tense moments. Would this be an ally, or an enemy who could take full advantage of her incapacitated state? A human shape formed a darkened silhouette against the cloud of ash. Soon Captain Lee could discern that he was one of her men, crawling toward her through the rubble.

"Are you injured?" called Lee. "Who is there?"

"It is I: Jansson," came a hoarse voice, "and I do not yet know how to answer the first question, Captain. Can you move?"

Captain Lee tried once more to shift the fallen timber. She could not.

"No," Noa Lee replied. "I'm pinned under this wretched mast."

"Very well," Jansson acquiesced. He was close enough now that Lee could see his mangled left leg and what appeared to be a penetrating wound to his abdomen. "Let's get you out of there."

"Fool!" Lee attempted to yell. She only coughed, inhaling a mouthful of wood-dust, "you're in no condition to help! Stand down!"

"Apologies, Captain, but not this time." There was no defiance in Jansson's voice, only an odd mix of compassion and determination. He would surely be promoted for his courage, Lee decided. First, both of them would have to survive to see the promotion. Captain Lee was less concerned with idle badges of shining metal, preferring to focus on reassembling what was left of her depleted fighting force.

Jansson took hold of the timber with both hands and forced himself onto his good knee. With a grunting cry, he brought the timber higher—nearly high enough for Lee to escape. Both were pushing with all their might.

Jansson gave a great yell, and even as the wound in his side tore open, he forced the groaning timber from the ground. Blood ran down his good leg.

The captain was at last free. Jansson let the plank fall where the Captain had lain, and both collapsed on top of the truculent beam. It simply lay there, gloating in its own defiance of the situation.

Using a shred of her torn greatcoat, Captain Lee tried to bandage Jansson's side. She met with little success, however. Evidently the Captain was far better at taking people apart than putting them back together. This fact had startled her in its alacrity over the past week. Maybe she ought to stick to cutting up enemies.

"We need to search for supplies and survivors," Lee decided out loud. Then, "Nay, I must do so alone. You are not even fit to stand."

"Just so," Jansson conceded, somewhat breathlessly and he pressed his hand to his side. He knew he would not be able to stagger far even if he made it to his feet.

Before the two could execute said course of action, they heard movement in the rubble. It was impossible to see more than ten paces, so they waited. A warrior's instinct warned Captain Lee against crying out. She motioned to Jansson to do the same, silently freeing her sabre from its sheath. Jansson drew a pistol and watched silently. Captain Lee hoped most sincerely that her weapon had not been mangled.

Through the smoke came several men in armour, brandishing futuristic looking guns and staffs. The Captain and Jansson would soon be surrounded. All time to hide was now gone, and the mist would not shelter them much longer.

The haze and ash was suddenly stripped away, fleeing before the advance of a woman or rather, the smoke and ash fell dead at her feet as she strode forward. The woman was clad in a black dress and seemed to tread over the ship's deck rather than upon it. A small contingent of men followed apprehensively in her wake. Captain Lee had the distinct impression the men would rather be anywhere else than where they presently found themselves.

Captain Lee and Jansson lay deathly still, barely daring to breathe, the two appearing as corpses to the searchers. Taking full advantage of their grime-and-blood be-smattered appearance, they certainly seemed as soldiers recently and entirely dead.

"Lieutenant, take your men and search the wreck. We have the manuscript; all we need is the writer. She was not on board the sloop when we intercepted, she must be here somewhere."

The only response was a warbled computerized blooping emitted from the helmet of the first spaceman. This noise was taken for assent, it seemed, as the armoured and artillarized acolytes adjourned in ambulatory fashion.

The words gave Lee a mad kind of hope. They had not captured The Wordsmith! There was still a chance that these wretched villains could be defeated. Suddenly her personal fate seemed but a small part of the role she had yet to play in the unfolding tale. Free of a written fate, absolved of the indelible trajectory that she was formerly bound to, Lee decided that the only thing to matter was doing her utmost to stop the spreading evil. Jansson suddenly gave an involuntary cough and a spasm, loosing an armful of clattering rubble. Captain Lee felt her own heartbeat quicken. The tall woman spun on her heel. Spying the two, the woman headed directly for them, her face contorting into something not dissimilar to a sly smile.

Lee decided her best mode of attack would be to lead her enemy to underestimate her state; she remained quite still, prone upon the ground.

She even coughed weakly for effect. For some moments, it seemed to work.

"Speak quickly," demanded the tall woman. "Who are you? My master grows impatient, and I look now for any scrap of flesh to feed to the wolves."

"Kill us or aid us, but do not talk us to death," Lee spluttered, maintaining an air of brute authority despite her compromised and injured state.

"Ah. You must be Captain Lee. I have read about you," the woman smiled. "How fortunate you survived the wreck—you might have died without giving me the chance to assist in that endeavour," the woman taunted, her smile widening.

"Then Perfuga was working for you," Lee inferred. "What do you want here?"

The woman stalked to within a few strides of the two wounded sailors. "Quite simple," she cooed, "we wish to continue doing exactly what we have been doing. But you are wrong. Perfuga, as you know him, does not work for me. It is I who serve him."

Having confirmed her enemy, and clearly unaware that she was beaten, Lee rose and rushed at the dark-haired woman, sabre flashing to hand with a pale, steely cry.

With a wave of her hand, the tall woman unwound the sabre as a scarf unwinds when one pulls a thread. What remained was a long, twisted shard of steel macaroni. It glinted in every iridescent pastel colour, suspended in the air.

With another wave of her hand, Ustrina twirled the long strand of steel about the Captain from her vantage place several feet beyond the reach of her would-be assailant. The steel began to sing, and before Lee could react, she was covered head to toe in shallow lacerations. A loud shot suddenly broke through the dust and smoke, and Ustrina staggered to one side. The steel fragmented then, or rather perhaps it evaporated, ending the Captain's suffering. Captain Lee collapsed, her face and bare arms streaming blood.

Ustrina gasped quietly, as if merely receiving an ungracious reproach. Indeed, an insult may have harmed her more than the ball from Jansson's pistol. She was soon recovered and striding toward the man lying on the ship's deck, Captain Lee fallen only a step beyond. A cold vapour rolled from Ustrina's wound, which in moments ceased to be.

Ustrina's attendants, stern in their dark armour, were now surrounding the Captain and Jansson. The sorceress was really quite certain she had won over completely the loyalty of the men from space, but then, she also believed she had every right to take over an entire world in which she didn't belong and force everyone else to do her bidding. The men's obedience came not from loyalty, but from fear, for we all know how insane it is to try to take over the world... well... most people know that, although the mental orientation of some politicians is a question for another discussion. The point is, Ustrina thought she was entirely right and completely invincible and now carried out her plan with irresponsible and impetuous impunity.

A sudden explosion of dirt and ice threw Captain Lee backwards. She landed in a pile of ashen timbers, smashing them and sending up a spray of splinters as she landed. For a brief moment, it occurred to Captain Lee that the boards that caught her may have, indeed, been the only two pieces of the *Aura* that had remained intact.

Before Jansson could hand the pistol to his second (who might have been dead somewhere nearby), or take the time to wonder how much shot and powder he had left, Ustrina had reached him. She bent her face to his and, taking his cheek in her hand as if she might have kissed him, merely exhaled upon his face.

Jansson felt immediately and most thoroughly chilled. His breath came as vapour on a mid-winter's night. It was all he could do to clutch his cloak tighter and attempt to warm his hands as the temperature about him seemed to drop drastically. He curled into a bloodied mass of flesh amidst the rubble and moved no more save to shiver violently now and again.

Just then, a deafening roar and the whoosh of mighty wings rent the air. The lion descended upon the spacemen, scooping one up in its muscular forepaws. The man struggled, but lost his grip on his firearm — the only thing that might have done him any good. The lion drove in its heavy teeth, biting through flesh, armour and bone.

Azalion leaped lightly from the beast's back, landing between Ustrina and Jansson. Reese raced to the side of Captain Lee, trying to determine if her heroine was still alive.

"How auspicious, my dear Azalion. You brought us the very person we would otherwise have had to go to great lengths to kidnap," Ustrina grinned, a sight which usually drove men to hesitate or swoon altogether. Ustrina knew the use and potency of her own deadly beauty.

Azalion, however, remained passive and unswayed, affecting only his usual sulky demeanour — evidently the antidote to Ustrina's charms. (A note to the reading audience here: do not try this at home. Countering female charms by any means, it must be cautioned, should not be attempted by mere mortal men. That would only get people (women, mostly) angry and upset and entirely wreck any book cred we editors still maintain at this point. Just don't do it.)

"Withdraw now, and I shall arrange a place to negotiate," Azalion was clearly buying time. That was bad, as Reese knew he would instinctively resort to action over words any chance he could get. We are already beaten then, Reese thought. No — wait!

Reese fumbled for her now-mangled notebook. The doodles Reese had previously meticulously rendered on the cover looked like some mad graffiti artist had got at it, really quite intent on his work, creating a good deal of havoc before being dragged away by his friends when they heard the police sirens. Reese fumbled for a few blank pages and, propping her notebook upon a conveniently flat plate of steel she found lying amidst the rubble, wrote: *And the earth clothed her champion in the finest of metal; the very ground produced for him his armament.*

Not too flipping bad for working on the fly, she thought proudly.

It worked marvelously; the impending duel was halted by a tearing, thundering rumble. The earth beneath the combatants shook and Ustrina, caught off guard, stumbled. The ground split and swallowed two of Ustrina's guards. Nearby, the lion toyed with a third — the remaining third of what might have once been a man.

With a great rumble, the ground beneath Azalion's feet yawned open. Yet he did not fall. Serpents of living steel, glowing a frightful and blinding orange rose from the bowels of the earth and coiled about Azalion. To his amazement, he did not feel the heat. Within moments the steel snakes cooled. Embraced in their thick coils, Azalion found that they had encased his body in a living, iridescent, stronger-than-steel armour. Finally, like a tree growing five hundred years in a moment, a small steel shoot protruded from the ground. Within seconds it had grown to the height of Azalion's chest. It produced merely two cruciform branches; Azalion drew his weapon easily from the molten earth. He hefted the beautiful sword, finding it lighter than any he had held before.

Reese struggled to help Captain Lee to her feet. If they could only make it to the winged lion, they might be able to escape! Yet Captain Lee resisted.

"Jansson is still here! He may yet be alive! Reese, you are of more import than any of us. Whatever befalls me, you must escape." Lee looked imploringly into Reese's eyes; there was no longer any brute authority or demanding of deference, Captain Lee addressed Reese as a friend.

"I won't leave you to face her alone," Reese objected, tears coming to her eyes. Recovering her resolve, Captain Lee pushed Reese away. The writer stumbled into the heavy smog and vanished. Captain Lee turned back to where she guessed the battle to be.

The clash of metal was clearly heard as Azalion fought with the men commanded by Ustrina. One by one they fell; their swords were no match for the super-alloy dredged from the depths of the earth. The pirates' bullets deflected harmlessly off Azalion's new glistening plating. Again and again he swung, and his foes could do naught but fall before him. Ustrina decided then that it was time to intervene personally. She strolled casually toward Azalion, who clearly had moral qualms about attacking an unarmed woman, sorceress or not.

"Stop. Withdraw now. I am loth to strike a lady, be she one in manner or nay," Azalion coolly delivered an underhanded insult.

"I have no time for you, boy. Get out of my way. I require only the labours of your literary friend." Ustrina knew pawns when she saw them. This boy had already stalled her progress for some time now and Ustrina had not missed the fact that Captain Lee was back on her feet. Ustrina drew a short, curved dagger.

Following a silent debate with himself, Azalion hefted his sword and rushed at Ustrina. She gave her head a tilt, seeming to consider for a moment, then sheathed her small knife. Azalion swung with all his might.

The blow never landed. Ustrina raised a hand, but not to fend off the attack. The air was rent by a tooth-grinding crackling sound. Ustrina had, by her magic, caused ice to obstruct every joint of Azalion's armour. In fact, the boy was practically an ice cube, though Ustrina mused that he would be far too large for any glass. She stalked idly 'round him, sporting a smug smirk, Azalion helpless to do anything but watch her gloat. Though the ice about him had already begun to melt, Azalion was at serious risk of hypothermia. He stood immobile, locked in a metal icebox. Ustrina put her cold lips to his forehead and he remembered no more.

Ustrina issued an order, and several

spacemen in armour, carrying futuristic guns, set off after Reese.

Reese, however, was presently lost in a thick blanket of smoke. If the pirates found her at all, it would be due to Sheer Dumb Luck. Reese did not have Sheer Dumb Luck on her side and she panicked, looking about frantically. The lion had vanished. Really? How hard could it be to spot such a large mammal? Yet it was most certainly gone. Reese took a moment then to wonder how, in two short days, she had gone from searching out a paper clip in her desk drawer to seeking with all her heart for a winged lion in the dense ash and wreckage of what had once been a majestic flying ship. Despite the situation, Reese laughed quietly and shook her head.

Regrettably for Reese, not only did she NOT have Sheer Dumb Luck aiding her, at that moment, Sheer Dumb Luck was, in fact, in the employ of the bad guys, having had a rather nasty quarrel with Fate and Destiny regarding an unrelated matter. Consequently, Sheer Dumb Luck was presently using Reese to prove a point.

A moment later Reese had cause for true concern as strange lights, like eyes, flickered to life one at a time, surrounding her. She came to the conclusion that these lights could only be the headlamps of the space pirates pursuing her, that they had likely been waiting for anyone trying to escape, and that there was no longer anywhere to run. It took an unprecedented evolution of thought for Reese to come to so many conclusions all in a row. By the time she had it all sorted, two of the men had grabbed her and were dragging her back to Ustrina.

"Now, my dear," Ustrina cooed, "there is no further use in running."

Reese glared up at her own creation, wishing her hands were free to retrieve her notebook from where it resided, rolled up in the pocket of her coat.

"Take her away," Ustrina commanded dismissively. Armoured men moved to obey.

"Stop!" came a halting voice.

"Back for more, Lee, you loyal fool? It would behoove you now to simply play dead and crawl back to your master," Ustrina balked. Her voice, smooth like honey, juxtaposed the harsh words she spoke.

Ustrina grasped Captain Noa Lee by the throat, pulling her close. Captain Lee, far from fazed, took the opportunity to draw Ustrina's own dagger from its sheath and plunge it up under Ustrina's ribs. However, the sorceress merely appeared annoyed. Drawing the dagger out, (the wound did not even bleed) she held it high. Condensation began to form and solidify upon the blade, shimmering in a deathly cold vapour. In moments, the dagger had become a gigantic, blunt longsword made entirely of ice.

The men hauled Reese from the wreck of the *Aura Regency*. The last thing she saw was Ustrina, holding Captain Lee still with one hand

and beating her unconscious with the blunt sword in the other. Reese turned away and let the men drag her from the wreckage.

The large spacecraft, posing inconspicuously as a mountain peak, was plainly visible from the hardware store parking lot. It loomed over the valley, like a majestic bird in its eyrie. None seemed to take any notice of it, despite the alacrity of its foreboding presence. A few distant figures moved over its hull, presumably doing maintenance or checking the solar panels. It is also possible that they were simply paid extras, milling about and attempting to look industrious.

The craft itself had been exposed when the daylight hit it in full. It also helped that it was not rushing about firing into buildings and generating large amounts of dust and rubble in which to hide. The hull was a dull metal; it was perhaps once covered in a heavy enamel, most of which had worn off. The exterior of the craft was pockmarked with many dozens of asteroid impacts both large and small. Though the prow was aerodynamic (a fashion must for any space-travelling ship), the stern of the ship was bulky and sharply contoured — something that spoke poorly about its speed and maneuverability (evidently no one looked at the rear end of the thing). This transport would surely have been some sort of cargo ship in its life prior to being captured by the pirate group. The ship had few windows and was fitted with many non-standard post-factory cannons. The pirate craft was truly a sight that would chill the bones of any honest spacefaring captain. A captain in such a position, facing down an enemy craft armed to the bulwark, would be better off appealing to God for support than to his battle-crew.

Behind the plate glass window in which this colossal craft was faintly reflected, Macy and Troy sat in a coffee shop tucked into one corner of the hardware store, very much aware of the ship. They sat quietly together, sipping their still-steaming coffee and glancing out the window occasionally. One or two other people occupied the dining area, and the barista was silently wiping a glass. It was the same glass he had started washing out an hour ago, but his wages warranted neither diligence nor productivity.

"How long do you think they'll be?" Macy asked Troy.

He watched her evenly from the other side of the small table.

"Who knows? I'm not even sure what Bainan wanted here." Troy took another ponderous sip of coffee, glancing dubiously in the direction of the hardware aisles.

After a valiant effort, Troy's small car had broken down while fulfilling its duty, dying a car's most noble death. Troy had been forced to pull into the small auto shop adjacent to the hardware store sporting a "Tire Mart" sign including a logo that vaguely resembled their country's flag. Troy had commissioned the establishment's finest mechanics to do anything they could to revive his car. A grease monkey who looked younger than Troy had volunteered. An adult human decided he needed supervision and went to help. Meanwhile, Bainan and his men had quickly disappeared into the store to have a look at the wares and perhaps do a little shopping. Troubling enough, they had been gone for some time now.

Troy and Macy had been sitting and drinking coffee long enough to cover all the basics: they had learned each other's favourite colours, foods, music groups, and movies. They had discussed books, and how shocked they had been when that one fantasy author had beheaded his only redeeming character (they had both, at that point, simply thrown the book across the room vowing never to read another word of it). Troy had looked close enough to see, to his delight, that Macy had several faint freckles about her cheeks and scattered across the bridge of her nose. They had commented on each other's eye colour until several single and bitter people had risen and exited the coffee shop with extreme prejudice. Overall, not bad as far as second dates go, although the circumstances may have been improved. Still, Macy conceded, she'd had worse.

The conversation had died down about ten minutes prior, each quietly content in the other's company. No words were necessary. Troy was the first to find the bottom of his coffee cup. Macy glanced up then.

"Do you suppose they got into trouble?" Macy asked.

Troy was about to reply with a fairly confident, "How much trouble can they get into in a hardware store?" when he was interrupted.

There appeared to be a bit of a row at cash register six. Macy could see their party of bearded warriors lined up to pay for their merchandise. Each man was carrying a veritable arsenal of hand tools: chainsaws, axes, saws, picks and sledges. One held a rather intense-looking gardening implement. They had also practically cleared out the sports section — each man carried a compound bow, multiple hunting knives, and a tactical machete. The warriors were arming themselves for battle, and would soon find modern steel much more to their liking than the iron-age heavy, low quality metal of which their ancient swords had been made.

"Oh boy, that isn't good," Troy murmured.

Macy and Troy got up to help their friends through the checkout.

A police officer stood with Bainan at the head of the line. The officer appeared to be questioning Bainan. Macy wondered with a fright what in the world Bainan was telling him. She was soon within earshot:

"… and the enemies of your fair townsfolk shall despair, they that hail from yonder flying craft of metal sleek —"

"Bainan? Hi," Macy greeted, interceding in a timely manner. She turned to the police officer. He wore an unreadable expression.

"Sorry officer. These men aren't from around here," Macy began, still trying to form a mental picture of herself successfully talking her way out of this one. It was a very blurry picture — a lot of soft focus lens use was involved. She quickly pasted on her most friendly smile.

"Yeah, we've met before," Jed replied. Turning to Bainan, he continued. "I'm not going to ask what you guys intend to do with all these tools," Jed said slowly, "because there's probably nothing I could do about it when you haven't done anything illegal yet, but how are you two mixed up in this?" He pinned Troy with a level gaze.

Troy was next to make an effort to explain. "We, er... that is, we sort of... Reese is better at explaining this than I am...," he trailed off.

"Right," Macy put in for good measure. "Reese could explain." Macy and Troy exchanged a nod, confirming their plan.

"Reese is the girl who bailed him out?" Jed asked, jerking a thumb in Bainan's direction.

Macy and Troy regarded one another, shrugged slightly, then turned to Jed, nodding. "Yeah," Macy answered.

Jed studied the pair for a moment before his gaze flicked over Bainan.

"You guys are going to find that flying saucer and take it down, right?" Jed asked

Bainan.

"As verily as the Western suns of Mordune set at the end of the first half-moon in autumn," Bainan returned.

Macy wondered if they had closed-ended questions where Bainan came from. She thought it unlikely.

Jed waved to the cashier and stepped aside.

"In that case, carry on, gentlemen. I see no issue with your purchases. In fact, your bill is on me. Just bring down that ship."

Macy thanked Jed, and the group made their way to the auto garage next door. The car had been miraculously revived, and now sat recovering in the parking lot.

It had been "nip and tuck" for a while. the car oozing a mix of neon-green and black fluid onto the garage floor, the motor stuttering, and one corner of the car perilously low to the shop floor. The mechanics had agreed upon a motor thoracotomy, plugging all leaks in the hoses then resorted to infusing copious amounts of intravenous fluids, turning over all coolant and replenishing near-death levels of power-steering and brake fluids. They had then restored oxygenation to the valves with a make-shift valve tracheotomy involving a drill and a metal tube that was borrowed from the middle of a ball point pen. Lastly, they had heroically employed booster cables, finally restoring the car to running order after several attempts at motor vehicle defibrillation.

The group had only to sort how to fit thirteen people and the entire hand tools aisle into Troy's small two-door hatchback. It took them ten full minutes to pile in. Troy was thankful that they did not have to use the chainsaws to fit the men into the car in smaller pieces. The trunk of the car bristled with their newly acquired armoury of gardening implements.

Azalion waited patiently until he began to thaw. It took quite a few minutes, during which he (with much frustration) witnessed the kidnapping of Reese and the defeat of Captain Lee. At last, he could hear the ice about him begin to crack. He struggled, but was not free yet.

The armour about him, its magic effects by now having passed, began to flake off along with the ice. Azalion struggled some more, and found that he had freed his arms. He could not turn to see if Captain Lee was alive, so he could only stand, trying to form some kind of plan. Nothing came to mind.

Within a matter of twenty minutes, Azalion was at last free. He was soaked head to toe, and plastered with the powdered-black carbon remains of his suit of armour. The only thing that had survived the freezing was the sword. Azalion touched it gingerly, as if expecting it to crumble. It did not, so he fastened the large blade across his back and decided to press on. He took one step then paused, having as yet no determined course.

He remembered then that Captain Lee was nearby, somewhere in the wreck of the late *Aura Regency*. He shook off the black, sooty remains of his elemental armour, and commenced to search the wreckage.

Azalion found her eventually, one among the many broken bodies that littered the area.

"Help me get a fire going!" Captain Lee rasped out as soon as she saw Azalion. He soon saw why: the still form of Jansson was curled into a shivering ball at her feet. She was trying vainly with tinder and a broken piece of flint to light a small pile of splinters. Her success to that point was less than stellar.

Azalion took the piece of flint from the captain. He clenched it in his fist, and it soon began to glow. Turning his palm down, Azalion crushed the flint like dust. He opened his hand, and molten stone dripped down upon the pile of kindling, which instantly ignited. Within a few minutes, a large blaze was burning, although admittedly consuming portions of the ship itself in the process.

The fire seemed to help very little; Jannson continued to shiver despite the fact that he was practically lying in the fire. Azalion felt the back of Jannson's hand and drew back sharply. The man's flesh was as cold as Arctic seawater. If only Azalion had been familiar with the Arctic he might have conceived just how cold that was.

Azalion nevertheless understood the man at his feet to be very cold and set to work; he knew every healing spell in the *Graeling* tongue. His master had carefully instructed him in the ways of healing and defending himself, but of human popsicles, he knew little. He hoped he could dredge up a warming spell from the dark recesses of years past and forgotten lore. At length he had it, and began to murmur strange words in *Graeling*, which as we have already established, was patched together from gibberish and pseudo-Latin that Reese had picked up from a terribly overrated book about wizards using pretend words and waving gimmicky wands about like two-bit stage performers.

Despite its grounds in unreality, the spell seemed to work for a brief time. Jannson opened his eyes, his lashes white with frost.

"Raise your head, Captain," Jansson stuttered through a shiver, "and you shall find your way."

Though Azalion chanted for several minutes, and Captain Lee fed the dwindling fire, Jannson slowly closed his eyes and ceased to move. Azalion looked upon the poor, frozen man and stopped his chanting. His spell had been overcome by the dark magic of Ustrina, the terrible sorceress. Azalion choked amid tears of frustration — or he might have been cursing incoherently. Captain Lee watched on, standing two paces away with splinters of the broken ship still clutched in her hands, ready to feed the fire.

These fell to the ground with an echoing, hollow clatter, and Captain Lee hung her head in defeat.

In the silence that followed, the captain took a moment to think over the last words of her comrade — why did dying people always speak in riddles? Clearly he had meant that by refusing to give in, she would figure out how to defeat the colossal odds that faced her. Jannson's last words were so fraught with weighty metaphor and hidden meaning that at last Captain Lee, weary of pondering what he might have meant, threw her tired head back and groaned.

That is when she saw the hot air balloon.

The balloon, navy blue with gold trim, and teardrop in shape, hovered over the smoking battleground like a wraith. It began to slowly descend. Of course Captain Lee had been unable to discern it before! The smoke and ash had prior to that moment precluded all visibility.

Captain Lee had heard stories of lighter-than-air elements, but she had never before seen the balloon ships of myth. The graceful craft, perhaps equal in size to a fifty-foot sloop, drew nearer and nearer. As the ship descended, mooring lines and anchors were cast from the bow; the ship intended to make port among the wreckage of her late mother ship. Captain Lee stood dumbstruck; she doubted the fidelity of her perhaps deceiving eyes, yet she held fast to hope.

Eventually the vessel was brought to a halt a mere ten feet above ground level; enough of the ascending gases had been expunged to allow for the craft to maintain a level altitude. Heavy anchor lines were let down, an agile sailor rapelling skillfully down each line. These men fastened the ship to trees, which were scarce and/or destroyed, or to anything else they could find.

A gangplank was lowered. Azalion, still on his knees next to the corpse of Jannson, watched with anticipation as a tall figure mounted the gangplank, surrounded by guards. As the man drew nearer, they discerned that it was none other than a rather ragged-looking General Quercius, his wound bound with reddened cloth. Quercius smiled weakly to see his best captain still alive.

Captain Lee collapsed, her duty fulfilled to its utmost, and knew no more.

The dirty rag tied about her head was removed, and Reese opened her eyes. For a moment her world was blurred, wiping her eyes slowly, she found she could see. It was like waking up after a wild night of hard partying with Macy; the two would go out, have two glasses of lightly spiked, heavily sugared and creamed coffee, stay out until 10:30 PM, and then collapse on Reese' two couches to fall asleep instantly. Waking up the next morning was dreadful and both would turn to "a hair of the dog" by making waffles and dousing them with flavoured syrup of the artificial maple sort and whipped cream — plus a cup of very strong coffee.

The heavy dose of sugar and caffeine generally set them straight.

This time, however, Reese woke to find herself in a long and very dark room. The only light came from a single, naked lamp. Great, Reese thought, it came to this after all. I must be on their confounded spaceship. Why did I even write that garbage in the first place? It didn't even do well in sales, and I'm still paying for it.

Not one feature or item could be seen in the room, save a water heater and the door. It was a wide room, and before the chair in which she sat was a small table and another chair. Nobody else was in sight. Did I write this location into the book? Reese wondered. This scene is way over-done. This is just bad writing.

Reese tried to rise, intending to quit the scene entirely, but the chair followed her. Realizing that she was cuffed to the arm of the chair, Reese sat back down with a heavy sigh. She had watched enough action movies to know that she needed a paper clip expressly for these situations. She had none on her — she never could find them in her apartment — so she tried to think of an alternative. She was a writer, for goodness sake — surely she could think of something useful for this situation. For some minutes her mind raced furiously. Sadly, despite her flailing ideas, Reese could think of no means of escape. She put her head in her hands, (which took considerable effort, cuffed by her wrists as she was) and ran her fingers absent-mindedly through her hair.

Wait! A bobby pin!

She quickly pulled a pin from her hair and un-bent the middle. One wavy lock of her dark hair escaped and caressed her face.

Reese had no idea what she was doing. She worked the bobby pin into the lock on the cuffs, trying to feel for a button or a spring… anything. She wrestled it around the lock almost as much as she wrestled with her growing frustration. Then finally: there it was! It felt like a small extrusion — she could feel it with the pin. She pulled hard, attempting to lever the device open, and her bobby pin broke off in the lock.

Fantastic.

At that moment, the door opened. Reese, startled, dropped what was left of the pin at her feet. The newcomer signaled to a guard outside the door, then entered the room. He sat down slowly, every move deliberate. Reese found herself, for the first time in her life, face to face with Jack Grendel, a creature of her own creation: superhuman in power, subhuman in morality. The blood drained from Reese' face and she watched Jack with a horror she hoped he could not read.

Jack Grendel glanced down briefly, taking in the broken bobby pin on the floor. He glanced at Reese, one eyebrow raised knowingly, but not in the least concerned.

Crap. How did he know to look at that? Reese wondered. She realized then that she hadn't really planned how to get out of the room, even were she able to free herself of the cuffs. A slow, sly smile spread over the face of Jack Grendel. He reached into his coat pocket.

Reese flinched, barely able to breathe and wondering what he might be reaching for—a knife no doubt, or something worse! All of her nightmares of danger and torture seemed to be distilling in this singular week—all tangled up with any multitude of nightmares involving two-dimensional characters, linear plot structures and entirely too much exposition.

Jack Grendel pulled his hand from his pocket and placed upon the table not a knife, nor any tortuous device, but merely a simple fountain pen. A small journal followed, and Jack pushed both of these items toward Reese. She stared dumbly at the book, trying to figure out exactly how Jack intended to use the innocent-looking items to inflict indescribable levels of pain. Jack reached over and silently thumbed through the pages, demonstrating to Reese that all were blank. Jack pushed the two items closer to Reese, who obviously did not reach for them, as her hands were still restrained following her failed attempt at escape.

"I want you to rewrite *Penultimate Graeling*," Grendel began, "so that Azalion lives. Give him the happiest of endings, let him have that princess he's lusted after for two hundred and forty-seven pages, let him have both kingdoms at his command, let him realize his full majestic powers—I don't really care. I need him to survive his story and stay in his world. I want him to stay out of this one. Only then will I be able to claim this world without interference. That boy has been a pain in my side since he arrived here. I want him gone with no possible chance of return. You will have him live on for eternity within his finite little world."

Reese had a sudden run on emotions: relief surged forward (maybe she wouldn't die in this scenario after all) but was quite suddenly blown out of the water by resentment (why was everyone insisting she re-write her book?!). Fear took the lead seemingly out of nowhere (what was Jack planning to do with the world anyway?). In the end, the race was a tie between grief (sending Azalion back felt wrong somehow) and longing (even Reese had to admit she would very much have liked to write a very happy — if rather mawkish — ending for her most beloved character).

Jack Grendel waved, and a guard entered. The man un-cuffed Reese hesitantly, then left the room. Jack rose. He paused, one hand on the door.

"Oh, and Ms. Richardson," Jack smirked, "the door is quite locked from the outside. No need to spoil your lovely hair." With a dry chuckle, he left the room. The door closed with a clack of deadened finality.

Reese looked down at the notebook. She tried to determine what to write but found herself confronted by a severe case of writers' block. She sat quite still as she often did when trying to conjure up an idea. She let a wave of improbable thought processes wash over her, tumbling her down one unlikely rabbit hole after another, yet she couldn't seem to get beyond the surf of her own mental turmoil and come up with a single thought to write down. Finally, she mentally laid down the cards in her hand one by one:

It first occurred to Reese, that if she did as she had been bidden, Jack would still need to kill anyone who had read the original manuscript in order for the change to be manifest—that included Macy, Earl, and Charles—and possibly herself, for all she knew of how the thing worked. That would not do. (He would also need a reader to instate the new plot into reality—something that was entirely difficult to procure for authors world-wide.)

Reese also understood she could not use this fortuitous weapon to destroy her enemies— they were already dead. That was, after all, how they ended up in the real world. Nor could she have the villians suddenly turn good, lay down their arms, and release their prisoners—they had not been created to be good and, more specifically, they had died being bad. There was no turning back.

That left Reese with only one card to play. Reese almost could not bear the idea, but it seemed the only solution. She sighed heavily at the prospect, rubbed her raw wrists and, bending to the disagreeable task with a heavy heart, reached for the pen...

Chapter 12.5:

Antecessum Librium

Bainan hefted a large wood-hafted axe and climbed over the last rocky outcrop. From there he could see the enormous metal craft perched on the mountaintop. It had taken one lengthy singing of a somber war song and two hours of raucous battle cries to get up the winding mountain road, not unreasonable given that Troy's car had been loaded well beyond its rated capacity. When the road had ended, the party had set out on foot, marching in time to the rhythmic clanging together of gardening implements and a background pulsing of an electric chain saw. Thanks to the quality mountain footwear department at Tire Mart, the group was adequately prepared for such a venture. The climb had taken three more hours, with frequent stops to quaff bottled water, and whatever else Bainan's men had in their flasks (most of which consisted of overly sugared post-workout beverages that the men presumed to be poorly made mead).

After hiking the steep incline for some while, the group decided it would be best if a small scouting party went ahead while the others remained behind sipping sports drinks. Mostly, the large men were becoming rather woozy, being unaccustomed to the copious quantities of sugar imbued in the drinks.

Bainan, Troy, and Macy, accompanied by two large, bearded men, scaled the remainder of the mountain.

They spied the space freighter, and each tried to think up a plan. Two guards were posted on the ground before the open gangplank, guns in hand. Troy was mentally reviewing all of the recent science fiction movies he had seen, trying to get ideas and now wishing he had purchased that copy of *The Survival Guide for Taking Over Enemy Space Craft* when he'd seen it on sale at the book store. Macy was watching an iridescent dragonfly buzzing past. Bainan's men were watching Macy watch the dragonfly. Fortunately, being back on the familiar ground of princess-finding, Bainan came up with a plan.

Following Bainan's lead, each warrior removed from his back a large, 370-pound compound crossbow. The warriors easily nocked a bolt and cocked the crossbows using only their bare hands and brawny muscles.

One of Bainan's men, Ugluf, signaled the rest of the group to join them. In moments, the rocky outcrop was bristling with chainsaws, axes, plaited beards, swords, and tacky fishing hats. The men awaited Bainan's command.

"Ordinarily at this point, my brothers," Bainan began, "I would deliver a rousing pump-up speech to invigorate our hearts and our sword arms. Yet I believe Macy, our fair lady-warrior, must dictate the plan on this, our day of victory."

One of the men gave a triumphant cry but was instantly hushed by all of his team members at once, each one informing him it was not yet time for raucous cheering. This was done through a secret hand gesture: a good cuff to his head.

Macy, somewhat shocked, attempted to do as Bainan asked. "Alright..." she thought out loud, "Reese may be on this ship, along with a few of our friends. Don't muff your shots, stick together and... let's just... go... get them back!"

With a wild, rousing cry, the raucous group set off. If the truth were told, those present would be forced to acknowledge that the secret to their success as a war party was mainly this: Bainan never stopped to ask "*how many* are the enemy?". Rather, the only question he concerned himself with (chainsaw whirring madly) was, "*where* are the enemy?".

The group advanced, unopposed, up the gangplank and into the open mouth of the ship. Macy and Troy followed close at Bainan's heels, much too afraid to stray too far from the protection of his might—that and the comforting presence of the chainsaw he wielded.

Bainan's party swarmed up the metal gangplank, and within moments, the sounds of bedlam and warfare could be heard echoing within. Chainsaws whirred, weed hackers whined, crossbows twanged, swords sung, and people screamed — there was lots of screaming — some yelling and roaring too — oh, yes, and an occasional whimper and sob. Think general chaos and noise.

The first ambush waited for them just inside the ship's doors, the pirates using the darkness of the hull as a convenient hiding place. As it turned out, however, heavy, high velocity medieval weaponry (and a few chainsaws) was superior to even the best and newest of space helmets, despite their high-tech, spacey design which, no matter how thoroughly explained, never quite conforms to the laws of science. Metal-tipped arrows, on the other hand, agree with the laws of nature very nicely.

With a wave of his hand, Bainan sent his men off to scour the ship and rout the pirates from their stronghold. As luck would have it, the pirates were really a fairly small lot — space ships being designed to be crewed by few men and rather overly dependent on computers.

The enemy force was entirely overwhelmed within the close confines of the ship's corridors. Bainan's men revved their chainsaws, brandished their pointy gardening implements, and made quite a remarkable mess. The crossbows also saw action despite the cramped quarters; with one group of warriors nocking bolts furiously, then handing off the crossbows to the fore group, who fired with definite skill. They made for a deadly, albeit excessive force given the small space in which they operated. Bainan's men were very disappointed with the paltry number of rounds they had to employ in order to defeat the enemy — such minimal effort did nothing to quell their fervor for battle. Their party suffered no casualties as they ploughed the ship from stern to prow save one: Ugluf accidentally pinched his little finger in the string of a crossbow, but they didn't count that.

Eventually the sounds of whining chainsaws quieted, the slinging of arrows stilled, and the chaos and screaming died down, although one sobbing pirate remained, his sobs echoing through the corridors like a far-away ghost. With a quick survey of the ship, and one hurried thrust of a machete when the sobbing man was found, it was determined that Bainan and his men had executed the entire ship's crew. The marauding men followed Bainan and regrouped in the large mess hall, the north end of which was now a veritable pincushion of crossbow bolts. They still held high hopes of participating in further mayhem and massacre.

Troy had looked around during the battle and had not been oblivious to the mayhem and gory violence he had witnessed during the assault. Ordinarily, that sort of thing would have deterred him from continuing with the company, however, Troy realized that these were, after all, fictional characters to begin with so really, what harm had been done by ending their miserable existence? If killing story-book characters were a crime, well, there should be no writers left loose in the world.

"We need to gain access to the brig," Troy directed. "That's where our friends will be. To do that, we likely need access codes from the bridge."

"How do you know all of this?" Macy asked, somewhat intrigued.

"I watch a lot of Space Check," Troy returned. "I never thought being a sci-fi geek would have any practical use."

"I guess today's your lucky day… Alright, let's go then," Macy agreed.

Troy led the way as if he had been born and raised on the ship. Indeed, he had read many science fiction books that had featured space ships and technologies similar to what they were now navigating. He had also read, not surprisingly, the science fiction book by Stella Cadenza featuring that very ship. Troy wondered briefly if all of the writers had once held a secret meeting at which they had determined an agreed-upon sci-fi space craft description then outlined said agreement in the *Top-Secret Handbook of The Rules for Writing* from which all authors drew formulated descriptions, characters, and plotlines — specific wording, elective. It would certainly save them a great deal of time and effort.

In a few short minutes the small party was at the bridge of the ship and found it barricaded shut. A large iron door loomed coolly before them.

It wasn't long, however, before the door's arrogant swagger gave way to Bainan's convincing arguments (although it may have been the persuasion of the sledge-hammer one of his men used on it that made the door cave — again old-fashioned laws of nature beat sci-fi malarkey).

Once the company had demolished the door, Perfuga was immediately propelled headfirst through the door at the insistence of a large leather hiking boot, courtesy of Tire Mart. He sprawled on the floor before Bainan and his band of brigands. At a signal, one of Bainan's men wrestled Perfuga into a kneeling position using Perfuga's hair as a convenient hand-hold, and placed a large bowie knife at his throat.

"Uthbert," Macy said, "can you give me just a sec to talk to him before you kill him?" Uthbert looked dumbly at Macy and Macy correctly determined it would take Uthbert a moment to process her request. While Uthbert was wondering why he had not already dispatched his enemy, Macy turned to address Perfuga directly.

"This is your last chance to call off your forces," Macy opened.

"There is no stopping what was begun," returned the kneeling man, "my name is Count Ignes, and I shall not be so defeated by a worthless band of thugs led by a piffling piece of —"

Count Ignes collapsed, and Uthbert calmly

cleaned his knife on Ignes' coat.

"What did you do that for?" Troy asked. "We hadn't even asked him where the brig is!"

"In neither this world nor mine own," Uthbert said, "do I suffer a man to insult a lady so blithely." Uthbert straightened and re-sheathed the knife.

"Cool," Macy put in with a smile and an approving nod at Uthbert. The man nodded once in reply.

Troy glanced between the two, then shrugged, not about to argue with the explanation given and only vaguely understanding why Macy had approved of the intervention. Troy would later reflect on the event and, rightly or wrongly, come to the conclusion that women like it when men do rash things on their behalf.

"Okay then," Troy said, "time for Plan B." He made his way carefully past Count Ignes, who was still seeping out onto the floor, to see what information he could glean from the ship's computer.

The captain was nowhere in sight. Troy concluded he must have deserted, taking what remained of his men with him. Troy considered the computer. He tapped a few buttons on the virtual key-board and a login screen appeared.

"Darn it!" Troy said. Then, remembering the secret writer's handbook, he quickly realized that there would be an over-ride code—every story-book computer had one and the code was always easily broken—but usually at the last second of the countdown. Having no countdown to race against, Troy simply typed in his email and password and the computer opened to the desk-top. Though the computer displayed only the Hiperbolic language, Troy clicked around until he found a map. Since the ship was equipped with all of the latest technologies, Troy was able to fax the map across the room to the nearest black and white printer / photocopier.

Retrieving the map, Troy marked a little red dot and wrote "You Are Here". He then began to lead the way through the bowels of the ship to where he guessed the brig might be.

The group walked an additional ten minutes until they found themselves back at the mess hall. That was when Troy realized they were lost. The party stopped. While Troy and Macy tried to figure out how to read the map, Bainan's men took to keeping themselves occupied in a very dignified and grown-up fashion—mainly by swinging from the zero-gravity rungs like they were monkey bars whilst tossing about swords and chainsaws.

That is when the captain of the vessel rounded the corner. He entered the large dining area, flanked by guards and hauling both Earl and Charles, along with a third man. Troy looked up from the map and the group turned to the captain—everyone except Bainan. Bainan had gone missing.

Not content to play on the zero gravity

rungs, Bainan had taken it upon himself to determine where they were. He had, by now, wandered back to the bridge following a vague inkling that he could retrace his steps from there. He was about to set off in search of the brig when a large blinking light on the console caught his eye. The flashing button displayed a hieroglyph of a spaceship (much like the one they now occupied) exploding violently. Bainan sat down to put to work his technical expertise and manly problem solving skills to efficiently determine what the issue was and why the red light was so angry. He surveyed the vast array of buttons that lay before him trying to determine the appropriate course of action in such a situation. A monkey might have had more luck typing out a ten-page essay on quantum physics using a desktop computer.

Meanwhile, the bald man advanced on Macy and Troy, holding a futuristic pistol to Earl's head. The thing looked like someone had squeezed together a toy revolver with a rectangular Taser (the gun, that is, not Earl's head). Immediately, Bainan's men-at-arms trained several compound crossbows on the bald man. The bald man and his guards stopped, but did not put up their weapons.

"Stip niw ind liy diwn yiir wiipins," the tall man stumbled through the English, which he was apparently having a hard time with.

"Who are you?" Macy asked.

"I im thi ciptiin if this vissil," was the

man's reply. Rather than offering more information, he simply primed his firearm in an effort to halt further discussion. A guard forced the third man to his knees.

"Sins this min is diir ti yii, hi will dii fiirst," the captain said, pointing the gun at dark-haired man who knelt before him.

"What?" Macy asked. "Wait. We don't even know him."

"Who the hell are you?" Troy asked the kneeling man.

"It's me. Matt Ferren," offered the kneeling man, his hands behind his head in a posture of surrender.

"They took his armour," Charles offered lamely.

"Ahhh…" Troy deduced brilliantly.

"Alright, boys," Macy acceded, "we'd better listen to him."

Bainan's men looked at Macy, appearing confused — this was a means of resolving a fight that they had never tried before. What sort of leader was Macy, anyway? Generally, at this point, Bainan would simply have rushed pell-mell into the thick of things and they would have followed him. Macy nodded at the men and the warriors reluctantly lay down their crossbows while glancing at one another uncertainly. They then lay down their chainsaws (all of which were still running), then their axes and swords, and finally the sharp gardening implements (one will note there was no laying down of hidden knives and short blades at that point).

The bald captain signaled to his guards who stepped forth to take Macy and her group into custody.

At that moment, the ship gave a guttural, jarring lurch.

The tall, bald man uttered the only word that he could properly pronounce in English. It began with an S. Matt said something that promised to be as colourful, if not more so, but his utterance was cut short when the momentum drove his cranium into a steel bulkhead. He collapsed.

Bainan's men immediately retrieved their weapons, and Macy grabbed onto Troy in an effort to keep her feet under her. Troy looked down at her and grinned. He quickly remembered his prior lesson (he was, after all, educable) and picked up a weapon. He then stood, wondering just what exactly he ought to do with it.

Having felt the sudden jolt, Bainan put the large throttle lever back where he found it. He wondered if it had been the wrong switch after all. But it was too late.

The ship had made a great hopping forward bound and had come down hard some way down the mountainside. It ground away its landing gear and began to slide down the mountain. The vessel then skidded sideways. Within moments it was pitching and rolling, crashing at high speed down the mountainside and leaving its occupants scrambling to maintain their footing.

Inside the mess hall, everyone present found him or herself floating freely within the falling craft, at the mercy of every flying object contained therein. A great deal of clanging, whirring, whining, and yelling erupted as chainsaws, axes and hand weapons flew about and ricocheted among the tables and chairs, Bainan's men having little success in keeping them all in check. Macy and Troy clung to each other.

"Don't worry, Macy. We'll be fine!" Troy called above the floating, still-whirring chainsaw that whizzed past them. Macy glanced at the chainsaw then gave Troy a dubious look.

The captain and his guards had lost their grip on Charles and Earl, who drifted about in a state of shocked panic, Charles flailing his arms madly as he floated mid-air. Matt, who much like occupants thrown from a vehicle during a crash, was likely the safest person present while conversely being at most risk of bodily harm. He hovered in the air, a peaceful sleeper among the maelstrom of chaos about him, oblivious to flying weaponry. A chainsaw approached him, but when Matt made no motion, it simply bumped into him sideways, disappointed by its inability to elicit a response from Matt. The malevolent machine then changed trajectory and floated back toward Uthbert who was scrambling to grab the handle (Predestination again seeing to those oh-so-important little details).

Had Matt been awake to either fight off the approaching death-weapon or make a grab for it, it should certainly have severed his hand. The chainsaw, bent on the anticipated action of battle, would then have dove off in an entirely different trajectory, moving to first relieve one of Bainan's men of his left thumb then continuing on to entirely shave Earl's head. But Matt had only slept through the incident and so the chainsaw was reduced to its impotent course.

Uthbert was the first to manage some degree of success in his efforts. He seized a floating chainsaw in each hand and pushed himself off a wall, grinning widely. He dove straight at the spacemen, revving the chainsaws into high gear with a loud roaring of machinery and an undertone of chuckling.

There was, however, still the problem of the multitudinous other floating implements of potential injury and dismemberment. Predestination had his work cut out for him, but Sheer Dumb Luck did drop in to give him a hand, perhaps in an attempt to get back on his good side — something Predestination rather resented.

Now, pay attention as this may take some explaining:

Macy and Troy, suspended as they were in midair, were completely safe during the whole disaster. As Troy had already stated, he believed that by Grace or Divine Intervention (Predestination's boss) or perhaps Sheer Dumb

Luck, the group would make it through their adventure without injury—this was, after all, a setting in one of Reese' stories and the good guys never died in her stories. Macy did her best to believe the same. Since they were both suspended and disbelieved in their own imminent demise, the course of the entire Narrative was directly affected and the group made it through completely unscathed. They would find out later that one fellow named Van Ugh had harboured one fleeting moment of doubt, and had thereby lost one square inch of his ear to a passing garden shear. This troubled him little, as it should you.

Captain Nat Dayman (all present had regrettably forgotten his name and needed to call him something, so they bequeathed to him the name of an actor who, incidentally, had taken on a number of roles as space rogues and Martian pirates—all present thought the name fitting) did not share the same belief. Consequently, every last careening weapon of melee and destruction in the mess hall (which by the laws of probability had to impale *someone*) ended up embedded in poor Cappy D and in his guards who, evidently, shared their captain's philosophy and failed to suspend their disbelief. Thus, it worked out in favour of Macy and company; their entire group was saved by Grace, Divine Intervention and Sheer Dumb Luck (as orchestrated by Predestination) while Cappy D and his men met their demise hand in hand with disbelief. Predestination, Grace, Divine Intervention and

Sheer Dumb Luck subsequently high-fived and left their day jobs for a well-earned night of revelry and celebration. They were well on their way to making up.

The ship eventually ground to a halt at the base of the mountain. Wide wounds had been rent in the hull, and many of the stabilizers were broken off. The ship would never fly again. A great cloud of vapourized dirt and powdered stone hid the vessel from view.

Earl, Charles, Macy, Troy, and their escort of men-at-arms picked themselves (and Matt Ferren) off the floor and checked one another for injuries. They found none, save the abraded ear of Van Ugh. This, however, was a minor wound and could wait as there were more pressing matters. Matt was still unconscious, and Uthbert hoisted his limp form easily over one shoulder, letting Matt come to rest there like a sack of flour.

Bainan bolted, bounding breathlessly before his brawny barbarian band. He appeared to have run the entire length of the ship to meet them.

"We must make haste," he gasped. "In moments this vessel shall be erased violently from existence!" When everyone present merely turned a questioning look on Bainan, he offered, "There was a blinky light with a picture that looked like this:" He mimed an explosion with his hands.

"That was you flying the ship, wasn't it?" Charles, hair disheveled, pointed an accusing finger at Bainan, who nodded, beaming proudly. He did not yet understand that his valiant efforts had indeed elicited a reaction quite opposite to that which he intended.

"You buffoon!" Charles shouted. Earl wrestled the smaller man away from Bainan with a sweaty arm. Charles made some kind of grunting, choking noise.

It seems that my valiant efforts have indeed elicited a reaction opposite to that which I intended, Bainan thought articulately to himself (and to everyone else present).

"Easy, Charlie boy," Earl cooed. "Consider to whom you speak." Earl tipped his head in Bainan's direction and cast Charles a cautioning look. Earl too, looked none the better for several hours spent in captivity; his eyes were rimmed with red and his voice was hoarse. Charles took several deep breaths.

"Where is Reese!?" Macy demanded. Earl's eyes went wide as he turned to her.

"She was taken elsewhere. The cell floor is empty," he concluded.

"I hope you are certain about that!" was Macy's reply. She was about to continue when Troy interrupted.

"We have to go, or we are all goners! Once the blast radius hits the twin ionized torsion drives, the abrasion repulsor fuel will ignite and this thing is the Great Canyon!"

All stopped to stare at Troy.

"What?" Troy objected. "I watch a lot of

Solar Star Battleship."

Macy and Troy raced to exit the torn-open ship, followed closely by the men under Bainan's command. Earl released Charles, who took a deep breath and turned to Bainan.

"I suppose I owe you my thanks, then," Charles mused once he had calmed down. "Those ruffians would surely have killed us if you had not unbalanced the situation. So... thank you, Bainan."

By that time, many of the more sane and forward-thinking people had completely evacuated the craft. They found themselves in a large field, with little cover to speak of. The few scrawny trees and rocks that dotted the field would not have hidden an anorexic rabbit from a blind coyote. A few seconds later, seeing the others already running for the hills, Charles, Earl and Bainan joined them in flight. A flapping, flailing Ferren floated along after them upon the brawny shoulder of Uthbert.

"There's the highway!" Earl pointed. "Head for the culvert!" He had spotted, with unusually keen eyes, a small drainage tunnel running beneath the roadway. All continued to run as fast as possible toward this point.

Perhaps they could make it yet!

Bainan had been unable to tell, during his brief glance at the ship's computer, precisely how much time remained until the ship would destroy itself. He had attributed the existence of the ship's computer, upon its attempt to communicate with him, to be a combination of sorcery and unnatural spirits. Their conversation was recovered centuries later on a partially burned manuscript. Archaeologists and historians studied the writings and finally believed it to be a biography of the life of Bainan, written by one of his men and later edited by someone else. The investigation into the origin of the document is ongoing, however, given that all of Bainan's men were illiterate. The conversation, recorded meticulously in a calligraphic hand, had gone precisely as follows:

BAINAN stands before COMPUTER. BAINAN presses buttons ~~idly~~ *heroically.* **He wears a** ~~confused~~ *heroic* **expression.**

Computer (in foreign tongue): "Ill In Ighin ist simis simili."

Bainan: "The demon speaks!"

Computer (in foreign tongue): "Inginin ich invin?"

Bainan: You have no power here, cursed creature!

BAINAN tears the monitor off of the console. He holds it aloft.

Bainan: "I AM BAINAN!"

BAINAN smashes the monitor full upon the floor and ~~flees~~ *exits heroically.*

The authenticity of this document has been debated, and the identity of the editor is both mysterious and absolutely impossible to guess.

However, it can be vaguely surmised that Bainan had thereupon smashed the monitor on the ground and fled the manifest den of devils. Thus, some moments later, the group had no idea if they could make cover in time. This was mainly thanks to Bainan and his inability to read a digital timer. They continued to run across the plain as fast as each could. They were perhaps fifty meters from cover.

With a tremendous, ground-shaking *BOOM*, the steel vessel erupted in a hail of metal, sparks, and dust. The group piled into the small cement cavity beneath the roadway just before the shrapnel began to rain down. They had cleared the wreckage in time, Predestination, Grace, Divine Intervention and Sheer Dumb Luck having paused their celebration to complete their task of protecting the protagonists as warranted by their collective goal and dictated by the Narrative. The large spaceship, along with Troy's aged sedan, was no more. Troy discovered the chrome badge, still attached to a broken piece of grill, a few paces from the entrance to their shelter, confirming its demise.

"Where do you think Reese has gone?" Charles asked.

"The woman," Earl panted.

"What woman?" Macy asked frantically.

"It's all right, Macy. We'll find her," Troy said, endeavouring to comfort her. Troy still fervently believed they were, ultimately, in a novel—perhaps around chapter 12, past the second act at least and, hopefully, nearing the climax.

"The sorceress took her from the ship when it made a stop." Having provided the information that was of use, Earl collapsed and continued to catch his breath in a more comfortable position.

"I heard something about a warehouse, that might be where they went," Charles offered. He sat upon the shoulder of the highway, shedding quite a bit of sweat.

BLLLGHGHGHGHGHGHGHHHHHHH.

This was the sound of Matt coming to, and subsequently emptying his stomach. Uthbert swung him none too gently to the ground, where Matt repeated his prior statement.

Chapter 13:

Sumus Superioris

Reese paced the small room. She had no idea where she was as the room had no window and the hurried car ride to transport her there had provided little navigational direction, in no small part attributable to the fact that she hadn't known from where they had departed. The door was of large, steel construction, with no defining features and offered no clues. It was remarkable in that it was completely nondescript. After some minutes of pacing, Reese sat down and stared at the notebook she had now held in her hands for the past ten minutes. She picked up the pen.

Reese placed the pen back down on the table at which she sat and resumed pacing for an additional ten minutes. She had the general understanding of what ought to happen next, but knew not how to proceed. Reese had already established that she could not, she was certain, rewrite Azalion's story. Jack Grendel was quite mistaken, and what he demanded was impossible. Therefore, Reese had come up with an alternate plan. As all of her friends had been scattered far and wide when the *Aura Regency Hide* had been destroyed for the second time in its naval career (this, Reese briefly acknowledged, must have been detrimental to crew morale) what Reese very much needed now was another hero — one that would save them all, most likely at the last possible moment in true deus ex-machina style.

Taking a deep breath, Reese sat down. She knew what she must do, but she bent to her work with a heavy heart. Her hand trembling, Reese penned one simple line. Reese considered the words she had shakily scrawled, then closed the book and placed it back on the table, shoving it away from her just a little.

It was done.

Some minutes later, Jack Grendel returned. He set before Reese a tray of cold, uninviting food. She looked at the bowl of rugged stew gratefully.

Jack Grendel scooped up the notebook, opened it with a cold grace, and read what was written there. Reese tried not to smirk as the colour drained from the killer's face. His expression changed from cold realization to hot fury, his lips going coal-white around their edges where he pressed them together. Without realizing that he did so, Jack drew a six-inch combat knife and began to spin it in one hand.

"What — How?!" he choked.

Reese sat very still.

"Do you have any idea what you've done?!!" Jack bellowed.

"I'm pretty sure I do," Reese answered in her coolest Stella Cadenza tone. "And now, being the only other person to have read the words, you have effectively sealed your own fate."

Jack waved the knife about but, realizing that he could not kill Reese then and there as he very much would have liked — she was needed to fix this after all — only embedded the knife deeply but impotently into the table. He threw the book down so that it splayed out in front of Reese, and stormed out of the room.

After the large door clanged shut, Reese ate her meager supper, grateful it had escaped unscathed when Jack's knife had killed the table on which it sat. The pages of the open notebook stared blankly at the ceiling, the sole line writ there still plainly visible, glowered at Reese accusingly:

"And Adriel, having learned his final earthly lesson, succumbed to bitter death and was carried by a whirlwind into heaven, where he was restored to his former power and place of honour."

Quite some miles away from where Reese sat and much closer to her now-destroyed apartment containing her half-finished manuscripts, traffic had come to a standstill. Many citizens, already tense from the spaceship fiasco a few days earlier, had quit their vehicles, looking cautiously to the skies then at the newly formed micro-car-sized hole in the street. A cloud of smoke billowed up from an intersection some way ahead. Already a large crowd had gathered and more onlookers were collecting.

Police officers had formed a perimeter of tape and orange safety cones (most of which had already begun the inevitable process of falling over, as though they had some agenda of their own or, perhaps, a silent arrangement with gravity) and stood trying to assess the situation. Through the smoke, they could see what appeared to be a crater several metres wide and maybe two meters deep. But what had caused it?

Jed scowled. It was a hot day, and he was already sweating beneath his dark uniform. The uniform continued to smugly absorb sunlight, slowly suffocating Jed as if he were shrink-wrapped. He had never met a boa constrictor, but this was one tenth of what he imagined them to feel like.

Jed was just beginning to wonder what sort of sheird wit he had gotten himself into this time when there was movement. Rubble clattered ominously, and the smoke began to rise from the centre of the crater.

The first thing Jed saw was the pair of very large folded wings: dove grey mottled with white. They seemed to glow radiantly for the briefest moment, then fade until they were no longer blinding. The crowd gasped. Rising from the smoke was an obscenely well-muscled, winged man. At first, his hair matched the mottled grey of the wings that adorned his back, but as the glaring light faded, the man's hair darkened to a deep chestnut colour. Jed had never seen an angel before, but if they were out there (and he rather fancied they were), this was certainly what they looked like.

The form took two steps forward and stumbled among the debris, dropping to one knee and supported by one very toned arm. Jed instinctively forsook the imagined safety of the police-tape barricade and went to help. The other officers seemed to be busy attempting to quell a miniature riot half a block down.

Jed helped the strange man to his feet.

"Are you alright? How did you get in there? Where did you come from?"

The man wiped a layer of dust from his eyebrow and accepted Jed's hand. The instant their hands touched, Jed felt a substantial jolt, as if the man were made of electricity. The man pulled Jed close, whispering urgently into his ear.

"I have a mission you would do well to endorse. Will you help me?"

"If you're trying to stop all the weird stuff that's been going on, absolutely," Jed replied. His arm was still being tasered by the firm grip this man seemed to effortlessly exert.

"I need to get out of this village as fast as possible," the man whispered.

"Take these keys," Jed said, not entirely sure why he did so. "That's the fastest car in our fleet." Jed pointed to the car he had driven up in.

The man took the keys from Jed, nodding a curt thank-you and ending Jed's session of electroshock therapy. Jed wondered if therapy would actually help him after this. The winged man turned back to the crater he had just exited. He bent and grasped something buried in the dust, then straightened and pulled steadily. He drew from the dirt a sword nearly two meters in length. Dust fell from the blade, leaving it a gleaming silver. Carrying the sword lightly in one hand, the man turned back to Jed.

"You may tell them I took the vehicle by force," he whispered. "That may make things easier for you."

"I'll deal with them—I just want all this chaos to go away," Jed replied. He figured at that point, it was simpler to ask his superiors for forgiveness rather than permission and, after all, rules were made for breaking.

"You are a good man, Jedediah. Tonight, you will receive a phone call from the state hospital to say that your mother has inexplicably recovered from her terminal illness." The man made his way to the car. Jed stood there speechless. "Oh," the winged man said, turning briefly back to Jed and flashing a small smile, "and the other one—she'll say 'yes' when you ask."

Jed was still trying to sort the first bit and had no context for the last. He stared stupidly at the strange man.

"Inform these dark forces that Adriel has been sent to reckon with them," the man called loudly from where he stood next to the car.

"Um. Okay! Drive safe," Jed was by now completely confused.

Adriel passed the sword through the open rear window of the police car. Even across both seats, the handle protruded from the window by quite a bit. Adriel next had some difficulty fitting both himself and his wings into the driver's seat. In the end, he reclined the backrest fully and the rear seat was filled with grey feathers.

Adriel surveyed the array of controls before him. How hard could it be? Once he had found 'drive' (quite by accident) a tremendous squeal heralded his departure. The crowd darted to the sides of the street, parting readily before him. By some quirk of Fate, nobody was hurt—again, likely through the timely cooperation of Grace, Divine Intervention, and Sheer Dumb Luck. However, it was also partly attributable to the driver's ability to (not on purpose, mind you) run someone over and then heal that person instantly. He muttered to himself about the incredulity of performing minor motorway miracles. It was like asking a civil war veteran to fire a pellet gun at the fair to win a prize.

The speedy inline eight engine purred uproariously, fueling Adriel's high speed journey. Adriel turned on the radio. He had quite a journey before him after all.

A hoarse male voice, well abused by cigarette smoke, alcohol, and quite possibly the consumption of gravel in lieu of breakfast cereal, screamed out "I'm on a road way that leads to hell," amid a chorus of screeching guitars. Adriel grunted and changed the channel. Ah. That was better; he had found an inspirational radio station (also known as Techno-Bible Jam).

A few miles later, Adriel stopped. There was one basic problem he had yet to think through: his present lack of any clothing whatsoever. This was not necessarily viewed as an impediment where Adriel originated from, however, as he had learned in the course of his Reese-written story, being clad in clothing was viewed as a must when working amidst Humans. Adriel pulled into a gas station / convenience store that was semi-attached to a small restaurant.

Adriel entered the gas station and selected from the shelves a pair of cotton pants, a t-shirt, and some versions of food and drink he thought were perhaps consumable. He immediately donned the pants, carrying the rest to the cash register. A corpulent man sat on a bar-height chair behind the register, completely engrossed by the comic book in his hand: Saskaman Versus Captain Gas.

"I require these items of clothing and these provisions," Adriel said, "yet this was all the money I could find in the glove box of the vehicle I'm driving."

The attendant looked at Adriel over the top rim of his spectacles and replied, "Yeah — caught that when you got out of the car..."

The man shifted his glasses and looked down at the two bills, three coins and one button.

"Eh," the man shrugged. "Close enough. A guy needs at least one good shirt," the man turned back to his comic, seeming not to notice the wings Adriel sported at his back (or, perhaps choosing to ignore them as a topic about which one did not ask questions).

"Cool sword, man," was the only further thing the man said, his gaze not leaving his comic as he spoke.

"Thank you. It is made of forged inconel."

"Sweeeeeeeeet."

Adriel exited the gas station. The man at the counter picked up the button, uttered a quiet "All right!" and from the plate on the counter began to eat a large frankfurter covered with chili and topped with cheese.

Adriel fueled the car (which took him a few minutes) and pulled out onto a blind gravel road shooting off the main highway where he stopped and exited the car. He opened the trunk of the vehicle. Finding a utility knife inside, he made two large incisions in the back of the t-shirt. This he donned with some difficulty. I mean really, mortal life had been inconvenient enough the first time, with no wings to contend with! How could these puny creatures stand it? They are eternal beings bound in temporary shells of dust. Like mud-covered vehicles entering a car wash, each would eventually be freed of its mortal shroud and become visible for what it had truly been all along—or rather, what it had managed to make of itself during the boot camp humans called life.

Yet Adriel could not merely fly to his

destination. For one thing, he did not wish to tangle with government aircraft carrying heat-seeking missiles or even power lines, for that matter. Aside from that concern, there were ten other reasons for taking the vehicle—and all of them were currently residing in the trunk of the car. Lifting a plastic cover, Adriel laid grateful eyes on a perfect arsenal of modern firearms and non-lethal grenades. He even found a grenade launcher with several anti-riot canisters. Fluent from the beginning of his existence in the language of warfare, Adriel sat on the rear bumper of the police car for some time, loading weapon after weapon after weapon after... well, you get the idea.

Captain Noa Lee awoke. That is, she had not opened her eyes, but she could tell that she was awake by the intense pain that encompassed her entire body. It was nearly an hour before she roused the will to move, and that was primarily due to the urgings of her ravenous stomach.

Noa glanced about and, looking out a near porthole, found herself in the comforting, wooden quarters of a sky-faring vessel. How could this be possible? The *Aura Regency* had been destroyed! Trying to think through her slowly passing headache, which continued its gradual decrescendo behind her temples, she remembered that the *Aura Regency* had indeed gone down. She recalled the battle with Ustrina, and the lighter-than-air schooner that had come to her rescue. General Quercius is alive! she thought suddenly, mentally rejoicing in lieu of attempting to do so physically.

The room was warm, sunlight pouring in through a closed porthole. At their present altitude, there was not even wind noise to be heard—naught in fact, but the slow creaking of the timbers in flight. The sound was home to Captain Noa Lee.

Clothing had been laid out for her, an officer's garb complete with a cloak and a fresh sabre. Blast. She would have to have a new one made, assuming she could find a worthy swordsmith to begin with.

However, it was not the clothes that first drew Noa's attention. Rather, it was the bowl of stew sitting on the bedside stand. She took up the spoon: the stew was still warm! The captain dove in hungrily.

Noa was halfway done the stew (mere seconds had elapsed) when a knock came without her door.

"Come in," Noa mumbled around a mouthful of potatoes and carrots.

The door opened and entered General Quercius himself. A wide grin split his face.

"General!" Captain Lee spluttered, snapping to attention. The sudden movement was premature in the Captain's recovery and she proceeded to pitch forward. The general quickly stepped forward, catching her with strong arms, but bandaged as he was, his efforts only caused the two of them to sag against the wall.

"Easy, my child. Rest now." Quercius helped Noa into a sitting position on the edge of the bed. She resumed eating her stew.

"My General," Lee rasped between mouthfuls, "how is it you are still alive?!"

"A story for another time, I'm afraid, Captain. Right now we are bound for a warehouse on the edge of the city. One of our prisoners has given us the location." Quercius gazed sternly out the porthole into the clear, bright sky.

"And there we will find Ms. Cadenza — Miss Richardson?" Noa inquired.

"I devoutly hope so." Quercius turned to the captain. "Noa, in your state I will not ask you to fight—"

"Nor will you have to ask," Lee returned, eyeing the sabre with a grim determination. She wondered then how much willpower it would take to raise a sword given her present condition.

"That is why you are my foremost Captain," Quercius chuckled. He turned to the door. "Judging by that empty bowl, I will have them send you more food and drink."

"Thank you. And sir—"

Quercius paused in the doorway.

"I'm sorry I failed you—failed to protect *her*."

Quercius drew a deep breath and sighed.

"You did not fail, Captain. You performed better than anyone could have hoped to, facing such a foe. As always, I am proud to have you under my command."

Noa simply nodded, and the door closed. The Captain collapsed into the warm sheets, exhausted. She slept deeply until the door opened and the cook brought her a fresh bowl of hot soup accompanied by a thickly buttered piece of toast.

The wizened farmer drove along the country road, his equally dilapidated pickup truck straining even with the slight incline. The antique radio squeaked out some new Taya Quick song. Or was that even her song? This was one old man who had too much going on to bother with keeping up with pop music. His mental collection of song lyrics included nothing past the year 1953.

Macy and Troy sat in the cab with the aging farmer. He glanced at them with a concerned, questioning look in his eyes. The truck grumbled and rattled; Troy surmised that the farmer had bought it new — a very long time ago. Regardless of the vehicle's age, it was still in better condition than the old man who sat at the wheel. His grey hair was sparse and a rugged white stubble coated his hollowed, worn face like an autumn snow.

"Thank you for the ride," Macy said sweetly (and manipulatively — she was very good at that, Troy had noted — something which concerned Troy on some level). Troy leaned one elbow out the open passenger window. He bit his lip, wondering how much longer the old man would let the silence drag on.

"It's no trouble, young'ns. How did you get so far into the country in the first place?"

"The car broke down," Macy offered.

"Broke down?" Troy laughed. "More like broke apart!"

"Maybe it's worth fixin'?" the old man suggested. "Ah used to tinker wit anyt'ing what had wheels, Ah did. Do you want me to have a look at 't?"

"Sure!" Troy laughed. He drew the hood ornament out of his pocket and slid it down the dashboard. "This was all we found of it."

"Well then," the old man laughed. "Guess 't answers 'at question!"

The truck drove on for some twenty minutes. The old man pulled the truck over in front of what appeared to be a payphone, miles from anywhere and years from nowhere. It was the only evidence of human technology in sight.

"'Ave t' drop y'all off here," said the old man, "could be Ah reckon you might figure t' call someone you know from town, leastwise then you might get a ride t'other half o' the way."

"Thank you very much, Albert," Macy purred. She turned to the open window at the back of the cab. "Alright! Everyone out!"

This directive was aimed at the box of the truck in which sat eleven rough men and one very pale Matt Ferren. His skin was completely white from years in space followed by weeks spent encased in the metal suit—that and a couple of heaving episodes. The man practically glowed. Even now he covered himself with a blanket to shade his skin from the burning sun. His muscles had benefitted from moving the armour about, and he appeared much the stronger for it. However, he still looked sick to his stomach, and the men had wisely placed a steel pail at his feet.

The men evacuated the box of the truck while the farmer watched uneasily from the cab, keeping a close eye on the proceedings in the rear-view mirror. He had learned quite some time ago through a rather unfortunate encounter with a hoe why it is best to stay clear of large men tending gardens with sharp implements.

Uthbert lent Matt a shoulder as he stumbled down from the tailgate. It took 6.5 minutes to unload all the heavy power tools that Bainan's men were misusing. The truck finally rumbled away, and the group was left standing on the road, looking around uncertainly.

Before anyone could ask "what do we do now", the payphone rang. All eyes turned to the phone as it rang a second time. No one moved.

RINNG

This time everyone turned to look at one another.

RIIINNNGGG

It was Matt who finally stepped forward and picked up the receiver, holding it gingerly to his ear lest it explode or perhaps spew forth a telemarketer.

SO YOU ARE A FISH OUT OF HIS TIN, came the voice. AND EVIDENTLY HAVE NOT YET BEEN CONSUMED.

"Seraiah!" Matt cried. He could hardly feature being glad to hear the steely, rasping voice that had tormented him for weeks, yet glad he now was. Matt had not heard that voice since his suit of armour had been forcibly removed by a rather intent space pirate wielding an angle grinder and a plasma cutter. The last thing he had heard from Seraiah was a fading "NOOOoo…" when the bolt cutters had cut the wire running to the helmet. Matt had been left to hope that the fiend had escaped into the mainframe of the pirated spaceship.

"How did you find me?" Matt asked.

INCONSEQUENTIAL, came the voice, WHAT YOU MUST NOW KNOW IS THE ADDRESS I AM ABOUT TO TELL YOU…

The subsequent conversation lasted 1.3 minutes. Matt rejoined the others, all of whom were sitting dejectedly by the side of the road.

"Good news is, we have an address," Matt said, "and using the private jet I keep in my back pocket we will be there in no time."

Bainan leapt to his feet. "Excellent! Let us make haste!"

Matt looked at Bainan, wondering how best to explain. He gave it a valiant effort, having some difficulty given Bainan's lack of understanding regarding the application of sarcasm. Once again, a sarcastic font would have avoided much confusion.

"So you mean to say that you do not indeed carry an airplane about your person," Bainan concluded.

"That's right. It was a thing you say that you don't mean," Troy attempted.

"Like a lie?!" Bainan roared.

"Um. More like a joke."

Nobody seemed to be laughing. It appeared (as has been evidenced in many awkward social instances throughout the course of history) Explanation relieves Sarcasm of any humour.

Captain Lee winced, for the second time in her life. The first time had been when she was twelve years old; she had gotten into a fight with a boy much bigger than she had been. She had entertained no alternative but to fight; this boy had been pushing about another small boy. Noa had used her agility and speed to get the larger boy into a deadlock. That day had been the first time she felt bones break beneath her capable hands, but it had given her a frightful pain to do it and she had subsequently winced. She had, after some toughening of both muscles and stomach, discovered that she liked the gritty, nerve-rending, snapping-twig noises her enemies made as she broke them, and had devoted her life to training in combat. From that day onward she had had it in her heart to apply to the navy, and later on, the Coasting Guardsmen. She had made it to the rank of captain a mere 2.45 years from the time of her enlisting.

The episode with the bully had been the first time she had winced. The second occurred now as Captain Lee attempted to don her uniform; she pulled the stiff fabric over her recent collection of lacerations, bruises and burns. Never in her life had Captain Noa Lee taken such abuse, nor indeed lost a battle. Her stiff, sore muscles cried out as she moved them. Nevertheless, it was not a bad feeling; Captain Noa Lee was eager for an opportunity to even the score.

She sheathed the sabre at her side, then a loaded pistol. A second loaded pistol followed, as well as a large dagger and then another. In addition to these, there were likely several more weapons of various size and purpose hidden about her person by the time she finished her toilette.

Captain Lee climbed the gangway to the main deck, the brilliant sun momentarily blinding her. She could soon see all of her men assembled; all were survivors of the *Aura Regency*. There were more present than Lee had expected. General Quercius had done an excellent job collecting them all. Many were bandaged and injured, a few seemed to be completely unscathed. General Quercius stood near the helmsman and greeted her with an approving nod.

"There are stories told of great heroes," Quercius address the men, "who go to sleep for many years, hundreds of years, in some unreachable mountain hold. These heroes sleep, but not in death, until their time arrives to awake and retake kingdoms! Gentlemen, sailors and soldiers all, our hero has awakened!"

A tremendous cheer rose from the sailors collected about, who smiled as they roared, welcoming their captain. A cold smile spread across the face of Captain Noa Lee, splitting a few of her cuts open. With these men at her command, with such a force of courageous warriors, the enemy would have sufficient reason to quake in their boots.

"Guardsmen!" Noa addressed them. "Let the sun of this strange land see the gleam of our unsheathed blades!" She held her sabre aloft, and a chorus of metal on metal resounded about the quarterdeck. The sun glinted on what seemed a small sea of polished steel.

"Make ready for battle!" Quercius boomed. "We are due to make port any minute!"

The men hopped to attention, scurrying to battle stations. Captain Lee took a deep breath, feeling at home in the whirlwind of action about her.

King Sven parked the hyper-expensive, excessively macho Maserini two-door, triple-turbo inline twelve sports car that he had acquired. It roared with a ferocity that flew in the face of any eco-friendly, fossil fuel protesting, environment-loving social movement. "The planet could burn in the combustion chambers of the 899 horsepower engine," said the engineer responsible for designing the metal monstrosity. Alternately, there may have been something lost in translation from the original Italian.

King Sven turned off the engine and entered the warehouse. Many other vehicles, some expensive, and some chosen by Grendel's men, filled the parking lot. King Sven mumbled something unintelligible, but because Ustrina was now paying him by the word, he said nothing. That is, Ustrina was paying him for every word he could keep to himself in the course of a day. He was so far making quite an earning, yet was decidedly sore at such an insult.

King Sven was knocked flat by a deafening explosion. He may have uttered a word or two in the sudden shock; however, Ustrina would not dock his pay due to the offensiveness of his vocabulary — there was also the fact that they both said the same thing at the same time, so it was difficult for her to argue the point.

The Maserini was no more. In its place was a smoking hole and a burned-out chassis. Regaining his feet, King Sven stared out the doorway. Hovering above the parking lot was a large ship, held aloft by an ovular, lighter-than-air sac of a rich navy coloured rip-stop nylon embossed with silver.

The ship's cannons fired a second volley, obliterating every vehicle in the parking lot as well as some on the near-by street (including

King Sven's motorcycle collection and a moped that had belonged to Count Ignes). This task completed, the crew of the gun-decks turned their attention to the flimsy, corrugated iron facade of the building itself. King Sven could hear cheers of triumph breaking out from the ship.

In mere seconds, the building was crumbling. All within flooded outside to the parking lot. King Sven had his sword to hand, but pushed his way inside the building as he was not in battle gear.

Ranks of Sven's men began to form up along the crumbled parking lot. Rank upon rank of sword, shield and spear waved upon the tarmac like a quickly grown forest of metal and bone. Written for the purpose of obliterating Bainan and his men at arms, these renegades would nevertheless be satisfied with taking on the Coasting Guardsmen.

The first response the vessel made was a heavy battery of cannon fire, all to deadly effect. The men upon the tarmac attempted to fire back with an array of large siege engines, yet all were soon obliterated by the ship's cannons. So readily did the ship's crew act that the vessel herself took minimal damage before the enemy's weapons were destroyed.

A hail of barbed arrows was the next taunt hurled from the deck of the ship. Shields were raised, but the casualties were numerous nevertheless, the weighty arrows having the benefit of a great fall and much momentum.

Whilst the enemy cowered under their shields, lines were unfurled from the airship; hundreds of warriors descended in a great torrent to the ground. The vessel gave one last volley of arrows and cannon fire, then ceased entirely to avoid injuring her own men. Quercius oversaw the entire affair from the deck of the small sloop.

"Godspeed, my brave Captain," he called after Captain Lee.

Noa Lee nodded, then hurled herself from the deck, rope in hand and fully armed for combat.

Reaching the ground, Captain Lee drew sabre and pistol amid a maelstrom of whooshing arrows and small arms fire.

"Guardsmen, to me!" she cried. With the entire remaining number of Coasting Guardsmen at her back, Captain Lee led the charge on the warehouse, intent on rescuing their Creator. The sounds of battle reached the approving ears of General Quercius.

Reese could hear the commotion outside — indeed, she had felt the building shake and heard it begin to crumble with a wrenching cry and moan. She supposed herself, however, to be underground, as the sounds were distant and rumbling and were more felt than heard.

Reese knew she had to do something. Surely she could aid her friends as they battled this formidable enemy, could she not? Grendel had made the fatal error of leaving her the notebook, a weapon more potent and dangerous than he had ever imagined. Reese sat down and, with a grim determination (and admittedly, a bit of a grin of anticipation), clicked her pen.

Outside, the battle grew very strange. The villains were suddenly wearing naught but their undergarments, and the swords and spears of Sven's force had become limp as wet yarn, hanging from the hands of those who attempted to wield them. Sven's hoard didn't know which to do first: cover themselves or attempt to straighten their swords. While they tried to figure that out, Captain Lee and her men led a merry slaughter, with nothing to stop them from doing what they may.

That is when the hair on each man in the enemy army was suddenly (and with a satisfying WHOOSH) set aflame. All stopped, dropped to the ground, and continued to panic. (They had not had the benefit of fire-fighting rules taught in middle school and, thus, did not know the Stop, Drop, and Roll method of putting out one's own flames.)

In the lot nearby, stood several units of heavy construction machinery: loaders and scissor lifts, as well as many small digging vehicles — one with a menacing drill for a nose. Each of these seemed to spontaneously come alive, wheeling themselves about and trying to run over the combatants. The mischievous machines did not stop there, however. They shortly sprouted mechanical legs and rose up, each one twice as tall as anyone present. The machines did what they were made to do; smoke billowing from their exhaust pipes, they scooped up the enemy bodies in their large shovels and forks and deposited them into loader-vehicle-automaton to be hauled away and disposed of (we, the editors, have deleted further exposition on this point, preferring not to say where). Soon the parking lot was clear of the dead, and a small street sweeping vehicle (which had seemingly joined the other machines in its sudden acquisition of sentience as it had driven past the mayhem, minding its own business) rose up on two legs and began cleaning the parking lot of all the blood and rubble, as a custodian might clean a school hallway of mud and forgotten lunches after hours.

From the top windows and ground floor of the warehouse came a sudden burst of an alarming amount of gunfire. Captain Lee signaled her men to take cover, and they dove behind various burnt carcasses of what once had been vehicles. The large robots crouched down in a neat row, providing cover for the guardsmen, understanding their superior metal hides would protect the flimsy humans from being throughoutly perforated.

Nearly a dozen men poured out of the building, Thompson sub-machine guns in hand. They wore long, dark coats and hats of the sort found in a 1940's film noire — all of them tilted rakishly over one eye for good effect. They were indeed members of the gang with which Jack Grendel had worked and coincidentally appeared in black and white — but mostly black — and lots of very dark grey shadow. They lay into Lee's force with their Tommy guns, amassing a fair count of bodies.

· Captain Lee and her men attempted to fire back; yet their arrows were few and their pistols were soon out of shot. They had downed one or two of their foes, but more seemed to be joining the battle from within the warehouse and Lee's men were hopelessly outgunned.

There was a brief lull in the gunfire as the gangsters withdrew momentarily, seeking cover and keeping Lee's men besieged while waiting for reinforcements. More black-and-white mobsters were soon gathering behind the covering gunmen. A few orders were shouted and the men began to organize themselves into groups. Lee and her men hunkered down behind what cover they could find, waiting to see what plan their enemy would unfurl.

Lee knew, however, that she and her men would not make it out of the situation given the loss of many of her force and the resulting sheer number difference between the opposing factions. They could only wait for their own demise.

Into this tension-riddled silence, a single police car rolled up, siren wailing and lights flashing. Everyone on both sides stopped to stare.

The car, seemingly oblivious to the current situation, parked boldly in the very center of the parking lot, right between the two warring parties. It looked as if it had driven through every ditch and bush for a hundred kilometers. The vehicle was covered in mud, brush, and every shade and variety of dirt. The tires were nearly bald, and the engine dripped onto the tarmac very slightly. A large cloud of vapour erupted from under the hood with a startling HIIISSSS.

After a few moments, and thumping the dash a few times with his fist, the driver appeared to have figured out how to turn off the lights and sirens—or perhaps he simply eradicated the mechanism. At any rate, the vehicle obligingly quit its wailing and flashing.

The gangsters tensed, aiming their Trench Sweepers at the car and watching closely to see what the driver intended. The man in the car reached down under the dash slowly, smiled politely at his enemies over the dash as he did so, then popped the trunk of the car.

"Fire, fire! Knock 'im dead!" shouted the leader of the small Mafioso. The mobsters opened fire on the car, the passenger side of which was soon a smouldering, steel art impression of Swiss cheese.

The gunfire ceased. The smoke cleared and the dust settled. Everyone on both sides could clearly see that the vehicle was empty. Also, rather disturbingly, the two-meter long sword had been removed from the backseat and was nowhere in sight.

With the grace of a large bird landing, Adriel touched down before the wreck of the police car. His sword was strapped to his back, for his hands were too occupied to wield it, being full of compact, automatic submachine guns. He opened fire and the gangsters each chose one of two options: flee or fall in the face of the sudden attack. Most did not possess swift decision-making skills, so chose the latter by default.

Moving swiftly, Adriel entered the warehouse, the dead and/or dying gangsters having fallen rather conveniently in an orderly fashion and leaving a clear path to the gaping front of the building. He left naught but bodies and brass shell casings upon the doorstep. Captain Lee had no idea who had rescued her and her men, but promised herself to thank him later. Her force regrouped, reloaded, and prepared to assault the warehouse, intent on dealing with whatever count of the enemy were left standing and thus rescue their beloved wordsmith and creator.

That is when a very bad thing happened: the ground began to shake.

Chapter 14:

Victerio illos Errare

Adriel did not notice the quaking of the parking lot. He was, by that time, a blur of fury, kicked-in doors, feathers and gun smoke. If he sustained injury he did not heed it as he blasted his way through the mosaic militia of Grendel and Sven, the combined force a juxtaposed mix of barbarian hoard and black-and-white mobsters.

Adriel made his way down the hallway where he knew (simply by some inexplicable innate knowledge that had been written into his character) Reese was being held. His folded wings barely allowed him entry to the crowded staircase as he descended to the basement.

Adriel reached an open workshop; there were none in that room save himself and one tall, thin man. Adriel paused, debating whether or not to dispatch the man.

"I knew you would be coming," the tall man said calmly. He turned to face Adriel, shuffling a large coat from his shoulders. This he folded neatly and draped lightly over a workbench, brushing it once with his hand to smooth a wrinkle before turning to Adriel with a small smile.

The tall man had dark hair, darker eyes, and wore several knives in a custom-made leather harness that hung about his torso.

"I suppose you are Jack Grendel, then," Adriel stated.

"You suppose correctly," replied the snake-like man.

Adriel placed his firearms upon the workbench alongside Grendel's coat, brushing at one of them with a hand to remove a smear of blood. There would be, Adriel knew, no bullets in this match. Good and evil require no weapons to mediate their conflict.

"If you want Reese, you go through me," Jack Grendel grinned, drawing a large knife.

"This is not a fight you can win," Adriel admonished with a shake of his head, "tell your forces to stand down and release the girl."

"I have no forces left to command. Whether or not I defeat you, I have waited a long time for this chance," Jack smirked then. "Tell me, Adriel, what were her last words to you? Can you ever outrun her ghost? Isabella trusted you and you failed her utterly."

"You have been studying. Very prudent of you, Jack. You didn't really think you could provoke me with that?"

"I thought it was worth a try. She did have such lovely eyes," Grendel sneered.

"Aye, she did. Now leave off with the torment. You can inflict no more pain on me than that which I already have taken on willingly.

Come over here, if you call yourself a man, and truly wound me!"

The wordplay evidently finished, the two men began to circle one another slowly, each a predator stalking his prey. Jack Grendel brandished the knife and made a satisfied hissing noise. Adriel held forth his empty hands, palms open.

Jack lashed out with a furious flourish of the knife. Adriel had time to deflect the blade with a wave of a hand, and the slash aimed expertly for his chest merely tore open his forearm. The two continued to pace.

Adriel countered another stab of the knife with a devastating right hook to the face. Grendel staggered back and raised a hand to his bleeding nose. He glared up at Adriel as both men bled upon the floor. Adriel was slightly slower than his opponent, having to maneuver with a large pair of wings on his back, but those wings also lent to the momentum of his swing.

Jack Grendel attacked again; this time Adriel caught the blade (unfortunately he did so using his left shoulder). Before Grendel could withdraw the blade and swing again, Adriel had him by the wrist. With his left hand, Adriel delivered a blow, bending Grendel's elbow ninety degrees—in the opposite direction of its intended movement. Jack cried out, but Adriel was not finished. Keeping a tight grip on Jack's now flailing arm, Adriel spun the wounded Grendel about. Grendel was firmly trapped, his back to Adriel, and a firm elbow crushing his throat.

"It's been a pleasure, my friend," Jack spluttered through a mouthful of blood.

"I cannot say the same," Adriel grunted back. Adriel hated killing, but he hated killers more.

"I'm glad to have met a foe like you," Grendel muttered, "a man of my genius becomes bored in a place like this."

"Notwithstanding, there is no world in which your plans succeed. You might have made a great hero, Jack."

"So might you have," Jack shot back with a gasp, "but I've already set in motion things even you cannot undo."

Jack watched as Adriel slowly drew the glistening, red knife from his own shoulder and held it before them.

Some moments later, Adriel picked up his firearms from the workbench. Not one to get blood everywhere (a bit of a neat-freak, really), Adriel forced his wounds closed with duct tape he found on a nearby counter.

Passing by the still form of Jack Grendel, Adriel noted a splay of papers, lying astrew on the floor beside Jack, evidently having fallen from his vest. Adriel glanced at the childish scrawls of writing on the papers, noting the jejune drawing of a bright yellow flower with a disturbingly vibrant smiley face boldly emblazoned on it. Thinking little of it, Adriel exited the workshop, leaving Grendel prone upon the floor, his own blade protruding from his lifeless body.

Reese looked down at the notebook. It was quite a sight, laced with frantic scribbles and half-thoughts. She felt she had somewhat aided in the battle. Or so she hoped.

A knock came at the door.

"Who is it?" Reese called, feeling slightly silly doing so, and wondering why her captors would feel the need to knock.

"Miss Richardson?" came a male voice.

"Yes?" Reese replied.

"You will want to stand aside."

Reese moved to one side of the room.

"Oh, and please step behind anything that might shield you from flying debris."

Reese upended the table and ducked behind it, perfectly confident in the ability of arborite to protect one from any projectile known to man.

"Ok," she called. "I'm good."

There was a brief moment of silence, followed by a substantial **CRASH**. The door buckled inward, its hinges flying through the table, past an astonished Reese who had only just been missed by the impromptu missile. The hinges imbedded themselves in the back wall. The door clattered to the floor in pieces in front of the table Reese hid behind. Reese peeked over the table's edge just in time to see Adriel lower one raised foot.

Reese was momentarily astonished. She recognized Adriel of course—she had created him. She knew his face, written from some vague place in Reese' memory—something conjured, perhaps, from an overly popular male model turned actor whose face had been plastered everywhere for a time. However, to see him standing before her was an entirely different sort of thing altogether.

His glinting, fog-grey eyes met hers from beneath his stormy brow. He strode toward her, but Reese stood entirely distracted by the way his muscles moved beneath the t-shirt he wore (she knew what hid there—she had written that too). His biceps flexed like powerful coils of metal. Reese forced herself to return his gaze, and nearly melted from its intensity. His black hair fell about his face in raven locks, framing a lightly shadowed, chiseled jaw. She could still make out the scar from an encounter she had written, a thin white pencil stroke running cheekbone to chin. However, the scar detracted little from his overwhelming appearance. In fact, it lent itself marvelously to enhancing the brooding effect of his very presence.

[Dearest and most valued reader: at this point we, the editors, must interject a word. Several words actually, formed into sentences that culminate in one strongly-worded paragraph. We wish to note that the above-written scene, including all of its excessively sappy adjectives and syntax, is not our doing. The writings, may we remind you, are the sole property and culpability of Ms. Richardson as outlined by the Writer's Guild. We cannot be held accountable for the gooey, platitudinous entirety of it. In addition, we are dismayed to note, her writings suffer an undeniable dearth in punctuation and pacing. Your sagacious understanding and persistence in reading is appreciated.]

"We have to leave," Adriel said, his voice like thunder over a distant, clouded hillside.

Reese failed for some moments to form an articulate response. When she was again able to form a coherent reply it went something like, "Uh, yeah. Sounds good to me."

Reese was not, in point of fact, responding to Adriel's directive. In reality, what Reese had heard Adriel say was, "Hey. How's it going? We should hold hands". This was what Reese was actually replying to.

Ironically, Adriel then took her hand and led her from the cell. Reese may have sighed slightly as she followed him through the dark hallway. They reached the workshop and gingerly circumambulated the still form of Grendel.

Suddenly the very building shook.

From a drain in the floor (a large, dank, wet drain covered by a sparse steel grate) came a small green shoot. A dark green tentacle of vegetation, sprouting thorns and leaves, began to grow at an alarming rate.

"Oh no," Reese gasped, noticing the small sprout. "It can't be... How did he even get that?!"

"What is this?" Adriel questioned.

"When I was ten, I wrote a story. In the story, I was playing in the garden when all of the sunflowers came alive and chased me." Reese stared in horror as the vine snaked across the floor. She stepped closer to Adriel, hugging his arm.

"In the story, you must have killed them — they are in this world after all. It might aid us to know how," Adriel returned, out-stepping the curling vine which appeared to be trying to make a grab for his ankle.

"I had Grandpa come out of the house and mow them all down with the tractor," Reese said. This story had been based on true (if heavily extrapolated) events concerning the garden at her grandparents' farm. Reese had been scared of the tall, looming flowers waving high over her head — menacingly, she had thought. On a few occasions, when the wind had stirred the sunflowers and their great heads had bent down over her, whispering in their shaky breathy voices, she had run inside to her grandparents in tears. Finally, her grandfather, tired of the drama, had rolled his eyes and gone out to mow down the troublesome plants with the riding mower. (He had always thought they were senseless and ugly anyway and was really somewhat grateful for the excuse to get rid of them.)

Reese looked down at the coiling plant,

taking another step back. The vine had nearly reached the wall.

"I'm assuming you did not, in fact, write the death of your grandfather into that story and, as such, we cannot rely on his assistance in this instance," Adriel murmured. "We must reach the exit before this place is overtaken."

Reese and Adriel ran, hand in hand, up the stairs. This was no problem for Adriel, as he was in top physical condition. Nor was it a problem for Reese, who did not mind holding hands with Adriel in the slightest and, in her distraction, was able to ignore the burning stitch that set up firmly in her side as she tried to keep up with her handsome hero.

Outside, the concrete of the parking lot lay in crumbled pieces like broken eraser bits. Large vines coiled about the pavement, and stalks were edging their way toward their victims—these included any human within reaching distance. One stalk had curled around one of Lee's men, circling his waist twice, and was hoisting him off the ground. Lee and several men were searching frantically for anything with which they could dismember the thick-stalked foliage.

"Why, in all my research pertaining to your writings, have I never read of this foe?" Adriel asked, again running headlong into a confrontation with frustration.

"I wrote the story when I was ten! It was a grade school project, and even I forgot about it."

"How do we destroy them?" Adriel asked,

turning on the spot and watching the twisting vines weaving amongst Lee's men and circling ever closer to where he stood with Reese. He holstered his firearms and hefted his gigantic sword easily (once he had disentangled himself from Reese' clutches).

"I don't know! I don't remember what I wrote!" Reese said. "Let me think for a minute."

"Make it a very brief minute," Adriel returned. The parking lot had by that time become a forest; indeed, it was difficult to see the assembled force of the Guardsmen, standing not far from them.

Adriel swung his sword. A dozen yellow sunflower heads dropped to the ground and burst into a spray of black, smoldering seeds. Like a hydra, several heads grew back swiftly in their place, ever more numerous than before.

After a few more efforts producing the same results, Adriel put up his sword.

"I think I wrote that they have to be killed with garden tools," Reese called. "That's why Grandpa could kill them with the tractor." Reese shook her head.

Adriel thumbed the handle of one of his firearms, wondering if it was worth a shot. Already the two were hemmed in, trapped in a small clearing. It was growing dark about them, for the stalks were so thick and growing so tall that they were crowding out the light. Large sunflowers loomed in over their heads, watching their about-to-be victims. All but a sliver of daylight was erased.

"What do you remember of these foes? Why were they so terrifying and malicious?" Adriel asked.

"Well, I think I wrote that they drink human blood," Reese offered.

Adriel cast Reese a concerned glance then kicked a small vine that was attempting to entangle his leg.

"That's good to know," Adriel grunted. "Anything else?"

Reese dug through the deteriorating scraps of recollections, trying to recall her grade school experience and attempting to light any remaining spark of memory. Perhaps the darkness helped her concentrate; perhaps an author always remembers their first story; either way, in a moment she had it. Reese recalled a picture she had drawn in grade one, an illustration to be turned in along with the two-page story. She wondered briefly why any teacher would subject herself to reading twenty stories written in the crayoned, paper-tearing, ham fisted writing of grade school children. Maybe she just got a kick out of the hilarity of it all.

The picture, Reese recalled, featured the scene she had described in her book: a young Reese running to the left side of the page, her stick arms flailing ludicrously, projecting four stick fingers each (counting had been a problem for her at the time, particularly since her actual count of fingers never did match her perceived anatomy). On the right side of the page, her handle-bar-mustached grandpa rode a purple tractor onto the scene (motion lines streaming out behind him in bright turquoise and yellow). The illustrated grandpa was smiling a maniacally large smile with way too many teeth, the caption above his head reading: "I will kil dem all". Leaves and sunflower heads spewed out from under the purple tractor as it mercilessly mulched the man-eating vegetative villains. Before the tractor was another sunflower — the leader of the marching floral force. It was reaching out and trying to grab a small fleeing Reese with its outstretched leaves. It wore an innocent button-eyed smiley face on its yellow blossom — Reese had also found smiley faces creepy at the time — those and ducks.

That was it.

"We need to destroy the flower with the smiley face!" Reese yelled.

"I beg your pardon?" countered Adriel, giving the head of a sunflower a harsh upper cut as it bent closer to Reese. It slunk away momentarily.

"The one with a yellow face, black eyes, and a black smiling mouth."

"That should give me something to do," Adriel said grimly. He drew one of the compact shotguns he had taken from the police car. A sawed-off would have been illegal for any police force to carry, but this one had clearly been modified with a cut-off disc and an angle grinder, so it was perfectly fine. Adriel had figured that, legal or not, the weapon would still fire effectively.

Adriel was correct.

The shot erupted from the short barrel with a significant amount of force, tearing a large hole in the foliage before them. Adriel emptied the shotgun, round after round; the plants seemed to give way before him, however, they were still surrounded. The vines continued to creep toward the pair.

"Get down," Adriel ordered. Reese obeyed instantly. Drawing the sword, Adriel swung. This time he did not let up; with vigorous swordplay that would have taxed an Olympic fencer, he was able to carve a path through the deadly forest. The two ran in the direction they guessed the ship to be, Adriel slashing all the way. The path closed behind them instantly.

CLANG

Adriel found that he had inadvertently cut through the ship's anchor line. Despite the solid links being made of four centimeters of steel, Adriel had severed the chain easily with one accidental swing.

The ship began to drift upward. Adriel sheathed his sword, making a grab for the chain and Reese both at the same time. With a firm hand-hold on one of the chain's rungs, and pulling Reese to him with his free hand, Adriel placed one foot into the lowest link of the chain. The two drifted up, out of reach of the ferocious flowers, as the ship floated away.

The anchor line was slowly reeled in. The helmsman, suddenly finding that his ship was freed of her mooring, leapt to action trying to maintain position.

Soon the pair was pulled to deck level. Adriel waited until the Guardsmen helped Reese aboard, then leaped lightly to the deck with a great SWOOSH of his wings, riding the downdraft to light on the ship.

To their extreme relief, their combined fighting force had retreated to the safety of the schooner and now remained safely out of harm's way on its deck. Captain Lee stood, wondering how best to attack an army of plants, now released onto the world at large from the imagination of a then 10-year-old creator. General Quercius and Azalion conspired nearby.

From where Azalion and Quercius stood, they could see the large robots, composed of re-ordered construction equipment, hard at work. The machines tore up dozens of flowers, piling their corpses into a dump-truck now turned robot. Despite the steadily growing numbers of dead flowers piled up, the robots never seemed to make any progress, nor did the plants seem to be aware of them. As the mechanized military contained no blood to drink, the plants did not acknowledge their existence. The scene continued for some minutes.

Then something extraordinary happened. A city bus pulled up to the curb.

The bus was far enough from the exponentially expanding forest that there was still a curb for it to pull up to. From the doors of the bus poured at least a dozen burly warriors, all carrying chainsaws, swords, varied gardening equipment and anything else they deemed useful in combat (Uthbert had picked up a pick-axe in the back of the farmer's truck which he intended to return when he was done with it).

Reese gave a small cry of joy to see that Macy, Earl, and Charles (and another guy) were alright after all — at least for the time being.

"Bring her about, helmsman!" General Quercius boomed, not missing any of the situation. "Civilians to the starboard keel!"

This indicated to the helmsman, of course, to make a course down and to the right. For in aerial sailing, there is not only port and starboard, aft and fore. There is the third axis, to be called keel or colours. Therefore, if the captain shouts, "Port to colours!" this indicates to lay a course left and upward ("colours" being the flag flying from the topmost mast of the ship, or "up").

Soon a rope ladder was hurled down to the group. Charles, Macy, Earl, and that other guy clambered up. Reese realized it must be Troy — whom she had met briefly once before.

Bainan made no move for the ladder. He simply shouted an order to his men, who fired up the chainsaws and reciprocating saws. One revved a Whipper Snapper into a high pitch and others hoisted their axes, hedge trimmers, rakes, hoes, and various other implements high. The dozen men dove into the forest, hacking and demolishing the overgrown sunflowers. Their choice of weaponry proving most providential. The sunflowers' susceptibility to gardening instruments meant they did not grow back when struck down. Bainan and his men roared with delight and pursued the enemy with great vigor. Warfare was, after all, their greatest pleasure, regardless of the foe fought.

Unfortunately, there was now a new problem erupting. The warehouse began to split and shake. This continued for quite a while before the building simply exploded, burst from within by a malevolent, powerful force. The party on the schooner fell flat upon the deck, hiding from the fragments of foundation that pelted the vessel.

Rising from the demolished building was a beast, a monster of colossal proportions. It was lithe and snakelike, with six powerful legs. The creature's iridescent coat of scales glistened, despite the lack of direct sunlight (clouds had hastened to shield the scene from the sun's disdainful view).

The large serpent had no wings, but did have a very long, lashing tail. For just a moment, it looked up at the vessel with a human face — a feminine face, in all likeness to Ustrina. With a great hiss, the human face was coated with heavy scales, the nose pulling up into a snarling snout.

Bainan let out a fierce roar. From the grisly meadow of vegetation, covered in seeds and sap from head to toe, Bainan held aloft a single sunflower. It was featured with a face that once had been smiling, but was no longer. Now it grimaced in the throes of death, the button eyes bearing only vacant X's. The rest of the plants withered in moments. Their leaves curled up and dropped to the ground, and the vines ceased to move.

That was the moment King Sven chose to exit the partially ruined structure. He was fully armed and armoured, and a handful of his men followed. Most were still in their underwear, with singed hair and eyebrows.

"Mein auld frind," Sven greeted Bainan, "so gud to see yoh."

"Thou iniquitous malefactor!" Bainan roared back. "I have been waiting for this day!"

King Sven hefted a large sword. He grinned at Bainan. "So güd of yoh. Forst, I tek your princess, now I vill tek yor life fur eh sckund time."

Bainan let out a ferocious battle-cry. He dropped his chainsaw to the ground, drawing a large sword from his back. His men at his side, Bainan charged. The swordplay began in earnest.

Meanwhile, the gigantic creature began to hiss out a stream of clear vapor. It gave vent to a colossal jet of visible gas which projected several hundred feet into the air. Several cotton-ball clouds suddenly froze, stuck together, and fell to earth with a tremendous, icy shatter. Miraculously, none hit the schooner upon which our fair friends presently flew.

"I'm withdrawing the vessel and taking our guests to safety," General Quercius called. He could not risk the remaining survivors—particularly the Wordsmith—by remaining so close to such a dangerous beast.

"A wise idea, General!" Adriel affirmed.

The helm was brought 'round, and the vessel changed course.

Yet the creature snarled and followed after them; chunks of structural steel and corrugated metal flying about as it burst from the confines of the roofless warehouse. It stamped after them, roaring deafeningly.

Reese looked about the deck, searching the gathered faces for Adriel. Adriel stood at the ship's rail, watching the distant building that now hatched into a dragon every square centimeter as awesome as Reese's rival writers'. Adriel's eyes were stormy. Reese walked over to him, wondering what emotions his gaze concealed. Adriel put his hand on the rail of the ship, preparing to propel himself overboard. Reese halted him with a hand on his arm.

"Do you really have to go?" Reese asked.

"Yes. It is my duty," Adriel responded solemnly.

Reese looked away. All at once she could feel a pain in her chest, as if her heart was fragmenting into a thousand tiny pieces. *That's really good*, Reese thought, *I ought to use that in a book sometime.*

Presently she returned to the present. Despite having met Adriel only a short time ago, the thought of being parted from him felt akin to having a searing clothing iron lodged in her heart. Reese had no time to think of a better analogy, as Adriel turned his stormy gaze stormily upon her. The words *I don't want you to go*, were on the tip of her tongue, but in place of words, Reese found the only input available was a dial tone. Reese wondered if anything she might say could ever have an impact on Adriel's resolve, anyway.

"Well, good luck," Reese offered lamely. She honestly needed a significant amount of time to come up with better responses — she'd always done poorly at writing dialogue. It seemed silly not to, so she quickly kissed his cheek.

"Thank you, but I don't believe in luck," Adriel said. Without another word, he gathered up his great sable wings, leapt over the ship's rail, and took flight, descending in a blur of fog and feathers. Reese stared after him and mentally kicked herself in the mental rear end for all the editing she should have done with that scene.

Chapter 15:

Ignis Anhelat

Reese wondered how long it would take for her audience members and followers to realize that she had just been BS-ing them all along. In grade school, had anyone asked her teachers what kind of career little Reese should pursue, writing (or anything creative) would have certainly not come up. Her stories, she felt, were only of moderate caliber in the writing world. The poor reviews had been many, and one in particular had classed Reese in the same genre as books by Everly Geyers, a B (or perhaps C) grade one-hit wonder whose dark teen fantasy-romance was generally viewed with extreme disdain. In fact, Reese had been through that exact conversation with Macy some time ago. Macy had asked whether Reese would simply invent a new bad guy to carry the story through the lacking exposition when it came to the penultimate chapter of one of her earlier novels.

"I don't know, Macy," Reese had sighed, "I have to write fiction! I can't just make crap up!"

As it would turn out, the two were essentially the same thing. Reese pulled out the notebook, several pages falling out of the failing thing as she did so. She thought frantically for a moment then scrawled a brief phrase.

Ustrina died suddenly of a heart attack.

She watched the gigantic monster as she lowered her pen; Reese waited for several minutes. Nothing happened. She had known it was futile — Ustrina had already died in her world, but still, she'd had to try. She could be of no help to Adriel.

Or could she?

Reese thought for a minute then began to write once more. This time she took a new tack.

Adriel touched down, righteous feet upon an earth tarnished with darkness. An empty expanse of the shattered ice of fallen clouds was all that stood between he and the monster. The noble warrior, alone, advanced upon the plain of frost and crumbled cement. A heavy snow began, emanating from the creature of cold cruelty.

Adriel drew his sword from its sheath, brandishing the righteous blade. It was of such girth and weight that no mortal would ever contain the strength to wield it. The brightly forged inconel, its surface worn smooth in the blood and bone of countless former enemies, glimmered in anticipation, reflecting its enemy in the cold air.

Slowly the creature climbed up, up over the ruined building, up into Adriel's sight. The monster, noting the brave and noble man before it, seemed to smile. Something began to happen then — something that proved most fortunate for

Adriel.

The ice beneath his feet, the thick covering of broken hail, had begun to move. Like a garden sprouting green shoots a hundred days in a minute, tall shafts of ice had begun to shoot forth from the frosty ground. These, in moments, grew into tall, icy trees with sharp, jagged branches. Thus, the hero had some cover from unfriendly eyes. He moved warily toward the monster amidst the shelter of the ice-trees.

The glittering trees grew taller and taller. Within moments, they had encased the creature completely, trapping it in an icy grip. The monster that was Ustrina roared and struggled, attempting to kick free of its restraints.

While it has been deemed wise, throughout the depths of time and the stories contained therein, to fight fire with fire, one must avoid fighting ice with ice — no one manages well on ice, as anyone in mid-Canada can attest to (and Reese ought to have known this). The ice could not hold a creature wielding that very element as a weapon — all power and sway over the ice was held by Ustrina. Soon the snake was free, blasting a clearing in the icy forest with its mighty forepaws.

Ustrina, her vision clouded with rage, looked about for her attacker, but he was nowhere to be seen.

Bainan staggered backward, Sven's dagger protruding from his abdomen. The King, knowing that he was completely outmatched by Bainan's swordplay, had resorted to trickery. He had feinted with his longsword, and with Bainan's blade momentarily out of the way, he had rushed in with his small dagger. It had been a cowardly attack.

"Thou makest a most cowardly attack," Bainan reiterated for the benefit of those trapped within, and not comfortably reading, this story. King Sven only smiled.

There were casualties on both sides; Bainan's men and Sven's had been fighting for some minutes. A number of wounded struggled to yet fight.

Bainan sank to one knee. He had known such defeat only once before; that time too, had been at the hands of King Sven.

"Sech a femilier sight, yoh und I," Sven chuckled. He advanced on the kneeling warrior with a raised sword.

"Thy cowardice may win you this day, but shall cost you your life," Bainan lectured from the ground. He had, at that moment, no idea just how quickly those words would take effect.

Sven only chuckled, now two steps from Bainan. He glared at his age-old enemy, savouring his victory. That was his first mistake.

"Hold!" boomed a voice from behind Sven. Sven turned, staring full into the wrathful face of General Quercius. The General stood with drawn sword in one hand and a loaded pistol in the other. "I, General Aloysius Quercius, permit no living soul to cut down any ally of the Coasting Guardsmen."

King Sven seemed to pale, taking an uncertain step back—which enemy should he attack first? Taking full advantage of this distraction, Bainan tore the blade from his side. He rose and began doing a fair imitation of first aid style abdominal thrusts on Sven—the only difference was that Bainan had a large dagger in his hands. The blade slipped silently under Sven's ribcage.

Striking Bainan with a steel-plated elbow, Sven attempted to flee. That was his second mistake. He ran blindly through the forest of ice-trees, losing himself in the mirrory maze and clutching his wound. King Sven began gasping for breath, one lung spewing air to the outside through the gaping hole in his chest. He spurred himself on, running with one final effort—right into the waiting weapons of Captain Noa Lee.

The duel was short: Captain Lee parried an ill-timed attack from Sven. She first severed his sword hand with a vicious slash of her sabre. Without waiting even a fraction of a second, Lee struck again. Something bearded, with gaping eyes and mouth, fell to the ground with a dull and bounceless *plunk* (while it landed solidly enough, it did go on to roll some distance). Captain Lee kneeled, cleaning her blade on her late adversary's cloak.

The forest of ice was yet growing. Captain Lee, General Quercius, and their men aided

Bainan and his companions to the schooner, their heading charted at a guess. They all boarded safely after quite a few suspenseful minutes spent aiding limping men and peering into the darkness, waiting to be attacked. No attack came.

General Quercius commanded that the ship repair to a higher altitude and sequester herself from further damage. This order was carried out swiftly. Though Adriel was still missing from their company, he possessed wings and would likely be able to reach them on his own — should he be allowed that luxury.

Jed stopped his classic Bevelet truck at the side of the road, leaned back on the headrest and sighed. He was finally out of uniform after a long day of policing pedestrians, public relations, and answering silly questions — some of those things occurring all at the same time.

It had been a long day. Upon returning to the station there had been the requisite filling out of paperwork and explaining why he had given the fastest car in the police fleet to some guy who crawled up out of a crater. Jed had gone with a rather elaborately falsified version, in which the man had wrested the keys from Jed violently and fled the scene. It sounded convincing enough, right? So Jed had thought, until he was subject to the stern, patented glare of his superior officer. Jed, sweating under the gaze, had felt that he was melting along with his flimsy alibi, like butter under a reading lamp.

Fortunately, though they thoroughly disapproved of his failure, the higher-ups did not once question his story. Jed sighed in relief and exited the office. By mid-day, Jed was certain that giving the man the keys had been the right thing to do. It was a belief he would never be able to quantify or justify, and yet it held firm.

As it turns out, for his next shift, Jed would arrive at the station to find the loaned car returned, sitting proudly in the station parking lot. Jed's eyes would go wide as he took in the bald tires, the flame-scorched paint, and the fact that half of the car had been obliterated by small arms fire. Jed wasn't at all sure if the presence of the vehicle would really help his position, but there was no use doing anything about it. Much later, the forensics team would pull a bullet from the shattered chassis and determine with some bewilderment that the rounds fired had been from a 1930s automatic rifle, but this was currently irrelevant since, at the present moment, Jed's world had a weighty probability of ending well before any of these events would unfold, given the current events presently being enacted elsewhere.

Jed climbed out of the truck, the ancient door creaking. He had spent quite a few years restoring the truck, why he did so he knew not. Perhaps he had been bored, or just liked the reliability of the old girl and wanted her to look a bit less "junkyard." In either case, the truck looked nearly new. Fresh rotary New-Year tires still gleamed black, giving off a brain-wiping rubber smell. Ahhhhhh. Rubber smell. Second only to gasoline or perhaps permanent marker (although mimeograph ink may have also made the list).

Jed entered the coffee shop he had patronized nearly every day over the length of his career. Joyce was, however, nowhere to be seen. Disappointed, Jed ordered his usual coffee from Javier (knowing, of course, that the large man wasn't quite as good at making it as Joyce was). In fact, Joyce had his order memorized by now and typically had it ready and waiting for him by the time he got to the till. Their conversations, by extrapolation of this fact, were less of "which roast do you recommend?" and more of "how has your week been?".

Jed sat down with his coffee. He was tired after the long day and resolved that instead of working out at the Jim (short for Jim's Gym and Running Track), he would simply take the night off. Besides, he had been to the Jim last week... at least, he thought he must have.

The fact was that Jed's Memory Lane was blocked off around Tuesday for routine roadway maintenance, and Jed could not find the detour route in order to reconnect to the remainder of Monday. Though it was about time someone did something — the cobbles were coming up out of the road like popcorn out of a kettle. There was a rather large sinkhole that had consumed most of last week — possibly due to the strange things that had occurred more recently. Jed was distracted from his trek through a rather dim and foggy Memory Lane by someone approaching the table at which he sat.

Jed looked up, with only mild trepidation—understandable given that, on that particular day, he was fully aware that anything imaginable might possibly turn up. He was relieved then when the figure standing beside him turned out to be Joyce.

"Is this spot taken?" she asked, indicating the bench on the far side of the table from Jed. Jed, somewhat surprised (pleasantly so), took a moment to realize that a response was required.

"Sort of," he replied with a smile. "I was saving that seat for you," Jed joked jestingly. Joyce smiled her lovely smile and sat down with her own cup of steaming coffee.

Joyce attempted to put a plastic lid on her own cup. She struggled with it for a moment, chasing the recalcitrant lid around the cup rim— the silly things never did like to be pinned down, due to their incessant fear of commitment. They were well aware that, once attached to a cup, there was no leaving it until they found themselves separated from said cup in the dumpster. Not a life they wanted to lead. No one ever asked what the cup wanted. Watching Joyce, Jed had an instant premonition of the coffee cup rejecting the lid, and with an angry tantrum, vomiting its contents all over Joyce.

"Here. Allow me." Jed reached for the

stubborn couple and deftly snapped the lid onto the coffee cup (he had years of practice). "Big hands," he said by way of explanation. "They're good for something. Besides, if anyone gets to spill coffee all over themselves, it may as well be me."

"Thanks, Jed," Joyce replied with a small laugh. "These cups weren't very well engineered! Not very cooperative, I'm afraid." The two laughed and with the ice broken (as well as the will of the obstinate coffee lid), they proceeded to converse late into the evening. They did not part before taking a long, cool evening walk, and when Jed asked, Joyce agreed to meet him for dinner the next week.

Jed smiled for the first time in some days as he drove home. The radio played his favourite country rock song by Here's-Your-Change-Back, causing Jed to practically dance in the driver's seat. The lead singer sounded as though he perpetually had strep throat, and the band had long outlived its popularity, and still, Jed listened to their first few albums. He resolved to thoroughly clean his apartment and throw out some of the junk that cluttered the place (which was mostly everything). He might have company for dinner sometime soon. Jed sighed happily.

Fortunately for Jed, the anticipated day would also unfold in the soon to be explained alternate universe where no weird crap happened at all. At any single moment, there were ten to the power of seventeen different Jeds, having different days. Some varied minutely, for example, wearing blue socks instead of black. Some varied entirely, such as the single parallel Jed who was currently polishing a revolver on the front porch of his expansive farmhouse, wearing nothing but underwear, a holster, cowboy boots, and a cowboy hat. In that reality, however, he would never meet Joyce, as he would be too busy chasing after Stacy and roughing up diner customers who looked at her for too long. Fate was kind enough not to perpetuate that Jed through the millions of possible Jeds that passed fleetingly through numerous daily decisions.

The beast's icy breath struck Adriel with full force. He felt his heart seize instantly, like a man who had just jumped into arctic waters. His wings iced solidly, saturated with frozen moisture condensed from the swirling fog surrounding him. He could barely move, burdened by the sudden weight. Sinking to one knee, Adriel waited for the end.

For the first time, Adriel looked full into the eyes of the monster as it leaned in close, relishing his tribulation. There was a fiery hate and a depthless darkness lurking there, but something else lay there as well. Buried deep in the brute's eyes was fear.

Adriel grinned at the grotesque face now only inches from his. The creature struck Adriel for his impudence, dealing a heavy blow with a massive paw. Adriel stumbled back in a shower of tinkling, shattering ice. The blow had, at least, freed Adriel's wings, breaking the solid ice so that it clattered to the ground. He could move more readily. He flared his wings and shook the weight from them. Adriel regained his feet; he must not fail to rid the world of such flagrant hate and malice. There would be no bounds to the evil and perfidy such a being could wreak should she ever reach the city, even in human form. Ustrina had a talent for playing upon weaknesses and turning allies against one another.

Before Adriel could leap into the air, the gigantic creature bent down, opening its jaws wide to devour him.

Having the advantage of reach, Adriel struck the creature forcefully upon the brow with his sword. Blood bubbled forth from the wound, blinding the creature. It screamed and shook its head, trying to clear its sight.

The beast looked about for Adriel, seeking the small man-creature that had dared to smite her. Too late did she look up; too late did she see the winged form of Adriel diving upon her, hidden at first in the fragmented and magnified blaze of the sun that still shone beyond the ice fog. Adriel drew back his sword arm, and with one mighty swing, severed the head of the creature. The beast collapsed. Adriel paused to clean his sword then noticed something strange.

Within the creature's mouth was a glowing metallic object. It sat in the abscess created by one large, missing tooth. The corpse of the monster put forth a horrid stench.

Adriel leaned closer despite the oppressive smell. He pried the beast's jaws apart and tore the object free. He turned it over in one hand; it was a metal casing of an unsettling trapezoidal shape. Adriel, reading the strange markings that glittered in silver letters upon the black, obsidianite surface, smiled with a knowing comprehension. This was the missing piece of the puzzle. It could have but one purpose, which Adriel had all but guessed.

Adriel took to the air, seeking the airship upon which his friends would be found.

He spied the ship after quite a while of flying about. It had set down in the wide river, all of its flying equipment furled. To anyone who did not know the vessel, it would seem an ordinary schooner. What on earth it was doing on a river, gliding through a landlocked province would be quite another matter of guesswork for any unfortunate observer.

Adriel landed on the deck; only one guard was posted. Locking eyes with Adriel, the guard dropped to one knee and ducked his head.

"Where are the others, good sir?" Adriel asked the guard, at the same time slipping the Artifact into the duffel bag he had retrieved. The bag was still one hundred percent full of guns, though the ammunition levels of the bag had dipped into a single digit percentage value.

"They dine below, sir," replied the guard, "you might just be in time to lunch with them."

"Thank you," Adriel replied. Adriel retired to the lower deck, the duffel bag at his side.

The guard slowly stood, watching Adriel as he descended the stairs. The guard returned then to his position. It was a duty he had oft performed, and the solace of guard duty gave him both time and freedom to let his mind wander.

Too late did the guard see the lone assassin climb the anchor line; however, it would not have made a difference if he had. You see, the assassin was dressed in a large, black cloak with an inconspicuously shadowy hood. Such a disguise would certainly have ensured his concealment absolutely anywhere, and the black robes he wore were designed to draw no attention whatsoever — not even in broad daylight. He was trying very hard not to be noticed.

The guard was thrown overboard, a dagger in his back. The assassin, rethinking the ordeal for a moment, frowned down at the floating body. He had neglected to foresee some aspects of the plan. Yes, he confirmed with himself, he should have stolen the man's uniform and *then* thrown him overboard. Not to mention retrieving the perfectly good knife now drifting through the brine, lodged in the corpse. It had been on the exam and everything. The assassin swore softly then looked around to see if anyone had witnessed his misstep. Nobody noticed that either.

Adriel joined the others; everyone assembled was eating a meal of reheated stew and bread. Bainan was deeply engaged in a conversation with General Quercius; listening intently but with rather confused expressions as Quercius explained the concept of lighter-than-air travel and the invention of gunpowder.

Matt and Azalion laughed as they sat together and ate. Captain Lee was instructing Macy regarding the use and maintenance of a naval officer's pistol (fortunately it was empty). Troy sat near to Macy, watching her and smiling to himself.

Charles seemed to have gotten over himself, eating with Earl and wondering if he ought to pick up his children from their aunt's house yet—and exactly how he would do so if he were so inclined. He peered over his spectacles at the faces gathered; his expression was uncharacteristically shadowed. Earl put down a half-eaten bowl of stew. Perhaps he had finally filled the void that comprised his stomach.

Even Seraiah was present, in a way. Matt had recovered a space gun and a communicator that had been among the debris of the wrecked craft. Somehow both still worked. Seraiah's voice crackled through the communicator whenever he had something to say. Matt and Azalion shook their heads at one another as they listened to Seraiah. The fiend talked of weaving some kind of web by which he would ensnare every computer and piece of technology on the planet. It sounded rather science-fictiony and far-fetched to Matt.

Bainan's men laughed with the officers of the Coasting Guardsmen, telling stories of valour and their loving women back home.

The conversations stopped and all looked over as Adriel entered. A cheer went up, and General Quercius himself presented Adriel with a victory bowl of tepid stew. Adriel realized how absolutely starving he was — the temporality of the human form never ceasing to catch him off-guard. He devoured one and then an additional three bowls of Lukewarm stew. The cook, Luke, was somewhat pleased that *someone* was enjoying it.

The meal lasted until the horizon was brimmed with a fiery red; the sun touched the water and flooded the galley with an orange haze. Pipes were lit, the party reclined with an air of muted victory. Each wondered silently what the future now held. Could they return to their own worlds? And if they could, what then? Each had died in his or her native realm. Going back seemed futile at best and somehow counter-productive at worst.

Adriel stirred. Something had gone awry. He could feel it — a stirring deep inside his chest making it difficult to breathe. Rising, he made his way to the upper deck. Adriel had the duffel bag with him, lest it leave his sight for even a moment. Matt trailed him; any upset in the winged man's disposition surely meant trouble. One guard stood on deck, his back to the approaching two. Matt approached the guard to ask him if anything was noticeably amiss. As Matt soon found out, the amissitude was indeed of noticeable proportions.

Swiftly, the guard spun Matt to face Adriel, at the same time putting a knife to Matt's throat. The blade was a double-edged, standard-issue, clipped-point, full-tang, case-hardened, and only slightly rusted assassin's dagger. It was specially made to penetrate, in particular, the rhomboid and latissimus musculature of the undefended back.

"The Artifact, if you please," hissed the assassin.

"Hey!" Matt objected, "you already lost! Your leaders are dead! Ah—" this last noise was an involuntary response to the tightening of the blade at his throat.

"Yes," the Assassin mused, "you could not have cleared the path for me any better. I was contemplating how to get rid of them all, especially Ustrina and that Grendel fellow. You have done me quite a nice turn. In return I suppose that, once the power of the Artifact is mine to wield, I shall make your deaths swift and even perhaps merciful. Nobody shall know of your acts of valour; indeed, I shall erase this entire affair from existence. Then, using my stealth, I shall infiltrate human society and take this country as my own."

"Wow, man," Matt complained, "give it a rest! That's the worst, third-rate evil scheme I ever heard! Ow, ow. Ok, ok, already!" The blade made a white mark on Matt's throat.

Adriel had, after sufficient rummaging, found the last loaded weapon in his bag. He was in luck! The gun was a powerful, eighty caliber revolver. Perhaps the police had used such a weapon to, for example, penetrate armoured cars or maybe stave off pesky polar bears? No matter. As long as the gun was in his hand and loaded. The ten-round cylinder responded to the priming of the hammer, chambering a round.

"Excellent," the Assassin hissed, "you've brought a nice new toy for me. These Guardsmen carry such outdated firepower." The Assassin, with his free hand, threw a naval pistol into the water. "Place the gun on the ground, or this man dies before you can fire."

"Matt," Adriel began, "I'm very sorry about this. Inasmuch as you are only the comic relief in this tale, you are therefore the most expendable one here."

"Wait—I thought he was with you," the Assassin argued quickly.

"Truly? This man doesn't even possess his armour anymore. He's no longer of any use to the team."

"Aw, come on… that's harsh, man…" Matt had no time to finish his complaint.

Adriel's revolver went off, and Matt hit the ground.

The Assassin was momentarily shocked. This wasn't in any of the text books and no professors had ever hinted this might happen. He reviewed the Assassin's handbook for the remaining two seconds of his life; let's see, take a hostage, everyone puts down their weapons, and the next step was…

The revolver sounded again. An eighty-caliber round split the Assassin's throat. He stumbled back, clutching the wound (even though *void* was the more appropriate descriptor for the hole in his flesh). Adriel stepped forth and executed a graceful front snap-kick, hovering lightly mid-air for a moment and landing the fiend in the water. The vile creature sank to the riverbed, taking his rightful place amongst the other bottom-dwellers.

Adriel turned his attention to Matt.

"You shot me," Matt complained. "I'm just dead now. I feel so utterly betrayed. Thanks."

"Your foot will be fine," Adriel informed Matt. "I just needed you out of the way."

"I have an idea," Matt barked, "next time let's *not* shoot Matt, we might just, I don't know, tell him to duck!"

"As you wish. Though I hope that was the last assassin we will have to deal with today."

"How about tomorrow?" grunted the injured Matt. "You seemed to like that. Wanna do that again tomorrow? Maybe without me getting shot this time?"

Matt continued to grumble from where he

sat on the deck. By now the entire party had gathered topside, weapons drawn. When they realized that someone had shot Matt, they all relaxed. Everyone at some point had wanted to do the same, having been subjected on the long journey to the alacrity of his smart mouth.

"It's alright," Matt jibed, "Adriel was just kicking my assassin," even injured, his comedic nature was rampant—and substandard.

Captain Lee held up the abandoned, black cloak. "I see. Nicely handled, Adriel." Captain Lee threw the black cloak into the water after its master. "Answorth was on guard. He will be missed."

The guardsmen removed their headgear and bowed their heads for a silent moment. General Quercius, after some time, nodded to Adriel to speak.

"We have a choice before us, each one of us," Adriel said. His wingspan, and his commanding presence, ensured that he had the attention of all present. He drew from his bag the Artifact, holding it high for all to see. The crimson sunset glinted on the otherworldly markings, and the object seemed to glow red in the light of the setting sun.

"This is what brought each of us into this world," Adriel began, "and this, too, has the power to send us all back. However, you know why you are here to begin with. If we go back, we return to the death that was written for each of us."

Adriel paused. Perhaps there was no way to escape their fates. Could one resurrect a character once his end had been written? It was a sea never before charted. Expectant eyes watched Adriel, waiting for more.

"Every villain we killed is now trapped within this Artifact. Therefore, as long as it exists, we face the risk of a mortal releasing them, even if only inadvertently. Our departed allies are trapped within as well, yet there is no way to grant them freedom without releasing our enemies. We have two choices. Either we use the Artifact to return each of you whence you came, killing us all and sending those in the artifact to the same fate, or we bury this thing so deeply that mortal man will never find it, imprisoning forever both our allies and our enemies and remaining in this realm ourselves. I myself will personally guard it for eternity."

"Wait a minute," Matt said as Captain Lee knelt before him, bandaging Matt's foot and doing a notoriously bad job. "There is the slight chance that, according to ancient prophecy, the Artifact will create a new world for those of us that have been displaced. Our loved ones will be waiting for us. It will be totally awesome," he concluded.

Adriel frowned. He looked over the Artifact for any writing he had missed. Reese cast a puzzled glance at Matt.

"Are you quite certain?" Adriel asked.

"No. I made that up. What would I know

about an ancient artifact?" Matt admitted. Nobody laughed.

General Quercius placed a hand on Adriel's shoulder, addressing the group. "Then we are left with two choices. We remain here, or we return and thus die. Yet we were never meant for this world, and we shall all find it difficult to remain here. I, for one, will return to oblivion. I am weary. I miss my wife and even in death, she will join me one day if I return to my own story, but not so here. We have all lived, my faithful Guardsmen, and in living we have done enough of valour. Each one of you, with this second chance at life, has proven himself time and again. If there be any among you that wish to remain, speak now."

A stillness descended. The group stood silent in the haze of a river sunset.

"We go with you, my General," Captain Lee finally said. Macy sniffled and wiped away a tear. Troy seized the opportunity to hold her close.

"Very well," Adriel concluded, "once I say the words, there is no turning back. The only way to send us back to our realities is death. Death brought us here, and so it can, with the right command, send us back.

BEING A COMPUTER-GENERATED PERSONALITY, I DO NOT BELIEVE DEATH APPLIES TO ME.

"Don't worry, Sera. You will be fine," Matt tried to sound confident.

The group spent the next few minutes saying their goodbyes. Tears were plentiful, as were strong embraces. Bainan had resigned himself to the fate that awaited, and stood eyes closed, bringing before his mind's eye his beautiful Tsarmina. Perhaps he would see her in another life, just as Quercius had said.

Azalion patted the massive lion that trotted by his side. It growled sadly, seeming to understand the situation perfectly. Azalion waited patiently to see what lay beyond the next mortal curtain. Each had been given a chance to live again — another chance to show their honour, and while each felt that their new life was a lot to give up, they all knew that existence in the modern human world would be meaningless. They would always be unwelcome aliens, their true purpose as set out by their Creator beyond all reach.

Captain Lee helped Matt to his feet, supporting him with her sword-arm. Both looked to have seen better days. They exchanged a frightened glance, each trying to comfort the other.

Macy could no longer stop the tears. Troy took her hand. Macy reached out with the other and took Reese' hand. Reese knew that her fictional friends had to leave, but all the same she felt a deep sadness at their going.

"What happens to us?" asked Charles, "we are still mortal."

"The command will send all characters

back to their realities," was all that Adriel said, looking from Charles and Earl to let his gaze rest on Macy, Troy and finally Reese. Reese nodded, seeming to understand—if she did, she was the only one.

Adriel held the artifact aloft, and in a booming, singsong voice, began:

> "Row, row, row your boat
> Gently through the sky
> Merrily, merrily, merrily, merrily
> Now we all must die!"

"*That* was your magical spell?" Matt asked incredulously.

"Not a *spell*—a command over Death. And, yes, it was. Why?"

The entire group burst out laughing.

"I suppose that's it for my writing career," Reese muttered gloomily, thinking over the trailing carnage that the past few days had caused.

"Perhaps," was all Azalion said as, with a faint smile, he handed her a perfectly typed transcript detailing the events of the past five days.

"You know what I like about fiction?" Reese pondered. "How little of it I actually have to make up."

The orange sunset grew brighter and then blinding. A shower of fire rained from the sky, destroying the ship and engulfing the Artifact,

obliterating it in a blinding flash of light.
And they all died happily ever after.

Chapter 16:

Finem Loquendi

Something miraculous had happened. Reese, trapped in a sweaty, unpleasant dream of villains and wanton, fictional carnage, had quite woken up. Reese had only 3.24 seconds to wonder what had woken her before the phone rang again, insolently demanding her attention.

What?! How did I get here?!

Reese leaped out of bed, or should have. The bedclothes catching her ankle, she clumsily tottered out of the bed in a landslide of pillows. With an involuntary "eep!" she was devoured by a cascade of navy velvet and pink cotton, narrowly escaping the 1 in 42, 000 risk of injury due to bedclothes.

Intermittent 3.24 seconds. RING. Intermittent 3.24 second. RI-

"Reese here," she answered, the phone cable trailing to an arm protruding from the layers of cushions.

"I have good news!" came the voice at the other end of the line.

"Earl? Where are you?" Reese shouted incredulously.

"I'm in my office," Earl fibbed from where he lay on his couch, "and like I said: good news. I have a new publisher lined up for your latest novel."

"What novel? What are you talking about? And how did we get off the ship so fast? Is General Quercius there with you?" Reese clambered out of the piling drift of bedclothes. There was a long silence at the other end of the phone.

"Are you all right, Reese?" Earl asked.

"I think so. Holy smoke! It's still Tuesday!" She had just noticed the readout on her bedside digital clock, complete with day of the week. It had been, she was sure, late on Sunday night when the meteors had struck the small schooner, sending them all (presumably) back to their respective worlds.

Wait a minute.

Reese had woken up here—the morning that everything had begun to go awry.

Did that mean—?

"Earl, did we meet yesterday?" Reese asked.

"Uh. Yeeess… You ate an omelet."

"And you don't remember what happened tomorrow?"

"How could I remember what happens *tomorrow*?"

"Good. Just checking."

"Riiiiiight. So er…. That manuscript? You need to have a copy printed. I set up a meeting for you tomorrow."

"Thanks, Earl. That's fantastic. But… um.

What manuscript?" Reese was now genuinely confused.

"*Read This Quickly or We All Die*, of course. Everyone I have spoken to loved it."

"Then we aren't publishing the one we discussed yesterday?"

"Trust me Reese, this one is the best story you have ever written. Besides, the editors are holding off on the other one. They're still hoping you will rewrite Azalion's ending."

"Yeah, I can do that."

"Really? What changed—"

Reese said goodbye, and hung up the phone. She leaped out of the bedroom, her hair in disarray. After hurriedly slopping some pancakes into the pan, Reese ate breakfast and opened her laptop.

On the screen was a file she had never seen before. The scenes outlined in it matched her hazy recollection of the past next few days exactly. It must be the one Azalion had handed her just before the ship had been demolished! Reese was about to wonder how in the world it got there when she had an idea. She scrolled down, attempting for some while to find the right page and cursing MacroFace Work at each mouse click. It was the most fickle, infernal, deplorable word processor Reese had ever used. She resolved to pitch the laptop as soon as she performed the Manuscript Extraction surgery (A.K.A. printing).

At last she found the page, with a cry of victory. She typed:

A shower of fire rained from the sky, destroying the ship.

And they all died happily ever after. The outcome of the matter was that, according to an ancient prophecy, the Artifact created a new world for those that had been displaced. Their loved ones were already there, waiting for them. It was totally awesome. They also quickly slaughtered all of the villains, for the third time, something which Bainan and his men quite enjoyed doing.

Stella Cadenza smiled widely and strode confidently out of her apartment, taking her laptop to get the story printed for editing. She was still in her pajamas.

"Stella Cadenza, right?" The voice barely penetrated the veil of euphoria that enveloped Reese. She looked up, for a moment alarmed.

"Yes?" She responded.

Before her stood a young man in clean, sharp clothes. His long, dark hair was restrained in a ponytail, and his dark eyes gleamed with something that could easily pass for friendliness.

"So it is you," the young man went on in a silken, rich voice, "what a coincidence. Did you know, I have here one of your works?"

Chapter Finito:

Post Script

Dear Reader:

In order to avoid a repeat of the afore-mentioned events, we, the editors, have made the executive decision to suspend further writing of this manuscript at this point. We are very grateful for your determined and grown-up-underwear-clad efforts in slogging through the rather uninspired writings of Reese Richardson / Stella Cadenza.

Having read to this point, you have assisted in cementing the restorative story into the collective consciousness of the masses — or, if not the masses per se, enough people to do the cementing. Whether or not that is a good thing is another matter and upon which any rational human being would not enter into debate. No further changes can now be made to the story. The universe has been set to rights — well, it has been put back the way it was at any rate. Fiction and reality are again conveniently sorted into their separate and confined dimensions and we should be able to steer clear of any further entanglements with Reese' characters and their destructive shenanigans.

One word of caution: you may notice you will see no newscasts, internet videos, or primly clad office workers standing by the water cooler discussing the destruction of a city, large spaceships cruising by, or imperial galleons hovering overhead. Having been undone entirely by the very responsible and diligent people who have read this book, prior events have been drawn back into the realm of fiction and, in essence, have never occurred in this version of reality (although in several alternate realities, things ended rather differently—a situation we will not be extrapolating on here—suffice it to say we are continuing to sort the matter). As for this reality, we advise you not to go digging about for evidence of their happenings. No decent person would want to look too closely at such undesirable proceedings. We suggest you leave that to the conspiracy theorists— they quite like an unprovable theory anyway.

Again, your efforts are very much appreciated. You may now indulge the urge to sit on a sunny beach with a drink in one hand and a smarmy romance novel in the other. Again: your choice.

Sincerely,
Steven

Made in the USA
Lexington, KY
19 April 2019